To Sharon —

YOU'LL BE SWELL!

Jim Dawson

YOU'LL BE SWELL

A NOVEL

JIM DAVID

TRUMBULL

Copyright © 2012 by Jim David

TRUMBULL PRESS
New York, New York

All rights reserved. No part of this publication may be reproduced, stored in a retrieval system, or transmitted, in any format by any means, digital, electronic, mechanical, photocopying, recording, or otherwise, or conveyed via the Internet or a website without written permission of the author, except in the case of brief quotations embedded in critical articles and reviews. For information contact the author at www.jimdavid.com.

This is a work of fiction. Although reference is made to real persons and events, the dialogue, actions, characters and context are products of the author's imagination only, and any resemblance to actual persons living or dead is coincidental.

Library Of Congress Cataloging-in-Publication Data
David, Jim
You'll Be Swell / Jim David. – 1st ed.
LCCN: 2012903290

ISBN-13: 978-1470116569
ISBN-10: 1470116561

Printed in the United States Of America

FOR MY FAMILY

AND FOR ALL WHO DREAM OF
SHOWBIZ SUCCESS

"The truth, the absolute truth, is that the chief beauty for the theatre consists in fine bodily proportions."

- Sarah Bernhardt

"There's no damn business like show business – you have to smile to keep from throwing up."

- Billie Holiday

"In case you didn't happen to notice it, you big Texas longhorn bull, I'm one hell of a gorgeous chick."

- Sylvia Miles, *Midnight Cowboy*

1

On a beautiful moonlit night onboard the elegant cruise ship *Seafarer* off the coast of St. Croix, as she sat alone in the Island Waves Grill staring at her half-eaten salmon filet, Lucy Dixon thought, *I may vomit.*

She poked her fork at the rubbery, overdone fish that was only fit to be eaten hours ago, if ever. A gourmet cook, she thought much of the ship's food could have replaced shellfish as an abomination in the Book of Leviticus. She glared at the limp asparagus lying on the plate and thought, *what a Godawful excuse for cuisine. Whoever cooked this should get a lethal injection of béarnaise sauce.*

Ironically, she wore a green floral dress with a bust line that seemed encircled with dancing asparagus, but was actually a vine. A knitted lime shawl draped her shoulders. Lucy had fussed over what to wear for twenty minutes in her stateroom, finally deciding on this springy ensemble that had been a

Christmas gift from her sister. She liked the way it comfortably caressed her curvy body without accentuating curves she preferred to disguise. The previous night, in her slightly too tight white pantsuit, she caught herself in a hallway mirror and feared she looked like a night nurse at a VA hospital.

At thirty-eight, round though she was, she was still in better shape than most of the women on the ship, who were on a vacation from fitness and fashion as well as a vacation from work. Lucy was plump, but these other women – whose breasts were so large that they surrendered to their brassieres only at gunpoint - made her feel lithe enough to strut topless in a thong on a Milan fashion runway. They stormed the buffets like GIs on the beach at Normandy. In swimsuits their thighs resembled cones of cottage cheese. Most had trouble holding a child in their lap, since few still had laps, but had no problem lying on lounge chairs balancing a plate of french fries on their stomachs.

Many wore form-concealing tracksuits with fanny packs tied around their waists, making them resemble large, cushy fire hydrants. Lucy saw so many with these growth-like accessories, probably containing nothing more than a room key and pack of cigarettes, that she wanted to start ripping them off and throwing them overboard, encouraging other passengers to join in a fashion police conga line. But she didn't.

She also thought, *leave the poor women alone. So what if so many American women are overweight? I'm one of them, and they are probably lovely ladies who feel the same as me. But dear Lord, please don't ever let me ever balance a plate of French fries. If I do Broadway again, it will be as the scenery.*

Lucy's lifelong struggles with her own weight had been a war that her weight was currently winning. She had punished herself over the years with a variety of diets, and was now about twenty pounds too heavy for her five foot seven frame. She was still very attractive by any standards, except perhaps hers, with gracefully styled shoulder length chestnut hair, big brown eyes that shone like headlights, pronounced cheekbones, and a beautiful smile and friendly face, on a good day resembling the singer Adele, and on a bad day resembling the singer Adele if she were married to the singer Ike Turner. If Lucy had been alive during the 1600s when Rubens was a painter, she would have been Antwerp's Next Top Model.

Lucy's keen, quick-witted mind tended to involuntarily zap between the present and the past, as if trapped in a time machine that kept belching. Snippets of past events, experiences, songs, movies and lines of dialogue continually invaded her brain. She looked around the restaurant and an old Talking Heads lyric popped into her head: *You may ask yourself - how did I get here?*

Lucy had come on this cruise after taking the unlikely advice of Taniqua Matthews, a cleaning woman at the Asheville, North Carolina Toyota dealership with whom she had struck up a conversation while having her Celica's front bumper repaired. Weeks earlier, while driving, she was distracted by a ludicrously hot man modeling underwear on a billboard and rammed into the back of a car stopped at a red light. She wasn't driving fast enough for injury but fast enough to do $3800 worth of damage, and the man she hit turned out to be a total dickwad who screamed at her like she had just taken a bowel movement on his porch.

She sat on the bench outside the body shop's office, surrounded by cars in various states of fragrant disrepair, and thumbed through a tabloid magazine that trumpeted, "Best And Worst Beach Bodies! Who's A Fox And Who's A Cow?" Curious to see the cows, while glancing at a candid image of a bikinied starlet with red circles highlighting her alleged cellulite, she noticed Taniqua having difficulty lifting an overstuffed trash bag out of the industrial plastic drum.

"They throw any crap they want in here and expect me to take it away with no problem. I'm a little woman and this is damn scrap metal," said Taniqua, as she struggled to lift the engorged plastic bag.

Lucy stood up and grabbed one side of the bag, saying, "OK, on three – one, two, threeeee, *aaaaah, woah,* how did they think a woman could *lift* this?"

"They didn't. They just fill it up with shit and think it walks away by itself. I hate people."

Lucy chuckled and their eyes met.

"'Scuse my language, ma'am, but *dayum*," huffed Taniqua, as she maneuvered the bag onto the garbage cart she had driven up to the office. "Thank the Lord I'm gettin' outta here soon."

"Oh, you're quitting?" inquired Lucy, envious of a stranger who seemed to be able to do something she wasn't able to do herself.

"No such luck, but I'm goin' on a cruise in the Caribbean. I saw that commercial with those cute young folks on the wave runners and right then and there picked up the phone. Next week. Yippee!"

"Oh, that sounds *fabulous*, where to?"

"Just outta here. Aruba, or somewhere."

"How *fun*! Do you have kids you can take?"

"They're grown, it's just me and the husband."

"Aren't cruises expensive?" said Lucy, wondering how a body shop cleaning woman could afford a week in the Caribbean.

"$350 and change, plus air, apiece. My husband was furious, but now he can't wait. We got a cabin down by the propellers, but I won't be in there much."

"I could use a holiday in the sun."

"Call 'em," said Taniqua, securing the bag in her motorized cart and climbing into the seat. "The *Seafarer*. 800 number. Charge it. America's trillions in debt, so you might as well do your part, *hee hee*. Thanks for the help, sweetie. Have a better one." She drove away to another section of the shop.

A holiday in the sun. *So much for that,* Lucy thought, as she sipped her decaf after the remains of the salmon and asparagus were mercifully whisked away to their proper home in the trash. She looked around the restaurant. Mothers berated their squalling children, couples lazily stared out the window, and humongous creatures refilled their plates with a smorgasbord of colon busting cuisine. Iphone and Crackberry addicts tried in vain to get a signal, their faces betraying a pathetic inability to be incommunicado with the outside world for more than two minutes. The loudspeakers broadcasted a ghastly aural mashup that might well have been Lady Gaga singing Swahili.

She felt insane to have come on this cruise alone. There had been a grand total of two hours of sun for the entire week. The rest of the time was spent avoiding Tropical Storm Mildred, evidently one nasty bitch. The drenching monsoons forced the ship to sit in the port of St. Thomas, Virgin Islands for two days, and when the rest of the ports were cancelled due to high winds, the captain had no choice but to sail back towards Miami directly through gasp-inducing squalls.

Frequent cruisers, who think they own the ship just because they have cruised more than once, complained as if the weather was the captain's fault, compounding their endless bellyaching. They complained so much that they complained about the length of the line to complain. Lucy had spent the bulk of her cruise playing bingo, reading a stupid romance novel from the ship's library, and viewing ancient situation comedy reruns on her stateroom TV in between a few bouts of vomiting. That someone on the ship considered a lamebrained sitcom like *Three's Company* worthy of a rebroadcast was enough to make anyone hurl.

She hoped that the cruise was going to break the chains of the depressing monotony that had become her life. Instead, she was out in the middle of the ocean, stuck on a floating Alcatraz, a woman literally adrift.

However, she had a great time singing at karaoke, at last doing what she loved doing after a long dry spell, and got lots of applause singing the power ballad "Defying Gravity" from *Wicked*. She thought. *Oh, right, this is what I do.* When performing, Lucy felt she was being of service to the audience, entertaining and providing a few moments of joy, able to convince an audience that they were all winners. That is, until she lost the audience applause poll to a huge black woman belting "And I Am Telling You I'm Not Going," using every wail and yelp of the Jennifer Hudson *Dreamgirls* version. Although she was a professional losing a stupid karaoke contest to an amateur, Lucy had to admit she was no match trying to turn the nightclub into a church.

And she enjoyed the Broadway style rev performed by energetic young singers and dancers wh still hopeful they could make a living singing and dancing. It recalled her beginning days in theater and her dream of being a great musical comedy star or, failing that, in the chorus as third girl from the left. When the cast broke into "Everything's Coming Up Roses," she instantly flashed back to her triumphant performance as Mama Rose in her high school production of *Gypsy*, which she pulled off in spite of competing with the rhythmically challenged student orchestra, more adept at playing Sousa marches than complicated show tunes. The high school audience, accustomed to amateur performances that made proud parents cringe, didn't know what hit them when she belted the climactic "Rose's Turn," crying, "Well, someone tell me when is it my turn! Don't I get a dream for myself?" She had asked that same question many days since then.

She had probably wanted to be an actress since she was a fetus, but definitely since she was mature enough to recite dialogue from the old movies and musicals she constantly watched, so addicted to *American Movie Classics* that when her parents considered downgrading their cable subscription and eliminating the channel she threw a scene-stealing tantrum. She watched most movies alone, since her friends didn't understand how she could watch something in black and white with old dead people, and she often wished she had lived in the 1940s. Sure, the women were in the kitchen, the gays in the closet and the blacks in the back of the bus, but onscreen it looked glamorous as hell.

Born Lucretia Emily Dixon in Asheville, she identified not with the contemporary Southern girl but with the wisecracking Hollywood dame of long ago – Ginger Rogers, Eve Arden and Katharine Hepburn. They all starred together, along with her idol Lucille Ball, in 1937's *Stage Door*, about a gaggle of smart-aleck actresses living in a Manhattan hotel. Lucy, born with the gift of sarcasm, saw herself fitting in with this bunch like a sex addict at a whorehouse.

She was named after her maternal grandmother, an alcoholic Alabama housewife whose husband had been a watch repairman and sometime member of the Klu Klux Klan, more for the social networking than the lynching. Grandma Lucretia had once commented that her retirement home employed "some real nice nigras." Even at age six, Lucy knew such a comment was sufficient evidence she should aspire to a more exciting life and get the hell out of there.

She also wasn't wild about her name. To her, "Lucretia" sounded like a church organist, nun or maid at a Motel 6. After she saw the 1954 musical *A Star Is Born*, where actress Judy Garland changed her name from "Esther Blodgett" to "Vicki Lester," eleven-year old Lucretia took the cue and debuted as "Lucy" in the program of her first school play, *Puss In Boots*. Her father Frank, who had been a hotel chain executive, and her mother Ida, a bank teller, never adapted to the name change. To them she was born Lucretia and would remain so until they forgot her altogether, either dead or in a nursing home wheelchair staring vacantly at a rose bush. As they repeatedly addressed Lucy as Lucretia, she wondered if Kirstie Alley's parents called her by her real name, "Gladys."

If *Glee* or *American Idol* had been on television in those days, she would have flown to Los Angeles and demanded a role at gunpoint, but she settled for being a valuable asset to the high school drama club. Performing in classic musicals like *Anything Goes* and *Cabaret* made her a lover of standards from the golden age of songwriting, making her feel even more that she could have been born in another era. She ignored contemporary pop and listened to Gershwin, Berlin and Porter, prompting one classmate to pronounce her musical tastes "retarded." Because of her arcane tastes and the fact that she looked older than many classmates, some of the more sadistic ones coined a nickname for her: "Grandma."

But whereas most drama girls were thin, flighty ingénues whose voices couldn't be heard past the fifth row, Lucy was a powerhouse whose personality rang to the last row of the balcony. She was always cast as loud, funny women at least twenty years her senior and always nailed the performances, secretly yearning to play the cute girl who gets the boy. Her talent, intelligence and wit masked massive self-doubt, and embarrassment that she was shaped more like a shot glass than an hourglass, more shop girl than showgirl.

When the high school presented *Fiddler On The Roof*, she lobbied for the part of Chava, one of the beautiful daughters, but was cast as Fruma Sara, the matronly ghost of the butcher's wife. She got a huge ovation belting her solo with enough power to force the pigeons from the rafters, but spent the rest of the evening backstage playing Scrabble and singing "Matchmaker, Matchmaker" in the wings along with the onstage "beautiful" daughters, hoping one of them would die so she could step in.

She was proud of her smarts and talents but wanted at least the option of being prom queen, cheerleader or high school slut. She knew that the prom queens and cheerleaders would probably become disillusioned housewives or pregnant biker chicks, but she couldn't shake the feeling that even if you don't want to go to the party, you still want to be invited.

It didn't help matters that her sister, Joan, was invited to the party frequently. Three years older, Joan was born sexy, a sexy toddler if such a thing is possible. She looked like Lucy but with a better figure, like a pile of question marks, and that indefinable "it" factor that distinguishes star from character actress. Their relationship had always been chilly and competitive; Lucy always won the talent competition, but Joan walked away with the swimsuit and evening gown categories. Boys paid attention to Joan from kindergarten onward, whereas Lucy felt like she had to lie down naked and spread-eagled in the street in to be noticed.

Not only that, everyone responded to Lucy's acting ambitions with a collective eye roll, smugly pooh-poohing her adolescent fantasies of stardom. Yet Lucy knew that performing was what she excelled at, the only time she truly felt alive, worthy, important and pretty. At that young age she felt what all true actors feel: *I have a gift I want to share with you all. Here it is. Enjoy.* But her teachers said that she should attempt a profession not so focused on one's appearance, like veterinary medicine or bricklaying. A classmate, Jolene, casually snapped over lunch, "You're too fat to be famous, Grandma," which prompted Lucy to impulsively shout, "Rubbish, you have no power here, be gone, before someone drops a house on you too, Margaret Hamilton," toss her Diet Coke into Jolene's face and then exit with an award-worthy toss of the head. All Jolene could manage to say in response was, "Who?"

Seventeen years later, Lucy enjoyed a welcome moment of schadenfreude as she pictured Jolene drunkenly tending a vomiting infant in some decrepit mobile home while watching the Tony Awards, as the Tony nominees included a beaming Lucy Dixon for her critically acclaimed performance in the Broadway revival of *You Can't Take It With You*. It was the peak of Lucy's life, major success at last after years of struggle, with the added bonus of doing what she loved eight times a week. But all silver has a cloudy lining, and close to the end of the show's two and a half year run, she received a four AM phone call.

"Lucretia, wake up," said her mother.

"Uh, I'm awake. What?"

"You have to come home. Daddy passed away two hours ago."

"WHAT?"

Frank Dixon had said goodnight to his wife, gone to sleep, and died. There had been no warning. Ida awoke to use the bathroom and had nudged Frank to move. He didn't.

Lucy was devastated, the floor beneath her yanked away as she fell into a pit. She had forgotten that life has a tendency to sprout crabgrass from out of nowhere while everything's coming up roses. She was crazy about her father, who for her entire life had offered nothing but love, encouragement and emergency financial support. That a sixty-nine year old man who had only brought happiness to the world should die for no reason, while there were so many available idiots deserving of death yet still walking the planet unscathed, infuriated Lucy at the injustice of it.

After the funeral as Lucy prepared to return to New York, she said to her mother, "I could take more time off from the show if you need me."

Joan said, "Don't worry, I'm going to stick around with mom for a while. It's quieter here than at my house, that's for sure." She laughed weakly, rolled her eyes and made a fart noise with her lips and tongue. Joan had always been a lively girl possessed with a droll humor, but her topsy-turvy family life had of late transformed her into a languid, world-weary cynic, resigned to a life of resignation.

Ida said, "You go back to work, honey. I know it's the only thing that makes you happy."

"Are you sure?"

"Of course. You go make people laugh."

"Thanks, mom. You'll be OK."

"I'll manage." The dead stare in Ida's eyes told a different story, the life sucked out of them. Ida was always gregarious and talkative but now, still in shock, seemed like a medicated zombie.

The remaining months of the show were a bit of an ordeal. The cloud of Frank's death hung over Lucy and she spent many days in melancholy, unable to reconcile how life, and the show, went on while her beloved daddy was gone. She struggled to give the same Tony nominated performance but it became increasingly more difficult, reminding her of the classic definition of insanity: doing the same thing over and over again and expecting different results. Like any performer stuck in a rut, she began to dislike the audience before the show even began, and would peek out at them from backstage before performances wondering, *who are these people? Couldn't they get tickets to 'Mamma Mia'?"*

When the show closed, she thought that surely as a celebrated star in a long running hit she would immediately get another job. She didn't, and was plunged back into Actor's Hell: the endless cycle of audition, rejection and disappointment that makes seasoned pros feel like scared children who want their mommy. She began to despair. *There should be a clinic for unemployed show folk, where we could all go to scream our brains out,* she thought. *Just a place where we could go, scream, and leave. I should have been a nurse.*

After six months of this madness came another late night call. Joan said, "Lucy, mom has had a stroke. You have to come home."

Mother of God in a horse drawn buggy. Not again.

The shell-shocked Lucy went back home to Asheville and began tending to the ailing Ida, and it became clear that she was going to have to stay. Joan could help out occasionally, but lived four hours away with a full time job and her own increasingly fractured family. It fell to the unattached Lucy to fulfill the dutiful daughter role, sublet her cherished New York apartment, relocate to her childhood bedroom and unceremoniously segue from actress to caregiver. In every family one person must assume the Rock of Gibraltar role whether they like it or not. She won.

Lucy's career, previously deemed "cold" by her agent Jared, now felt like a wooly mammoth frozen in arctic ice. Ida's stroke was severe enough at first that she seemed like a stranger Lucy was visiting while volunteering for the Red Cross. But this was her mother, and Lucy's precious *career* would just have to wait.

She had dreamed of a life as an MGM musical, living in a stylish Manhattan penthouse with a handsome doctor or venture capitalist, tending to a couple of children between Broadway engagements and hosting fashionable soirees. She realized those fantasies were indeed just fantasies, but now even the hope of simply performing again seemed likely as winning the Mega Millions Jackpot. Her life had become driving her mother to and from physical therapy, cooking, and working the fruit and vegetable inventory at the Piggly Wiggly grocery store, where she was forced to endure an endless barrage of unsolicited social opinions from simpleminded co-workers newly empowered by wingnut talk radio and the reactionary ravings of religious fanatic politicians, or as Lucy called them, "Talibangelicals."

The gentlemen callers were not pouring into her parlor; she had not performed in three years and not had sex for four. She felt she was in the twilight of a mediocre career, the bachelorette who missed the bouquet, the fourth runner-up in the Miss Beer Goggles Pageant.

Now, on the final night of the cruise as the ship sailed back towards Miami, the weather had finally changed to crystal clear perfection. The bright crescent moon commanded attention amid the surrounding blue black with a goofy face that said, "Folks, I'm back, how y'all doing?" The wind was calm enough for one to walk along the decks without hairstyle damage. Had the weather been this pleasant for the entire cruise, Lucy might have indeed gotten the revitalization promised in the advertisements.

At the very least, she had hoped to get some rest, a break from her mother, some sun, and meet new people. At best, she would meet an available man and strike up a shipboard romance, but the ship was overpopulated with elderly couples, families, teenagers on winter break, the overfed and the under read. Her jaw hit the deck when she asked a twentysomething girl the time, and the girl replied, "I'm sorry, I can't read this watch. I only wear it because it's pretty." Lucy couldn't help laughing, thinking, *not only does this generation have no idea who Ella Fitzgerald was, they can't even tell the freaking time.* The girl had no clue what she was laughing about.

She exchanged pleasantries at a piano bar with one agreeable man in his forties, but he had the protruding ears of a Teletubbie, a lopsided toupee and excessive nose hairs, any of which was a deal breaker. Another night a handsome young man approached her at her dinner table, where she sat alone.

"Excuse me, but you look just like that actress, Lucy Dixon."

Lucy's expression changed from nondescript to joyous in a millisecond. "Drat! I've been recognized!" she exclaimed with a laugh.

"Are you really? I saw you on Broadway in *Rag Trade*. You were great. I'm a dancer in the show here. I'd love to talk to you about working in show business, if that's OK."

"Sit right down, young man, and I'll tell you the tale."

Lucy recounted her career highlights and struggles, answering the kid's questions as best she could, careful to be encouraging and ignore her present career flatline. Her heart bled for him when he told of coming out to sea to get away from his family, who couldn't deal with his sexuality. Lucy had an affinity for gay men because they gave her the time of day, and around them she was funny and secure. Around straight men she had all the confidence of a one-legged woman attempting a tap routine.

Tonight, she dined alone yet again. When the West African waitress came to her table and said in an exotic accent, "Can I get you anything else, ma'am?" Lucy wanted to snap, "You can get me a vodka and tonic, a naked lacrosse player, and a career." Instead, she forcibly smiled and said a polite "No, thank you." Her eyes suddenly filled with tears. They had been doing that a lot lately, at random, her fears and insecurities taking the driver's seat.

Lucy momentarily locked eyes with the stunning waitress, who had a shaved head and looked like she should hightail it off this ship immediately and become an international fashion model. Lucy had always thought that a black woman could pull off a shaved head, but a bald white woman looked like a member of the Manson family. Schooled in reading the emotions of guests, the waitress could see that Lucy was in some sort of private hell and thought it best to smile crisply, turn and walk away.

As Lucy walked out of the restaurant and onto the open deck, she inhaled the fresh air, finding it pathetic that on such a beautiful night someone could feel sad at all. Life could definitely be worse than on a luxury liner in the Caribbean with endless food and drink on a gorgeous evening, but there you have it. She was a good time girl, and it seemed forever since she had actually had a good time. She knew that life as well as her chosen career has its up and downs, but she had just had up to here it with the downs. Her mind was completely at odds with the serene surroundings, like a person with Tourette's syndrome screaming obscenities at a cemetery.

She saw an attractive young couple leaning against the railing feverishly necking, the man devouring the woman as if he had crawled across the desert and she was the oasis. When they noticed Lucy, they abruptly stopped kissing, smiled awkwardly, took each other's hand and started moving towards the door. The woman grinned at Lucy as she passed by. Lucy instantly thought, *gee, I remember that, back in my salad days when I was green in judgment.* How a line from *Antony And Cleopatra* had just popped into her head, she had no idea.

The deck, a long walkway on the starboard side flanked by doors and windows on one side and railing on the other, was now empty of other passengers, compounding her sense of isolation. She stood at the rail looking out onto the open ocean with the sliver of moonlight shimmering on the water. As she did, a scene from her one of her favorite movies, *Titanic*, popped into her head, where Kate Winslet got up on the railing to jump off the ship only to be saved by Leonardo DiCaprio. Lucy, knowing that no Leonardo, Alfonso or even Floyd was onboard to save her, burst into tears.

As she wept, she looked out over the water and thought, in an embarrassing rush of self-pity, *maybe the dreams have died. I'm not a working actress. I'm single and childless. I have a mother who could care less that I ended my career to take care of her.*

I'm not acting or singing anymore. I'm not only not doing what I love to do; I'm not doing much of anything.

Maybe I should jump. They would be miles away before they discovered –

Wait a minute – naah.

How dare you, Lucy? Spare us the pity party and get a grip. What if things suddenly get better in a week? They won't, but what if they do? What would your mother do if you tried to kill yourself? She'd kill you. Stop it. You're funny and talented and people like you. You're a nice girl. Have a cocktail and shut up. Sing "My Favorite Things" or something.

No, she couldn't possibly jump. For one thing, she hated getting wet, since fabric clung to her wet skin like plastic wrap and accentuated every bodily crevice in explicit detail. In a wet T-shirt she thought she looked like the Michelin Man. And this was only deck four, too close to the water to knock her out on impact, unlike jumping from the top of the ship. The thought of floating alone in the ocean treading water for hours and screaming, only to be slowly picked apart by local sea creatures in search of a large white lady, was not appealing. She momentarily shuddered that she had even thought of such a thing.

But whether she was swept away by an unknown psychic force, the emotional drama of the moment, or just for the hell of it, she lifted her left foot and put it on the bottom rail, gently grabbing the top rail doing the same with her right foot. Like Miss Winslet in a happier and sunnier scene, she carefully balanced herself, held out her arms, closed her eyes, and let the wind blow over her to create the same sensation of flying it did for the fortunate Kate.

It felt refreshing and liberating. As the warm breeze enveloped her, she took a deep breath and then exhaled. *There. This is not so bad.*

She carefully moved each foot up to the second rail from the bottom, her thighs touching the top rail. She took another breath and let out a long, low sigh, as if to exorcise all the frustration she had held in for the past six days. Just as she inhaled for a third time, about thirty feet down the deck, a pair of sliding glass doors opened and two crewmen emerged to have a cigarette.

One of them saw Lucy and yelled, "Ma'am! Get down!" Lucy, startled to be interrupted in her private movie moment, let out a yelp and suddenly lost her balance. As she looked over at the crewmen running toward her, she panicked, and her arms made large circular movements as she attempted to regain her balance and grab the rails. She yelled, "Wait, I didn't..."

The crewmen came closer, but just as they were within eight feet of her, she pitched forward, her feet flew up in the air behind her, her legs spread and her dress hitched up to her waist, and she let out a confused scream as she tumbled over the rail, fell through the night air, and splashed into the dark, deep ocean below.

2

As soon as Lucy hit the water, the current pulled her perilously close to the moving ship. Fortunately, the seas were calm and the ship was cruising very slowly rather than barreling along, or she would have been sucked underneath and ripped to shreds faster than an absentminded squirrel that wandered into a wood chipper. After she surfaced, spit out a mouthful of brine and gained her bearings, she swam away from the ship with every available ounce of energy. Skilled by her acting training to be in the moment, she realized she was definitely in the ocean and definitely in hot water, even though it was freezing.

Her shawl was gone and so was her right shoe, but they were cheap and she hated them so she kicked off the left one. The cold salt water splashed into her eyes and mouth. She kept swimming, gasping for air, and as soon as she felt at a safe distance she treaded water, turned and looked back at the white ship illuminated by the moon. The ship had already moved several hundred feet away. Since it had been ages since she had been swimming, she was impressed with her aquatic skills. She just didn't want to be using them for much longer.

Of course, Lucy's flair for the cinematic kicked into overdrive, and the theme from *Jaws* immediately invaded her brain. She screamed, "Oh, not that, shut UP," and then she tried to yell towards the ship. What came out was a pathetic whimper: "H...elp!" Realizing she needed a hell of a lot more lung power than that, she took several deep breaths and summoned every ounce of vocal prowess in her arsenal: "HELLLLLLLLLLLLLLLLLP!"

On the ship, both of the panicked crewmen leaned over the rails and watched her as she floated away. "Do you see her?" said Victor.

"Yeah, I see," said Raj.

Victor screamed, "Don't let her out of your sight!" and grabbed his deck phone, dialing 911. When the bridge answered after what seemed an eternity but was just one ring, Victor barked, "This is Victor, guest relations officer. I'm on deck four. Woman overboard, starboard. Repeat: woman overboard, starboard. We saw her jump. Or fall. We still see her, kind of. Deck 4 starboard. She's out in the water now. We see her."

Remembering his crew training, Raj found a life ring hanging on the outside of the rail and threw it in a Frisbee motion with all the power he could muster. Victor said, "Keep throwing them in." Then the two crewmen quickly went down the length of railing and threw every life ring they could find far out into the water, doing their best to keep Lucy in their sights.

After all of the rings were in the water, they looked out, and she was gone.

"Do you see her?" Raj said.

"No."

"Shit, me neither."

"Maybe she's just in the dark and not the moonlight, maybe she's not under yet," said Victor.

"Will we get fired if we don't find her? I have a mortgage," said Raj.

"No, but keep looking anyway."

They both stared out into the water, the shaft of moonlight slicing the surface of the ocean like a neon knife. They were sure she was dead and that they would both be sent away to some hellish island gulag, denied food and sex and tortured for the rest of their incompetent lives. Suddenly, a shadow on the surface bobbed into view, and they heard a distant cry.

"That's her. You see?" said Raj, pointing.

On the loudspeakers, the First Officer's voice boomed, "Oscar, Oscar, Oscar, starboard. This is not a drill. Repeat, this is not a drill. Oscar, Oscar, Oscar, starboard."

"Oscar" was the ship's code for "Man Overboard," not a suggested award for Lucy's water performance. Several deckhands, crewmen and assorted passengers poured out of the doors and began swarming on the deck, looking out to sea, drawn to the sudden real-life drama.

The Captain put on the brakes and the ship stopped moving forward, remarkably quickly considering its massive size. The ship then fired floodlights out on the water, temporarily blinding Lucy, who momentarily thought it looked like a *Close Encounters Of The Third Kind* alien spacecraft. Her eyes took a few seconds to adjust, stinging with salt. In the light, she saw something white and round floating on the surface. She swam toward it, powered by adrenaline and fumes.

This was too much. One moment she was on the ship feeling the wind in her face and minding her own business, and the next she was in the middle of the ocean, soaking wet. A few minutes ago she was anonymous and now she was the hottest thing on the high seas.

The Chief Safety Officer, along with another officer who had been rudely awakened from dreaming of naked Asian women, ran down the deck and jumped over the railing onto the rescue speedboat, which was quickly lowered into the water on its motorized cables by four deck hands. The officers were from Nepal and the deck hands from the Philippines, so the whole event felt like international breaking news. The crew, most of whom had never actually experienced an event like this for real, suddenly went into overdrive, as if competing for Oscars themselves.

Shortly, the whole population of the ship knew something major was up. "Some lady tried to kill herself," one large man in his sixties said. His wife, standing next to him, flicked her cigarette and said, "How rude. The cruise is almost over, and now someone has to be all dramatic. She could have waited 'till she got home. I hate people."

Crewmembers began to shoo the passengers back inside to the center of the boat. Otherwise, the boat might tip from the extra weight on one side, and the crush of passengers would prevent the crew from doing their jobs. In an emergency like this the crew was able to order the passengers around and not put up with any unwanted lip, which the crew loved because for once they didn't have to be deferential to these entitled, ungrateful idiots, many of who deserved to be pushed off the boat and join Lucy in the water.

Two moving spotlights began to search across the sea. Lucy, who had grabbed onto a life ring with her left hand, draped her arm over the edge. She saw the spotlights and briefly imagined a drum roll and an overture, but soon came to her senses and started waving with her free right hand. "Over here!" she screamed in her loudest Broadway belt. "Over HEEEEEEERE! HELLLLLLLLLLLLP!!"

But then she felt something rub against her foot. "AAAAAH!" she screamed, and then she saw what seemed like the shadow of a fin on the surface in front of her. Her heart pounded violently against her rib cage to be released, like a prisoner during a jailhouse riot. "Oh, my God, a shark! HELLLLLP!"

Her voice quickly eroded from a scream to a snivel. About three feet from her face, the large fish stuck its head out of the water. She saw the deep blue silhouette of the fish's sizeable head. It was a shark. Suddenly, Lucy was frozen in terror, certain that this was the absolute end. She was about to be eaten. *By. A. Shark.* It wasn't enough that she was single, stuck at home or had a stomach churning cruise with horrible asparagus. No, she was also about to be fish food. A cruel and unjust universe was saying, "Take that, bitch."

Then the animal made a noise, a familiar sound to any kid who watched TV Land, as Lucy had. She recognized it instantly. *"Oh my God, it's Flipper,"* she screamed. "You're kidding. Aah!"

The dolphin made a sound that seemed like a laugh, as if it were saying, "See what a mess you got yourself into, mon, feeling sorry for yourself? Ha, ha ha!" In her panicked and salt waterlogged state of mind, the dolphin had a Jamaican accent. Lucy let out a huge laugh like the dolphin, and tears streamed down her wet face. She was still unsure what Flipper was planning on doing with her. After all, this was its territory. The dolphin then swam to her, rubbing up against her side, and somehow Lucy grabbed the fin, remembering a childhood trip to Sea World where she had swam with one of this guy's relatives.

The dolphin stated swimming *away* from the ship, not towards it, and Lucy let go immediately. "Wait, wrong way, buddy, this way!" The dolphin, as if on cue, miraculously turned around and came back, rubbing on Lucy's left side. She grabbed the fin again, and the dolphin swam towards the ship, with Lucy in tow.

She still didn't think she had been seen by anyone on the ship, so she screamed, "HELP!" as loud as she could as the dolphin slowly swam along. She held the fin tightly, but carefully, to avoid hurting the benevolent creature that was in the process of saving her life.

She realized she wasn't very good at yelling, but she was *very* good at singing. Knowing she stood a better chance of being heard by singing than screaming, she took a huge breath and broke into her Act One closer from *Gypsy*.

"I had a dream, a dream about you, baby, it's gonna come true, baby, they THINK THAT WE'RE THROUGH, but babyyyyyyy.....YOU'LLLLLLLLL BEEEEEE SWELL, you'll be great! Gonna have the whole world on a plate..." She absurdly belted the song as the dolphin pulled her closer to the ship. Her voice rang through the quiet night air, and she thought she actually heard it echo when it hit the ship. She felt like Ethel Merman singing in the bathtub. Now one of her stupid dreams had come true, at least.

From the speedboat, which sped away from the ship, one of the officers moved his searchlight across the water. He then heard, at about eleven o'clock from his position, something that sounded like a song.

"Do you hear that?"

"Yeah, I hear it. Someone's singing."

"Listen. Listen. It's a song from the show. Is it one of our cast members?"

The Safety Officer searched with his floodlight in the direction of the sound, and after a few sweeps back and forth, caught Lucy in the light, moving rapidly. *Wow, she can swim fast.* "There she is." The officer immediately swung the speedboat into action and powered toward her, arriving about fifteen feet away from her within seconds.

As the boat slowly pulled up next to Lucy, she blared the final triumphant lyrics, "Honey, everything's coming up roses for me and for YOUUUUUU!" Then, the officers noticed the dolphin bobbing up in front of her.

Expecting to see a panicked passenger on the verge of drowning, they were treated to a bizarre water ballet complete with a sea creature and a show tune. The stunned officers shone the floodlight in her face, and she shouted, "Here I am. You see me?"

"We see you, ma'am," the safety officer said through his bullhorn. Lucy swam towards the speedboat, still holding on to the life ring. The dolphin, still on the surface, seemed to enjoy the spectacle.

"Take it easy, ma'am, we've got you."

Slowly moving the boat within range, the officer positioned the aluminum stepladder on the outside. Lucy swam to the ladder, grabbed both sides, and the officers helped her up and onto the boat.

"Aaah. oh my God. Thank you, thank you," she panted. Her soaking wet dress clung to her skin, embarrassing her.

Turning around, she looked out into the water and saw the dolphin bobbing up and down. She let out a sigh, waved to her newfound leviathan friend and said, "Keep in touch." The dolphin actually cackled, seeming to answer, "No problem, mon." Then it swam away.

One of the men took a large blanket out of a box in the rear and wrapped it around Lucy. The other took his bullhorn and screamed towards the ship, "We have her. She is safe." In the distance, Lucy heard the ship break into the sound of applause. Lucy, not knowing whether to laugh or cry, did both, and then did a little curtsy. Then she fainted.

"Oh, shit," said the officer. "American. She'll sue."

3

Once the officers had revived her and brought her safely back on the ship, Lucy was put on a gurney and wheeled to the medical center on deck one. Passengers and crewmembers jockeyed for a view, some actually flashing pictures. *Paparazzi? Out here in the ocean?? I didn't get this kind of attention on Broadway.* She felt like Britney Spears being hauled to the booby hatch. The crew then wisely transported her through the restricted crew elevators to avoid onlookers and possible autograph seekers, which was, absurdly, not unheard of in shipboard dramas.

  The ship's medical center looked like a doctor's office crossed with a morgue. Lime green, white and silver steel walls enclosed desks, hospital beds and assorted medical equipment. The nurse, Biljana, a plain woman from Macedonia who resembled a young Auntie Em, had been aroused from her sleep and summoned to tend to the emergency. She helped assist Lucy out of her wet clothes and into a terrycloth bathrobe.

Lucy, suddenly wide awake and more alert than she had been all week, felt like sitting on a divan, lighting a cigarette, nursing a glass of champagne and holding a press conference. This was the most excitement she had had in years. But she was chagrined that all this commotion happened because she was a klutz with an overactive fantasy life. Realizing she was going to have to explain herself, right now, she summoned from deep within all available poise and charm and smiled a strained grin, all the while thinking, *I just fell off a freaking ship.*

The two officers who had rescued her were in the corner filling out a report and speaking to Victor and Raj, the crewmen who had first discovered her. Two of the ship's security guards were there as well, anxious to begin the thing they were most skilled at: questioning a suspect.

As the nurse attached her to an IV drip and began to take her blood pressure, Najeem, a security guard wearing a blue shirt with a gold badge, said, "Are you all right, madam?"

"Yes, I think so, just a little shook up," said Lucy. *Yeah, just a little. I was just rescued by a Jamaican dolphin.*

"Are you able to tell us what happened?" said Dijan, the other guard. They both had thick accents that she couldn't place, dark features and scowls, and suddenly she felt like a prisoner of war negotiating with her captors.

"Well, yes. I was standing on the railing because I wanted to feel the wind. I had my arms out like this –" she demonstrated – "and then the two guys came out and yelled at me to get down and I got all startled and I lost my balance and the next thing I knew I was in the ocean."

"Why were you up on the rail?" asked Najeem, suspiciously.

"Well," Lucy was embarrassed, but thought the truth was best, "You know that movie, *Titanic?*

Najeem said, "I never saw that."

Dijan said, his scowl unexpectedly morphing into a smile, "I did. You mean when the girl was on the front of the ship, pretending to be flying?"

"Yes, that's it."

"I loved it. I wanted to be her," said Dijan. Najeem eyed him warily.

"Yeah, me too," said Lucy. "And it just happened, I didn't plan it or anything, I just got up on the rail and held out my arms, and then those guys, um, yelled at me to get down, and I got nervous and fell over."

Najeem had his doubts. "Could you please tell me, have you been feeling sad or depressed lately, ma'am?"

Lucy's smile suddenly faded. *Of course I've been depressed, moron. I've been a wreck for the last three years, and this week on this ship I wanted to put a bullet through my brain, it was so boring. Wait. They think I tried to kill myself? Please. End this, now.*

"Well, I would never...I wasn't trying to kill myself, if that's what you mean."

Najeem looked at her. He considered himself as a good reader of people, and this woman seemed a little too glib for someone who had just fallen into the ocean, had an encounter with a dolphin, and fainted on the rescue boat. But he was unacquainted with professional actresses, who can seem glib while being manhandled by King Kong.

"Ma'am, jumping off a moving vessel is a violation of international maritime law."

"I didn't jump, I fell," Lucy said, "If I had been trying to kill myself, why would I have been screaming 'help' out in the water? Or singing, for heaven's sake? Didn't they hear me singing? I was *belting* out there."

Dijan and Najeem stared at her. Had they supernatural powers, their eyes would have seared her flesh. She felt guilty because, after all, she *had* thought about jumping off for about a second. She had not only thought about it, she had weighed the pros and cons, scolded herself, forgiven herself, and forgotten it in the millisecond it took to say, "Forget it."

"Really, it was an accident, and I'm OK now, and thank you very much for saving me, especially those guys over there," she said breathlessly. She wanted any possible confusion to be cleared up now, this second, and wanted to get out of there and back to the safety of her stateroom where she could order room service and have a good cry. Actually, she wanted to go back home and crawl up into her mother's womb.

The guards wanted to close the matter. She was, after all, American, and any time an American had an accident on a ship, a lawsuit was as sure to follow as a burp after a swig of club soda. All Americans did was complain and try to get things for free.

"Please say again, ma'am. You fell because these two crewmen startled you, is that correct?" asked Najeem.

"Yeah."

"So, do you feel that they were responsible for your falling into the water?"

"Well, yes, but it wasn't their fault, I mean, I was up on the rails, they were, um, just doing their job and trying to keep me from ... " She immediately saw what they were fishing for. "I'm not going to *press charges*, if that's what you mean. I'm not going to sue," said Lucy.

"Please understand that we must follow required procedures and file a report with the appropriate authorities in Miami, and you will need to be questioned by the police upon arrival tomorrow."

"Oh, God, no, I just want this to be over. I want to go to the airport and catch my plane home and forget the whole thing. Can't we just drop it? I'll pay any charges I need to, or my insurance will, or something. It was all my fault, no one else's, really, I swear. It was just this weird thing."

Najeem looked at her, and then said in a clipped, professional manner that sounded as rehearsed as any lawyer, "Would you sign a document to that effect, stating that your accident was your responsibility, and that you will release the *Seafarer* from any liability?"

"Oh, God, yeah, right now, sure. *Give* it to me. I'll sign it. Let's do it. Hallelujah," exclaimed Lucy.

Najeem said, "You would say the very things you just said to us to the Captain?"

"Oh, hell yes, bring him down," Lucy said, breathlessly.

Dijan said, "We will draw up the necessary documents. You will need further examination before we can release you. I am sure you understand."

The guards walked away to speak with the officers. At this point there were eleven people in the medical center, not including Lucy, who half expected a crew from *Entertainment Tonight* to show up. She felt simultaneously like a star, a defendant and someone about to be locked up with the criminally insane.

She then saw a man she hadn't seen before, wearing a green hospital short-sleeved shirt, speaking to Biljana. He had a stethoscope around his neck and an assortment of pens in his shirt pocket. He wore a gold watch on his left wrist. He turned and looked at her. He had long jet black hair that came over his ears and along his neck, deep black almond shaped eyes, eyelashes she could see across the room, a smooth, tanned face and square jaw, and his dark, striking features made him resemble a grown up Aladdin. He turned and walked over to her, seeming almost in slow motion, and stood about a foot from her bed. His eyes burned a hole in her. She felt herself blush.

"Hello, I am Dr. Bejravi, and you are…Miss Dixon?" he said, in a smooth, velvety voice that could charm the cobras right out of the baskets.

"Yes, Lucy Dixon, hello." She sat upright on the bed and adjusted her hair, realizing it probably looked like she had just stepped out of the ocean, which she had. She hoped it contained no unsightly shells, seaweed or jellyfish. With her luck, a license plate would be in there.

"I would like to look at you a little, is that all right?" said Dr. Bejravi. Lucy's heart rate rose, which she feared would cause an incorrect diagnosis.

"Oh, sure, knock yourself out," she said.

As he put the stethoscope in his ears and started listening to her breathing, he said, "Deep breath, please. Again, and again." He moved the scope to various places on her bare skin, which suddenly seemed to heat up the cool instrument.

"Very good. So, I understand you had a little adventure." He took the stethoscope out of his ears and to rest around his neck, put two fingers on her wrist, looked at his watch, and checked her pulse.

"Yeah, well, it was something, but I'm OK now."

"Yes, you are very lucky. If the ship had been going faster, or had the moon not been out, we might not have found you."

"Wow."

The doctor then took a penlight out of his pocket and came close to her face. Goosebumps competed for space on her skin. He turned on the light and said, "Look up there, please," and shone the light into her left eye, then her right. She then shifted her eyes from the ceiling to his eyes, and for a second they were staring at each other, making Lucy feel like Lois Lane gazing at Superman.

As far as men, her "type" had always leaned towards the All American Boy such as Ryan Gosling, even though he's Canadian. Her Southern upbringing had not been diverse, and she tended to go for what she knew. Her New York years had also broadened her types to include Italians, Jews and the occasional Latino. Lately she had lowered her standards, and her current type of man was one who had a full compliment of limbs.

But here was this exotic thing who looked like he had flown in on a carpet from ancient Baghdad, and she thought, *Ryan who?* Dr. Bejravi continued to look in her eyes.

"Please, where are you from?" she said.

"I am from Casablanca, Morocco," he said.

She gasped a strangled laugh, and said, "Of course you are."

Oh, my God, he wasn't from *Tangier* or *Marrakesh,* he was from freaking *Casablanca.* The most romantic, mysterious place on Earth! Instantly, "As Time Goes By" popped into her head, and Humphrey Bogart planted a whopping 1940s kiss on Ingrid Bergman before discreetly closing the door.

She looked at the name badge on his chest, which said, "Dr. Perooj Bejravi, Morocco, Medicine." Her friend Nancy had recently returned from Casablanca, and said that because of the traffic, pollution, overcrowding, dusty heat and endless torrent of beggars, it was an intimidating and unpleasant shit hole, and she would shoot herself before she ever returned. Lucy wanted to move there at once, redecorate the doctor's home, make him homemade baba ganoush, and work to improve Muslim - American relations.

"I'm from North Carolina, I've never met anyone from Morocco," she said, her speech suddenly starting to slur. She felt high. All she could then manage was, "So, how long, uh, where did, um, have, you….been….on…. big boat?"

The doctor smiled, flashing the whitest teeth in creation. "My contract is six months, and I have one month remaining," he said.

"Oh, well, have you ever been to North Carolina?" she asked.

"No, I have not been to America, only to Miami," he said.

"That's not America, it's Miami," she said. "I could show you my part of the country. It's beautiful. Maybe you could come see me when you are done here."

She was astounded at her forwardness, but the sight of him involuntarily revved up her inner motormouth. "Really, it would be my pleasure. You could come visit and eat Southern food. I'm a great cook."

Dr. Bejravi grinned, and said, "Why not?"

He was used to this. He had long become accustomed to his effect on female patients. He was also a professional and it never went anywhere. Still, he couldn't help but see that, despite her messy appearance, a beautiful woman lurked in there somewhere. Having checked her identification, he saw that she was three years older than he. Not too much.

After this contract was over, he had two weeks before returning to Morocco, which he dreaded more than a face full of camel dung. He wondered for a second. She had beautiful eyes. Something in them made him want to save her. From what, he didn't know.

But it had been so long since he had felt anything at all for a woman that he had no idea how to proceed. He had shut off that part of himself years ago. Yet here was a woman who seemed to …

A distinguished man appeared at the foot of her bed, interrupting the doctor's thoughts. He wore a white naval short sleeve shirt and white trousers. "Miss Dixon? I'm Captain Henrik," he said, in an accent that sounded Scandinavian.

"Hello, Captain, I'm Lucy, and I'm sorry for the trouble. It was a total accident and it was all my fault and I'm not going to hold the ship liable. I'm just sorry it all happened and it was such a *huge* scene, my *God.*"

"Well, we are all very glad you are OK, that is our primary concern and you do not have to worry about anything else. We are just happy we were able to help you before things got too difficult."

"Oh, I'll never forget it, believe me. I'll remember this trip forever," she said, smiling weakly. *Get me out of here, now.*

"And I hope you have enjoyed the rest of your cruise, up until this unfortunate incident," the Captain said.

Are you kidding? Until tonight it was a nightmare. But now there's been all this drama, all these interesting people with all these cool accents are talking to me, and I've just met the most gorgeous man in creation. "Oh, yes, it's been wonderful," she lied.

After a few more pleasantries, the Captain excused himself. Dr Bejravi was about to do the same, but then Lucy said, "Uh, doctor, is there any way I can, um, write you, to say thank you?"

The doctor paused. He thought an innocent note would not be a problem. "Of course, you can write to the company, including the name of the ship, the *Seafarer*, and my name. I will get it."

Lucy just couldn't stop staring at him. That face! *Woof!* "You will hear from me, I am so grateful, thank you," she said.

The doctor flashed her the most stunning smile she had ever seen, a smile fit for display in a glass case in the Topkapi Palace in Istanbul. A smile that could cause an entire harem to spontaneously orgasm with an accompanying chorus of singing

Arab children, a smile that was seductive, mysterious, safe and deadly. Just one smile like that before Congress would end all fears of terrorism, if they weren't such stupid, racist old white men.

He did a quick bow, and was gone. She sighed. *Oh, well, that's that.* Then the guards came up and explained the procedures she would have to go through in the morning before she disembarked. She was torn between returning home and regaling people with stories of what happened or saying nothing at all, especially to her theater colleagues. She didn't need to be the laughingstock of Broadway.

When she was dismissed, one of the security guards escorted her back to her stateroom. She kept her head down so as to not be noticed by too many passengers. Since she was wearing a white robe, barefoot and carrying her wet dress in a white plastic bag, being anonymous was difficult. But she didn't care, and felt, in a weird way, like she had had a complete experience for the first time in years – in fact, the most complete experience since she dated her old college boyfriend in her drama major days - and at this moment no one could hurt her.

As they passed by one of the bars, she saw two young men leaning against the bar, both laughing and loudly carousing. One of them looked like said old college boyfriend. He said to the other man, "Hey, what do you call a fat girl with a pretty face?"

"I don't know, what?" said the other.

"Fat."

4

Eighteen years earlier, Lucy had majored in theater at a medium sized University in Dallas. The faculty immediately knew she was the real thing and cast her in most everything she auditioned for, such as a Pigeon Sister in *The Odd Couple*, Lady Bracknell in *The Importance Of Being Earnest*, Miss Adelaide in *Guys And Dolls,* Martha in *Who's Afraid Of Virginia Woolf?* and, in a rare dramatic and classical turn, as Euripides' child killing mom from Hades, *Medea*. But for the first time it dawned on her that a legitimate theater would hire a much older actress for parts like these. Her professors assured her that there were plenty of parts for someone of her talent, but she had a TV, and knew that most of the parts her age were going to thin, flighty ingénues whose voices can't be heard past the fifth row.

The faculty was overpopulated with those who had scored a few professional hits, more than a few flops, and retreated, exhausted, to the security of academia. The head scenic designer had enjoyed a brief Broadway run until his designing hand was severed by a circular saw. One acting teacher had appeared in the same Broadway musical for nine years and 3700 performances, and then opted for teaching over bombing the theater.

Some teachers toyed with the budding, raw emotions of the students. In one acting class, the teacher, Nicki, had each student stand in front of the class and say nothing until the student became uncomfortable. Nicki would say things like, "I see your right hand is shaking, and telling me a story. What are you feeling right this second?" The student would then have his "true" feelings yanked out by repeated questions from Nicki, usually resulting in tears. In fact, crying in class became a status symbol, like sleeping with a football player.

Students stood in the hot spot, repeating phrases like "I hurt," or "I need, I need, I neeeed," until they were a blubbering mess. Nicki would rise majestically, guide them through their tears and explain how important their feelings were. Afterwards, students would crowd around whoever had had a "breakthrough" that day, saying things like, "Good *work*. Bravo." Even though all the student had done was to cry in front of the class with no idea whatsoever of how to translate it into an actual performance, he or she was congratulated like they had just performed *King Lear*.

One of the most riveting, and horrifying, moments in class came one day when Nicki asked a shy country boy, Zack, about his childhood. Zack was a lanky and charismatic kid who reminded Lucy of a young Brad Pitt in *Thelma and Louise*. He had broad shoulders and a thin waist. Right out of a Marlboro ad, he was good at playing small character parts like a bartender with dialogue like, "No, Officer, ain't seen him around here lately, I reckon."

He stood in front of the class awkwardly, in a torn T-shirt, jeans and cowboy boots, and Nicki kept insisting that he let his hands hang at his sides rather than escaping to the safety of his pockets. He told a roundabout tale about how he and his buddies would hang out at a barn, smoke dope and bring over the occasional girl. When Nicki asked what else went on there and he replied, "Nuthin," she said, "Well, tell me the worst thing that had ever happened to you there."

He shot a threatening look at Nicki, his hand shaking and his lips quivering. He adjusted his stance in his boots, and said, "Well, uh, one time…" He trailed away and looked to the side.

"Just tell me," said Nicki, in a soothing, manipulative voice.

"Well, we was playing poker one night and we got drunk and one guy said we should play strip poker, so we did, and uh…"

"And?" Nicki leaned forward, as did the rest of the class, in anticipation of something hot. A bunch of country boys getting naked in a barn was bound to lead somewhere.

"And, uh, when it came my time to take off my underwear, I didn't want to, and Willy Jay said, 'C'mon, don't be a pussy, you can do it,' and I said no, and before I knew it the others had grabbed me and…"

He was starting to shake with the memory. "...And they stripped off my drawers and they was laughing, and they tied me to a bunk bed, face down, and they pulled out their dicks and, uh..."

Dead silence. His face slowly rose to look at the class, his eyes like one of Jack Nicholson's sketchier moments in *The Shining*. The students were spellbound. Tears began streaming down his cheeks and he quickly moved to wipe them away.

Nicki stood up next to him. "Don't wipe them, no, just let them come, Zack. What happened then?"

"Oh, no, forget it," Zack said.

"There are enormous things going on inside you, Zack. You feel them? Those are *real feelings*. You'll be a greater actor."

"What the fuck, lady?" Zack pleaded as he turned away to avoid the faces staring at him. He thought he was being violated, that this was all for nothing other than the sick curiosity of the class. Trying to be helpful, one girl, Nicole, said, "Oh, come on, Zack, I told about my breast implants." A couple of students snorted uncomfortably.

Zack turned with a face of enraged, angry defiance, which would have been riveting had it been photographed up close and projected on the big screen. Directors pray for a face like this. He looked like a sexy psychotic about to hack his mother to pieces and then enjoy a martini.

Zack said, "OK, you asked for this shit. Bobby Lee who was real drunk got his dick hard and lay down on top of me and he...I told him to stop but everybody was egging him on. They were whooping it up. Then he got out and Willy Jay came in. And it was hurting me, and then..."

His face shook and tears poured out as if a garden hose had been inserted into his rectum, but his voice remained a low, controlled quaver, spitting out the words in fury: *"And then the rest of 'em did it, and one of 'em liked it and did it again. And I was screamin,' and finally Bobby Lee said, "Let him up," how it was all just a joke, and they untied me, and I got up, and there was sawdust everywhere, and my face was wet and I was sweating, and a stupid dog was watching the whole thing, and then I stood up and Willy Jay said don't worry Zack we wus just havin' some fun, and I pushed Willy Jay down and then I grabbed a big rock and I smashed it over Bobby Lee's head."*

Zack looked out at the class and saw a group of open mouths and slack jaws, like a pile codfish on ice in a market. The students were speechless. All of the pins that had ever been dropped in the history of the state of Texas could probably have been heard at that moment. It was certainly the most riveting thing anyone had seen on a stage at that school. Beat the hell out of *Cats*, that's for sure.

Nicki was utterly flummoxed as to where to go next, but she managed, "So, uh, um, what happened after that, uh, John? Uh, Zack?"

Zack wiped his face and said, "I put my clothes on and got my bike and got the hell out of there."

"But what, um…" Nicki struggled. "What happened to Bobby Lee?"

"They took him to the hospital, he got all slow and never walked again right after that. Needed crutches and he drooled a lot."

The class stared at Zack like he was about to pull out rocks and do the same to each of them. A few of them thought that, if they had ever considered running for their lives, now was the time. "That's why I didn't wanna tell nobody. None of us never did, cause we'd have to explain the whole thing. They all had something on me, but I had something on them."

He pointed his finger at the class, the veins from his muscular arm about to burst. "You guys gotta swear this ain't going no further than this room. If it do, somebody gonna get hurt."

Lucy was flabbergasted that her usually entertaining acting class had suddenly become a hostage situation, but she said, "Oh, no, Zack, I'll never tell anyone, never." Other class members chimed in quickly. "Me neither." "I won't tell." "I swear."

Nicki had heard plenty in her classes over the years. She was used to tales of parental traumas and childhood disappointments, but this was the first time she had heard a male white trash rape victim confess to attempted murder. Struggling to remain composed, she thought that she, and what remained of her career, was about to be hauled away in the back of a police car and that she might shit purple twinkies en route.

She clasped her hands, took a nervous breath and said, "What did I say at the beginning, Zack? What is said here stays here. That's the only way we can do good work. You're safe. No, uh, threats are necessary. Um, how do you feel now?"

"Like I wish I'd just gone ahead and killed Bobby Lee. He started the whole fuckin' thing. But he's no good for nothing now, so that's cool."

"Aah! Well. My goodness." She took a long pause, turned a looked at the class with frenzied eyes and a forced smile, applauded and said, "Great work everybody! Let's just leave now and think about what we've witnessed, uh, seen, uh, learned! See you Friday!" She then fled the building and frantically lit a cigarette.

The class began to awkwardly disperse, some no doubt in a hurry to lock themselves in their dorm rooms, but Lucy stayed behind and went up to Zack. When the other students had gone, she spoke.

"You OK, man? That was really brave. You did a great thing."

"Oh, yeah? How's that, I wonder?" he said, wiping his eyes with his T-shirt. When he lifted up his shirt, Lucy stole a glance at his eight-pack abdominals, which looked so hard they could grate cheese.

"Well, you told something that you're ashamed of, but you got through it, and maybe if you're in a play where you have those kind of emotions, you can call on this stuff, you know? To help you really feel it."

"Yeah well, unless it's a play where I get raped by a bunch of drunk rednecks, I doubt it. I don't get all this shit, anyhow. Seems like a big jerk off to me."

"Well, it will make you a better actor if you learn how to use it."

"How?" Zack said. Lucy could see that his no-nonsense country boy routine wasn't an act; it was the real thing. And he had natural talent, too, like she did. People noticed them even when they weren't trying to be noticed. Lucy had always liked him, but now she wanted to take him home, bathe him and nurse his wounds.

He continued, "What's to acting? I just come on the stage, say the lines and mean them, and that's it. If I'm mad, I act mad. If I'm sad, I don't do nuthin'. If I'm happy, I smile. For the Shakespeare I get rid of this hick accent. I read about some actor who said, 'I just learn the lines and pray to God.' Well, that sonofabitch had it right. All this emotional shit just confuses you."

Lucy knew he had nailed it. He knew that simplicity was the key, and all these emotional histrionics might help out a little, but in the end you just walk onstage, say the lines and mean them, and then leave. In all her best performances, that's exactly what she had done. She hadn't thought about it. From that moment on, she couldn't take her eyes off Zack.

But "The Theatah" consumed Lucy's college career twenty-four hours a day, as it did for most drama majors. The college theater experience deludes one into thinking that a professional career will be the more of the same, an endless succession of shows from Shakespeare to Sondheim, when in fact the only way to repeat the college theater experience is in a career teaching college theater. Students are never taught how to cope when the realities of the professional theater chew them up and spit them out on the Manhattan sidewalk.

Lucy also tried directing, helming a well-received production of Edward Albee's *The Zoo Story*, starring Zack. Lucy chose the play specifically for him. As a young actor, it helps if you're sleeping with the director.

After Zack's acting class meltdown, Lucy saw him in a different light as strong and sensitive, as opposed to some hick below her social class. They started hanging out in the typical "buddy" way she had always done with boys, but one night when she showed up at his off-campus apartment for dinner,

Zack surprised her by giving her a big sloppy kiss at the door. After he finished, she said, "Hold that thought while I put down the lasagna."

From that moment on she was all over him like a piranha attacking a submerged cow. Suffice it to say that the lasagna did not get eaten until eleven-thirty. The earlier hours were spent celebrating the triumphant demise, at long last, of Lucy's virginity.

Zack proved to be the perfect choice for this once in a lifetime event. When she saw him naked, she finally understood the term "brick shithouse." Underwear was meant to be modeled on him. His body looked like the Statue of David if it had spent years operating farm equipment. Both a knockout and a sweet guy, he could have become the first porn star suitable for the entire family.

Opening night of Lucy's post-virginity life was both exciting and funny. Zack had a way of licking Lucy's breasts and saying things like, "Nice, tastes just like my grandmama's waffles." And Lucy had no idea that cunnilingus would make her want to simultaneously laugh, scream and sing Gershwin.

Lucy and Zack spent their first months together exploring the wonderful world of healthy lovemaking. He taught her to think she was hot and ignore the parts of her body she didn't like. She taught him how to accept his strange past sexual encounters, which had begun that torrid night in the barn and continued with various women. Zack thought she was the classiest girl he had ever met, a hell of a lot finer than the trashy skanks he picked up at bars who then stalked him for weeks.

As physical as they became, they saw each other as friends first and lovers second. They were discreet, lest the drama department have yet another source of juicy gossip, but once another student caught them making out on a pile of costumes in a large backstage closet, their affair might as well have been on *The Tonight Show*. Lucy didn't care. Zack was hot, and so, by association, was she. Finally.

Being with Zack was like being with any other friend, with the added benefit of orgasms on demand. Every time she touched his naked body, the sun rose, set, and rose again, twenty-four hours of experience crammed into two seconds. Little cartoon birdies sang Disney ditties with dirty lyrics.

One of the surprising things they had in common was a huge affection for *I Love Lucy*. Lucy Dixon reminded Zack of Lucy Ricardo, which was a great coincidence since Lucy had taken her name from the comedienne. They each had a favorite episode. Lucy's was the one when Lucy Ricardo brought twenty-five pounds of cheese on a transatlantic flight disguised as a baby, and Zack's favorite was Lucy's drunken performance in the "Vitametavegamin" commercial.

On their first Thanksgiving together, Lucy took him back home to Asheville. He was the perfect gentleman and even bought some suitable "meet the parents" clothes, leaving his usual gas station attendant wardrobe at home. He hit it off with Lucy's dad and they talked sports for hours, a subject Lucy knew diddlysquat about, being exclusively a movie and musical fanatic. Frank was just as no-nonsense and unpretentious as Zack, which may have been a reason Lucy was so attracted to him. Most young women date their fathers, and men usually marry their mothers.

Lucy's mother liked him, even though she said that she found him "common."

"Common? Mother, who are you all of a sudden, Blanche DuBois?"

"Well, he's just sort of...he reminds me of my uncle Roy. That man used to beat the living daylights out of aunt Mary Kathryn. Daddy always had to go over there and pick her up. I was hoping you'd date someone who wasn't one step out of a trailer park."

"Oh my God, his family has a house. When did you get so snobby? Look at how he's taken to dad. He's so cute, don't you think?"

"Well, in a *Hee Haw* sort of way, I reckon."

"I am ending this conversation."

Zack returned the favor and took Lucy home to Waco. His family was cordial, but depressing. Their front lawn had been replaced by dirt and old plastic chairs. His father sat on the front porch all night with a scotch on the rocks and talked about his years in the war and his bursitis. Zack's drawn, haggard mother looked like a *Grapes Of Wrath* sharecropper's wife and forever fussed about the house assuring Lucy that no one appreciated her cooking and cleaning. While they sat in the living room waiting for dinner, she screamed from the kitchen, "This is the last time I knock myself out for you people!"

His brother drove up in a decal covered Firebird, grunted a few incomprehensible syllables to his dad, a "hey" to Lucy, and drove away. His younger sister sat in a chair in her room, bounced a ball attached with a rubber band to a paddle, and drooled. Their beagle had an expression that said, "Please kill me." She knew Zack was resourceful enough to someday break free of this dusty existence, but it wasn't going to be a cakewalk.

As their graduation neared, they both knew that the end, or something like it, was dawning. Lucy was determined to move to New York to seek her show business fortune, but Zack was expected to return to Waco to work in the family's hardware store for at least a few years before starting his own life. He asked Lucy if she would consider moving back to Waco with him. Lucy only needed to hear the word "Waco," and picture Zack's living room with the frayed hook rug and backache inducing couch to know that making such a move was the equivalent of hanging herself, then putting a shotgun in her mouth and pulling the trigger after she had stabbed herself. She loved Zack, but here and now, not on a front porch in the sticks surrounded by landfills and nursing homes.

Their impending separation seemed harder on Zack. Lucy was headed for the glamour and excitement of the big city, but Zack was headed back to square one. Lucy was not only his girlfriend, she was his only friend, and he knew that he was in for a lot of lonely Waco nights with a remote in one hand and a bottle of Jack Daniels in the other. He knew that he would never meet a fun, smart girl like her who thought he had talents beyond operating heavy machinery, who didn't assume he was stupid because of his accent, and who would make him western omelettes and sing show tunes after he had just screwed her brains out.

On one of their last nights together, they lay in bed and promised to keep in touch and see what happened. This was in the final days before cell phones and email, when "keeping in touch" required the skill of writing a letter, putting it in an envelope, stamping and mailing it, and free night and weekend minutes didn't exist.

Lucy said, "What the hell am I going to do? I'm used to a hot country boy traipsing around in his tighty whities fixing my door hinges."

Zack said, "The yellow pages is right over there, under the phone. Look under 'Nekkid Help.'"

Lucy hugged him and said, "I love you, you hick," and then Zack held her tight and said, "Don't do this, babe, you're breakin' my heart," which was the best declaration she was going to get out of him. She said, "Zack, you made me feel pretty, and I never did before." He said, "Aw, knock it off, babe, you're as hot as any Playmate, you're a damn pistol, and don't you ever think you're not, you promise me that, now."

It was, of course, advice that would go right out the window once she was on her own.

5

Before she left the *Seafarer*, Lucy visited the medical center to leave a discreet note of thanks and contact information for Dr. Bejravi. She thought it would be a riot to host a dashing Moroccan doctor, even though it seemed as likely as hosting a dashing Amish. But if she was to see him again, he needed to know how to find her. As the New York Lottery commercials reminded her, *If You Want To Win It, You've Got To Be In It.*

On the flight home, she did some serious soul searching, finding her soul gasping for breath at the bottom of a well. That jarring experience on the ship had been a warning. She had been wallowing in her unhappiness so far past the expiration date that the universe just had to be telling her to get off her fanny and make some changes, right now. Or, the next time, the universe was going to let her get eaten by sharks.

On the afternoon of the day she returned to Asheville, sun poured into the den. Lucy looked at her mother sitting on the couch, the cat curled on the couch, and a steaming hot cup of tea on the coffee table. Ida looked much better these days, her hair styled and face lightly made up, resembling the actress Cloris Leachman. And her sarcastic spark seemed to be returning. She looked at Lucy and said, "Well, Lucretia. That was some vacation. I didn't realize how much you had missed the spotlight."

Lucy didn't have to break the news of her shipboard shenanigans, because it was *on* the news. A reporter for a Miami station was onboard and called in from the ship before they reached the port, where a small TV crew was waiting. Lucy managed to don sunglasses and duck the cameras, like a celebrity sneaking out of the hospital. But several passengers were interviewed upon arrival at the pier, none of whom had the faintest idea what had happened, their inane comments instantly part of the public record.

"Oh, yes, I saw her, she was wearing jeans and a blouse and she jumped," said one woman. A man said, "I had dinner with her and she was depressed, and fat. Can I say hi to my girlfriend? Yo, Denise, I'm on TV."

The story, entitled "High Drama On The High Seas," made it seem like a suicide had been thwarted and that the valiant *Seafarer* crew had saved the day. Ida was informed of the story with a call from her friend Valerie, who said, "I guess she really doesn't want to be home taking care of you, does she, Ida?"

Lucy and Ida watched CNN for over an hour waiting for the story to be repeated. It had been a long time since they had watched so much news and were amazed at how much was useless filler. There was a story on people who named their pets human names, an expose on politicians who text messaged pictures of their genitalia, and a story about a cow tipping epidemic by redneck teens on crystal meth.

And then, her story. Her heart raced as she watched the first ever news item starring Lucy Dixon. It was a strange, out of body experience, watching a story about some crazy person who just happened to be you, broadcast to the entire world. She imagined people in Paris, Shanghai or Sri Lanka wondering just who was this nut case who jumped off a boat. She wondered if terrorists were watching and resenting her for being a rich white infidel, providing yet another reason to attack America. She wondered if Taniqua Matthews, the body shop cleaning woman, was watching and worrying she had inadvertently started a chain reaction leading to a suicide attempt.

It wouldn't have been so bad had the broadcast not used her name and a picture of her on the gurney taken by a passenger, which the shutterbug had provided to the reporter in exchange for a few moments of TV coverage. The report also said, "Sources say Miss Dixon was disturbed." Maybe this was the cruise line's way of avoiding a lawsuit: public humiliation.

Fortunately, she was identified as "Lucretia Emily Dixon of Asheville, North Carolina, who was unavailable for comment," rather than "actress Lucy Dixon." She hoped that the discrepancy would prevent the New York theater community from putting two and two together. After her story finished, a panel of blond and Botoxed experts moved onto more important matters and debated the significance of Paris Hilton's trip to The Sudan, followed by a commercial for a disposable douche.

But within minutes, her phone started ringing with calls from Manhattan friends, and she explained the story over and over. The beginnings of her life in New York bombarded her memory. She thought, *did I spend all those years struggling to have a career in showbiz, only to be humiliated on the freaking news?*

Fifteen years earlier, when Lucy arrived in New York after college, she had resided in a sleeping bag on the floor of her classmate Paula's fifth-floor walk up in a ramshackle East Village neighborhood. New York neighborhoods like this one were gradually transforming from bombed out danger zone to gentrified tourist mecca, and it was typical to see a sparkling new building next to a vacant lot filled with broken glass and discarded furniture, like a tuxedoed socialite standing in a garbage dump. It was easier to get rid of undesirable real estate than undesirable people, so many residents found themselves with a luxury apartment in a building that featured a toothless junkie acting as a doorman.

Lucy was plunged head first into this urban obstacle course. Her first weeks in town were spent adjusting to her surroundings, seeing shows, and staring into the mirror squeezing blackheads on her nose. She spent a few tearful nights making the jarring transition from college star to nobody, remembering a line from *Stage Door* where a producer had said, "These girls would be so much better off at home washing dishes."

She scanned show business trade papers for auditions. One was for an Off-Off Broadway musical version of Alfred Hitchcock's *Psycho*. She wasn't cast, which was just as well; when the show opened, one review called it "A musical abortion that holds the audience hostage. The composer should be stabbed to death in the shower."

Paula, who said Lucy could stay as long as she liked, conveniently spent a lot of time at her boyfriend's apartment, so it worked out well until Lucy discovered Paula and a strange man cavorting in naked carnal gymnastics on the floor. That night, Paula took her aside and sputtered how it wasn't working out with her boyfriend and this was a new broker who needed to be welcomed into the firm. She also told Lucy to find her own place. Paula had become as hard as the neighborhood.

Fortunately, Lucy had made a habit of hanging out at Martell's, an Upper East Side piano bar frequented by the theater crowd. When she sang she was a hit and met lots of people, becoming chummy with a chorus girl named Amanda, who needed a roommate and invited Lucy to move in to her spacious two bedroom. Lucy happily said goodbye to the East Village and hello to West 88th Street. One of the first people she called was Zack, to catch up and strongly hint that her naked body was waiting should he be horny enough to get on a plane.

Amanda was appearing in a Broadway musical and was able to arrange a meeting for Lucy with her agent, Jared, who was impressed. "You're a belter with a strong presence. I'm not promising anything – your type is difficult to cast since all they seem to want are gorgeous girly girls, but let's see if we can make some money."

So I'm not a gorgeous young girly-girl. Thanks for pointing that out. But I like the money part.

Jared insisted she enroll in a class to keep her acting chops fresh. She found one at the TP Studios, a revered theater school founded by a Polish director named Tadeusz Paczula who was famous for avant-garde productions like a non-musical adaptation of *The Sound Of Music* staged on trampolines: "The hills *are* alive!" said one review.

Lucy enrolled in the musical comedy class taught by a former Broadway dancer named Hal, in a basement room with black brick walls, chairs, and a piano. It seemed more appropriate for a sadomasochistic orgy or torturing political prisoners than musical comedy, but to Lucy it was pure New York. Her singing was met with raves from Hal. While flattered, Lucy wanted to know how she could improve, polling her classmates. A student named Brian said, "You plant yourself center stage and belt it, like you're trying to blow us away. We know you're great, just show us a real person in there."

"He's right," said Hal, snapping to attention and remembering he was the teacher. "We know you can sell it, let's see you feel it. Pick something that scares you, or even pick a man's song."

Lucy invited Brian out for coffee. "The problem is, I've played these roles that I'm too young for. I'm a character actress and there aren't that many parts for someone my type at twenty-three."

Brian said, "The only limitations are in your mind. No great person has ever listened to the negative voices in his head who told him he couldn't do it."

Lucy, whose negative voices in her head were loud enough to wake the neighbors, said, "Wow. Where did you learn this? Therapy?"

"Nah. *Star Trek*."

From then on, Lucy came to class with challenging material. One of her best performances was singing "My

Defenses Are Down" from Irving Berlin's *Annie Get Your Gun*, usually sung by the male lead. Her smoky, sexy rendition of the song would have made Berlin ejaculate in his top hat and tails.

Lucy planned on finding an equally original up-tempo song, but at the moment was preoccupied with finding a job to avoid spending her future at the Salvation Army. Most young actors don't traipse into town and start working in showbiz. There's a reason why New York and Los Angeles have the world's most glamorous waiters. Sandra, a girl in her class, recommended that she interview with the outfit that Sandra freelanced for, Eastern Onion Singing Telegrams.

Singing telegrams? What? Well, it was performing, sort of. And it sounded just goofy enough to be fun. She went to the office, a second floor walkup on 14th Street, to be interviewed by the boss, Vinnie.

As she walked into the office she stepped back thirty years in time, which is when it looked like it was last cleaned. Three desks looked randomly plopped wherever. The typewriters were old black Smith Coronas that seemed abused. Spindles with papers stabbed through them were what amounted to bookkeeping. An obese, middle-aged man seemed to grow directly out of a desk.

"You Lucy?" said Vinnie.

"That's me."

"Sandra says you're a great singer. And loud. Let's hear it."

"OK." She thought, and then began belting "Everything's Coming Up Roses." After three lines, Vinnie said, "OK, fine, you're loud and you're hired. See if you can fit into this." Vinnie reached for a bag and pulled out what looked to be a large yellow shag rug. "It's the chicken."

She had pictured doing a telegram dressed in a smart pantsuit, like a 1940s bellhop, not this mustard monstrosity. She said, "Uh, is there a bathroom?"

"Sure, down the hall." Lucy walked to the bathroom and went in. It smelled like ten people had eaten a dinner of salmon and Gorgonzola cheese and then vomited. Lucy gagged, ran out, slammed the door, sat on the grimy hall floor and awkwardly pulled on the suit.

She walked back into the office and Vinnie said, "Ha! Look at you, you were born for it. Try the head." He produced a huge chicken head that looked like a football game mascot. She put it over her head, and could only see by looking out of the space in the chicken's open beak. She figured she could navigate about five steps in this thing before an orthopedic disaster causing accident. It was also stifling hot, so she would soon be a baked chicken.

"Can you go to East 67th Street in an hour?"

"Uh, OK."

Vinnie produced an invoice. "Go to this address at 4:30. You take the costume in one bag and the balloons in another." Vinnie directed Lucy to the tall brown canisters of helium, standing in the corner like a group of bombs awaiting detonation, and instructed her how to fill one balloon after another with helium and attach a long ribbon. He did all this without moving from behind his desk. From that moment on, Lucy never saw him stand. For all she knew he had no legs, like a downtown Jabba The Hutt.

At 4:30, she nervously stood in the hallway outside the 67th Street apartment and took the chicken suit out of the bag and stepped into it. As she held the balloons in one hand, with the other she picked up the huge chicken head and donned it. She felt like a deranged burglar.

She checked the invoice for the name of the birthday boy and rang the doorbell. The door opened revealing a disheveled man in a soiled grey bathrobe. Through the chicken's mouth he stared at her with a disdainful glare, like she was a Fed with a search warrant. He rolled his eyes to the ceiling and begrudgingly invited her in.

She bounded into the room, almost knocking him over. She couldn't see much but was able to smell Vick's Vap-O-Rub, perfume and powder, recalling the smell of her spinster piano teacher. In her best chicken voice she said, "Hello...there! I'm here for Little Willie!" Dead silence.

After a few uncomfortable moments, a woman who sounded like a Golden Girl from the Bronx said, "Well, aren't you going to...cluck, or something?"

"I'm waiting for Little Willie," she clucked.

"This is Little Willie."

Realizing that the telegram was for this disgusted old man and not a kid, Lucy raised her arms and said, "Oooooohhhh, hellooo, Little Willie! Hap-py birthday to youuuuuuu! From Carla!" She then sang "Happy Birthday," but with chicken clucks at appropriate moments. She ended and handed the balloons to Little Willie. There was no applause.

Little Willie said, "Uh, thanks," escorting her back into the hall and slamming the door behind her. She took off the chicken head, and from within she heard him say, "What the hell was that about?"

"But…I thought you would like it, dear," said the woman.

"Aaaaah, phooey. What a waste of money."

"Well, happy birthday anyway, you old sack of shit. Jesus. The thanks I get."

Lucy's heart went out to the poor woman, merely trying to inject a little fun into a marriage gasping for breath. Having witnessed this, Lucy could only wonder what surreal domestic dramas awaited her. She was pretending to be a chicken in someone's home, a skill previously the property of deviants and schizophrenics. She doubted she could stand many more of these telegrams.

But stand them she did, for almost a year, in the offices, homes and assorted bowels of New York. Only a call girl could have visited so many places. She made decent money and it was flexible, but she grew to detest it. She was an actress, not a chicken, and every time she put on the ludicrous costumes her self-esteem went down a notch. Although covered head to toe, she was as embarrassed as if naked. And the situations became increasingly hazardous.

Once, dressed as a French maid, she entered a catering hall in Little Italy right out of *GoodFellas*, filled with men who looked like they had just returned from burying a body and women whose hairstyles were out of fashion by 1970. After singing to the cadaverous birthday boy, an ancient man who coughed as if expelling a wet softball, a morbidly obese man with greased black hair took her aside.

"Hey, c'mere," he whispered. "You do this for a *living?*"

"Yes," she nervously replied.

"Na'ah, c'mon, you gotta be a prostitute or somethin.' Tell you what. See that guy over there? Next to the fat dame. That's my uncle Joey. I'll give you five hundred bucks if you let him fuck you in your maid suit."

"Oh! Dear. Oh my. No thank you, I have to be going," she nervously stuttered. She started towards the door as the man grabbed her arm.

"It'll be easy. He don't take too long."

"Uh, no, but have a good evening and thank you for using Eastern Onion Telegrams," she blurted, gently pulling her arm away from the man, who looked like he beat women for exercise and was about to use her for a workout. She walked out briskly without seeming to run for her life, cursing the day she was born.

But the final straw came when, dressed as a pink gorilla with balloons, she entered a jewelry store in the midtown diamond district. Glass cases filled with jewels surrounded the perimeter, and bullet proof plastic went from the top of the cases to the ceiling. One small opening was in the center atop a case. Behind it stood a thin, bespectacled man who eyed her suspiciously through the thick plastic.

"I'm here for Rodney, to wish him a happy birthday," she said.

He calmly went to a drawer, pulled out a revolver, and aimed it right at Lucy.

"Get the hell out of here or I'll shoot," he said.

"But…" Lucy's heart pounded the opening drumbeat of Benny Goodman's "Sing Sing Sing." She let go of the balloons, held up both hands, and said, "I'm just doing a telegram! Don't shoot!"

"You got ten seconds to get out. Ten. Nine. Eight." Lucy didn't hear the remaining countdown, because she fainted. When she came to, she was lying on her back and being lightly tapped on the cheek by a police officer kneeling over her. Her mask had been removed and lay at her side.

"Are you all right, ma'am?" the officer said.

"What happened?" she said, groggily.

"This man says you were trying to rob him. Is that true?"

She snapped awake as if doused with ice water. "WHAT! No! I was doing a singing telegram. To a Rodney. Wait, I have the order." She unzipped the front of the costume, reached into her jeans, pulled out the yellow receipt and her driver's license, and handed them to the officer. "Lucy Dixon, I work for Eastern Onion Telegrams. I came here to sing *Happy Birthday* and this guy pulled a gun on me and said he was going to shoot. Call the police. Wait, you're the police. I'm unarmed."

"I know, I frisked you."

"You did? Where?"

"Why did you draw your weapon, sir?" The officer jumped into instant police drama mode. Lucy, from the floor, was impressed.

"I thought she was a burglar," said the jeweler, looking paler than the diamonds.

"In a gorilla suit? What are you, some pussy? Did you do anything to alarm him, ma'am?"

"No, I just walked in and asked for Rodney. Then he pulled his gun. Call my boss, the number's there. Can I go?"

"One moment. Let me verify." He then took his walkie-talkie and barked the Eastern Onion number into it, with instructions to identify a Lucretia Emily Dixon. After a few tense minutes with Lucy and the jeweler engaged in a staring contest, the distorted voice of a dispatcher said, "She checks out, but he said her name was Lucy."

"It's my stage name. I'm an actress. I do this to pay rent."

"Hell of a job," said the officer. "All right, you're free to go, ma'am, but if we need you for further questioning we'll call your office." The officer then turned to the jeweler and said, "Please come with me."

Lucy never found out what happened to the jeweler, nor did she care, because she fled the store, ran down the subway steps and rode back to the office in tears. Passengers stared, thinking that a crying woman dressed in a pink carpet was yet another homeless mental patient about to burst into song and beg for money, an unfortunate trend in the subways: spontaneous entertainment whether the audience wants it or not. Lucy felt like she could fill the bill, but there were no requests.

Arriving back at the office, Lucy slammed the mask on Vinnie's desk with a thud and a cloud of rising dust, and said, "That's it. It was a jewelry store and he held a gun on me. I quit. I've been propositioned and pushed around more than a hooker in the meatpacking district. I'm smart and I'm talented and I deserve better."

Vinnie took a breath, looked at her, and said, "Sorry to lose you. I guess it's a jungle out there. I just take the orders. You guys are out in the trenches. Here, take this." He counted out

$100 in twenties, paused, and then added another $100. "Severance."

"Thank you," Lucy said, suddenly moved at the sight of this lonely man trying to keep his struggling business afloat. "I appreciate it, really, I just can't do this anymore. I need to either do what I came here to do or go back home."

"I hear you," he said. "You should hear some of the stories the strippers come back with. People suck. I haven't figured out how to change that."

On the way back to her apartment, she decided that the dream might well be dead. After a year of telegrams, classes, piano bar performances and a mere ten auditions, she had experienced no indication whatsoever that she might have anything resembling a showbiz career. Not only was she not in demand, she could have vanished from the planet and only a few people would have noticed, who after a few days of mourning would go on with their lives as if she had never existed. Her default state of languishing in fear, disappointment and, God forbid, oblivion, subsumed her.

Long held fears have a way of perennially sprouting, like tulips, annoying relatives and herpes, and they were in full bloom today as she watched the story of her fiasco at sea on CNN, having no idea whether her humiliating moment in the spotlight would quietly blow over or inflict irreparable damage to what was left of her reputation.

"That was really you on the news, right?" said Brian, her actor buddy. "You seemed like the last person to jump off a boat. Look, Lucy, show biz ain't worth it."

She breathlessly told Brian the real story, which she would repeat so many times that day she felt like just sending out a press release. And then her actress friend Dee, who had gotten roles after posing nude in a men's magazine and appearing in the aforementioned disposable douche commercials, suggested that Lucy milk the story for all it was worth. Lucy said, "Absolutely not."

"But Lucy," said Dee, "It would be perfect. You weren't trying to kill yourself, but they think you were, and if you did an interview on CNN with Doug Johnson or somebody, you could explain it with your charming personality and make it seem funny, like a big goof, and get million-dollar publicity. I guarantee you might get an offer out of it. You could talk about how you suspended your successful career to care for your sick mother and come off like a saint. People eat that bullshit up. This is showbiz, baby."

Lucy demurred. "I'd look like an idiot."

"You're adorable and funny and if you did it right, it could make you famous. Why not? All Kim Kardashian had to do was make a sex tape. Remember when Lorena Bobbit cut off her husband's dick? She could have had her own reality show by now."

After Dee hung up, Lucy thought. Show business was all about exposure and recognition. She needed both, currently without either. And TV exposure was not only one of the most important things in American consciousness; it was something she seldom had. Exposure mattered more than talent. Everything, including the news, had become show business. War, tragedy and natural disaster were just entertainment, reduced on TV to the significance of disposable douche.

After a couple of vodkas that caused Ida to say, "Is that *another cocktail?*" Lucy decided she was indeed going to milk this for all it was worth. Why not? What else was happening? For months she had lain awake staring at her bedroom's peeling wallpaper wondering how she was going to get her life back. This might be the jump-start she needed.

The next morning she called Jared and told him to contact the Doug Johnson people at CNN, saying that she would like to talk and that they could have an exclusive. Oh, boy – the exclusive story of how a middle-aged fat woman avoided a watery death. CNN must be salivating as we speak.

But after Jared reluctantly made the call, CNN surprisingly *did indeed* salivate, and yes, they would be very interested in having noted theater actress Lucy Dixon appear on *Doug Johnson Live* as soon as possible while the story was still hot. They would like to fly Miss Dixon to Los Angeles for the interview at her earliest convenience, preferably in two days, which happened to be *their* earliest convenience.

Ida said, "Lucretia, TV people are vultures, picking the skin off your dead carcass for a ten minute story."

"What? Mom, Doug Johnson is an old man who asks softball questions. The whole world thinks I tried to kill myself. This way, I can have a laugh about it. And it will be nice to be in on TV, even if it is the news. Maybe someone will see me and think of me. Stranger things have happened. I'm going to have to go back to New York at some point, you know. I can't stay here and keep working at the store and taking care of you forever, because then I really will jump off a ship. I know you get it."

Ida got it. She knew she well enough to have to let Lucy resume her life. The umbilical cord needed a director's cut. "Well, get your hair done and wear something dark, it's slimming," she said.

Jared phoned to say that they would like her to appear on Thursday evening. A driver would pick her up on arrival at the Los Angeles airport and take her to the hotel where a segment producer would be waiting. There would be preliminary questioning to determine the direction of the interview – after all, Doug usually interviews celebrities and world leaders. He can't be expected to know everything about every nut job that jumps off a boat.

Lucy found a dark blue blouse and gold necklace with matching earrings. She would only be seen from the waist up, but opted for a black skirt and heels that made her feel dressed up. She experimented with makeup. This was to be her first TV appearance in years and she wanted to glam it up as much as possible, especially if she was to appear in high definition.

She called her friend Rick, a New York comedian. A TV interview wasn't a real conversation and you were an idiot if you went on a show unprepared. Lucy was naturally funny, but she wanted to be sure to have decent backup material. Rick came up with lines like "I was trying to be Kate Winset but I became Buster Keaton," "The theme from *Jaws* playing in my head turned into the theme from *Flipper*," and "While I was treading water I was thinking, 'I can't die here in the ocean, I have car payments.'"

The next day, while packing, she picked up the phone and was startled to hear a voice she hadn't heard in many years. "Hey, babe, you done gone and got famous," said Zack.

6

"We're joined by noted Broadway actress Lucy Dixon, Tony nominee for her performance in the Broadway revival of *You Can't Take It With You*. But her recent headline-grabbing role had nothing to do with the stage. Welcome, Lucy, nice to have you," said Doug Johnson, live to the world on the CNN TV Network.

"Thanks, Doug, great to be here," said Lucy.

She was remarkably relaxed for someone who had gotten no sleep the night before, tossing and turning in her childhood bed, worrying what she was going to say to the entire world about her stupid accident. She had slept a bit on the plane, but her connection from Atlanta was two hours late so she was whisked directly from the airport to the studio for the six PM show instead of first going to the hotel. She had no time to shower or get her hair done, but the hair and makeup staff of the show were used to emergencies, having done bang up jobs on Joan Rivers and Camilla Parker-Bowles. Lucy made them laugh so they did an extra fine operation on her, while the segment producer briefed her in the makeup chair. She was to open the show and have up to 15 minutes, after which the remaining 45 minutes were to be filled by the Governor of Alabama, who had recently been caught text messaging pictures of his genitalia to a woman in Albuquerque.

She was also doing well considering that she had met Doug Johnson thirty seconds before they went on the air. A stagehand positioned her at the desk, and then the man himself emerged from the surrounding darkness, sat down, shook her hand, and the lights came up and they were on the air. Bingo. She surmised that someone like him only really lives when they are on camera. Being a stage actress, she understood. She looked at him with a perky smile, and tilted her head upward so that her double chin would seem minimal. Up close, he looked like a friendly reptile.

"So it was reported that you attempted suicide by jumping off a ship, but what you're saying is that you were just minding your own business and the next thing you knew you were in the ocean, right?" said Doug.

"Well, not quite," laughed Lucy, "It was after dinner, and I was walking along the deck looking out at the ocean, and then I was having my own little Kate Winslet moment..."

"Your Kate Winslet moment?"

"Yes, my Kate Winslet moment, pathetic, right? I was standing at the rails looking out at the beautiful night, and then I got up on the rails a little bit to feel the wind wash over my body, like Kate did in *Titanic*, I plead guilty to having a flair for drama," she laughed again, "but I got a little too high on the rail, you know, I didn't have Leo DiCaprio holding me, and then these guys that worked on the ship came out and started screaming, 'Ma'am, get down,' and then I got all startled and leaned too far forward and before I knew it I was in the ocean. Surprise, splash. So my Kate Winslet moment turned into my Buster Keaton moment."

Doug laughed. The line worked. Thank God for Rick. "So then what did you do?"

"The backstroke," she laughed, remembering the punch line to the old joke, "Waiter, what's that fly doing in my soup?" "I started swimming like mad, away from the boat, I thought I was going to get sucked under it."

"What went through your head?"

"Water," Lucy laughed again. "My ears filled with water. I had to shake my head. Then I was just hoping that the people on the ship had noticed what had happened and would come and get me. Fortunately, they did."

"What about the people you were traveling with?"

"I was by myself."

"You were cruising by yourself?"

"Sadly, this was the case," Lucy said. "You see, I had been taking care of my mom, and I …"

"You took time out from your busy acting career to care for your ailing mother, isn't that right?"

"That's right. My mother unfortunately fell ill a while back, and I stopped working and went back home to take care of her." She was pleased with herself for using the euphemism "fell ill." It sounded so much more pleasant than "had a stroke."

"Well, she's a lucky woman, not everyone has a child stop working to come take care of them, I mean, you had a very hot career going, right?"

"Things were going very well, yes," she exaggerated. Actually, things had been at a dead standstill for the six months she was twiddling her thumbs before Ida's stroke. She had gone back home to mom not just to care for her, but also to alleviate the boredom.

"But look, she's my mother, and she's a great lady and needed to be cared for. I think, as a child, you owe your parents." She suddenly felt like a beauty pageant contestant trying to curry favor with the judges and had crossed the line into outright fabrication, but this was, after all, television. "She's been doing very well lately, and I felt I needed a little vacation, so I went on the cruise just to indulge myself. Obviously, I over-indulged."

"So, you're in the water and the boat is sailing away from you, what then?" This guy wasn't the leading interviewer in the world for nothing. He knew how to get right back on topic.

"I thought I was done for. I thought they were going to sail away and leave me in the Caribbean."

"Wow. Did you think you were going to die?"

"I didn't know. And all I could think was, 'I can't drown, I have car payments.'"

Doug laughed a big laugh. "Could you see anything happening on the ship?"

"Well, obviously they noticed what happened because all the lights on the ship came on, very dramatic, and they started throwing life preservers into the water, and I was able to latch onto one of them. That's when I saw the dolphin."

"The dolphin."

"Right, I saw a fin in the water and thought, oh my God, it's a shark, I'm dead, and the theme from *Jaws* popped into my head, but then I saw it was a dolphin, so the theme from *Jaws* became the theme from *Flipper*."

Doug laughed again. This girl was good. "So then what?"

"Well, after I got over the shock, I remembered when I had swum with the dolphins at Sea World or somewhere, and I grabbed onto his fin and he pulled me towards the boat."

"He pulled you towards the boat."

"He pulled me towards the boat. Like he had been choreographed, like it was a movie. He was obviously a union dolphin."

"In the dolphin's union," chuckled Doug.

"Right. It was so surreal. I had just had dinner, *by myself*. I was walking on the deck, *by myself*. It was the most uneventful evening. I was completely relaxed…" – another fabrication – "and I think I was probably thinking about some movie I saw or some show I had done, or maybe thinking about what to plant in my mom's garden, who knows?"

She was really laying it on thick now, and hoped that savvy viewers weren't screaming "Bullshit!" at their TV screens. She remembered exactly was on her mind: panic, depression and self-pity. Her mental state was below sea level, so no wonder she fell in.

"And then all of a sudden, boom, I'm in the ocean."

"So, why do you think it was reported as a suicide attempt?"

"Well, what else were they supposed to think?" After she discussed it with Rick, they both decided that, naturally, people were going to assume was a suicide attempt. People don't just fall off luxury liners willy-nilly, so Lucy should calmly acknowledge the obvious without being defensive. "I mean, someone falls into the ocean, of course they jumped off. But I didn't."

"I see. You're very understanding."

"I have to say, the crew of the ship was incredible – "

"They did a good job?"

"Incredible. They came out and saved me. I was screaming and hollering and – "

"I heard you were singing."

Where did he get this? She had never mentioned it to the segment producer. He must have a source on the ship. Very impressive.

"Yes, I was singing, in the water, because I thought that was the only way they would hear me. I have a *very loud* singing voice."

"A real Ethel Merman. I read that you've been compared to her."

"Man, you do your research, don't you? Very good."

She sensed she had suddenly gone too far, because the look on Doug's face said, "Don't mess with the illusion, bitch." But, ever the professional, he continued.

"I *know* people. I have friends out in the ocean. So you're singing, and then they heard you?"

"That's right. They heard me, and the dolphin pulled me towards the ship, and a motorboat came out and picked me up."

"What was the song?"

"'Everything's Coming Up Roses.' You know, 'You'll be swell, you'll be great,'" she sang. "And so on."

"From *Gypsy*. Hilarious. You played Mama Rose at some point, correct?"

"In high school. Wow. I'm impressed."

She wondered how much other information he knew about her. Maybe he had even managed to get a stool sample. "I must admit, I sang the song better in the ocean than I did in high school, probably the salt water helped, " she laughed. Doug laughed. Touchdown.

"How long did this all take?" Doug said.

"Gosh, about twenty minutes, I think. But the whole ship came alive in an instant, boom, it was amazing. It went from being a quiet evening to this huge drama, and they rescued this clumsy nincompoop who fell into the ocean."

"But if the crewmen hadn't seen you fall, no one would have rescued you, right?"

"That's probably true, but if the crewmen hadn't come out and startled me I probably wouldn't have fallen overboard in the first place."

"So, it was their fault."

"No, no, no, it was all my fault, I was the one who was standing too high on the rail. They startled me, true, but I certainly don't hold them responsible."

"I know some others who, if this had happened to them, would be the new owners of the *Seafarer*. Your honesty is refreshing."

"Well, what would I do with my own cruise ship? I can barely keep my own car out of the body shop."

"You could sing on your own ship."

"No, thanks, I'm going to stick to dry land from now on."

"That's great. We'll be back to talk more with Lucy Dixon, the loudest singer on the high seas…" he chuckled, "about what she does when she's *not* treading water, right after this."

Doug paused, staring into the camera. Then the lights on the set dimmed and Doug looked at Lucy. "Good job, honey, you're a natural."

"Thank you so much, and it's an honor to sit here with you."

Suddenly, Doug seemed to be switched off. His eyes closed and he looked like he went to sleep on the spot. Two makeup women came over to the set, one started powdering Lucy, and the other went to work on Doug while he sat there, immobile.

"You're great, very funny, he likes you," said Lucy's makeup woman.

"How can you tell?" said Lucy.

"He never laughs unless he's enjoying it, he just plows through it."

"Is he OK?" Lucy asked, looking at the sleeping Doug.

"Oh hell yeah, he always snoozes during the commercials. I think that's how he's been doing this a thousand years. Every guest thinks he's had a stroke. Good thing he doesn't drool. OK, you're done. Just a little sweat. "

"I'm used to the stage, but these lights are hot."

"Please, you should see Donald Trump. He sweats like a horse that just finished the Preakness."

The makeup women then vanished into the surrounding dark, and Lucy sat there for a few uncomfortable moments with the sleeping Doug Johnson. She thought it might be funny to reach over and rearrange him so he would wake up and wonder what had happened.

"Five seconds," a voice boomed over the speakers.

Doug snapped to attention, the lights came up and he was suddenly in action like a string in his back had been pulled.

"We're here with actress Lucy Dixon, who fell off a cruise ship and lived to do damage control." They both laughed. Lucy said, "You got that right."

"So, what's it been like, all this attention?"

"Very strange, like it was happening to someone else. It's only been a few days, and I didn't even have time to really digest what had happened before it was all over the news. Usually, when I get press attention, it's because of a show I'm in, and I've picked out the pictures they use."

"And you didn't here."

"There was only that one picture they showed that a passenger took, where I looked like some crazy lady being wheeled around, and then there were those people they interviewed who had no idea what had really happened, you know, you just want to jump into the TV and kill them."

"Kill them?"

"Oh, well, not kill them, but you know." She instantly felt she had misspoke and that the next news item would be "Lucy Dixon Wants Passengers To Die." "When someone is saying something about you that isn't true, it's very aggravating, I guess this is how a really famous person must feel."

"Which you are now."

"Oh, please, Doug, I'd rather be known as a halfway decent actress than as some nut who fell off a ship."

"But you already are – Tony nominated actress, musical comedy star, so what's next for you?"

She imagined Doug interviewing Hitler and saying, "So, Adolf, now that you've invaded Poland, what's next for you?"

She could either tell the truth, that nothing was happening, or lie and say that she was "considering some offers," when there were none. She went for humor. "What's next is that I'm going to continue to dry off. I'm still finding seaweed on my body."

"Still with the seaweed," Doug chortled, slipping into Brooklynese.

"After that, I'm not sure. My mom has been doing great and I think it's time for me to go back to work. Maybe someone would like to make a movie of my accident, and I could play myself. I already know the lines."

"I'm sure you'll do great, you're a fun lady, and good for you for suspending a happening career to take care of your mother."

Wow, this guy was the greatest press agent imaginable. "Thank you so much, but I wanted to say how grateful I am to the crew on the ship, and how professional they were, they were just great. Especially the very handsome doctor who checked me out. I almost want to have another accident just so he can take care of me," she laughed.

Doug looked into the camera. "So, doctor, wherever you are, you have a great bedside manner and one satisfied patient. Thank you, Lucy."

"Thank you, Doug."

"And we'll be back with Governor John Seymour of Alabama. He says the text messages were not pictures of his genitalia, but Flotilla Ramierez of Albuquerque has come forth with her own alleged photos of the Governor that match, down to the pimples. Stay with us."

The lights on the set dimmed. Doug reached over to shake Lucy's hand. "Very good, lots of fun. Come back when you have something else to plug."

Lucy was taken aback, like her accident was a career move worthy of advertising, but then she understood. "Thank you so much, did I do OK? I've never been on a show like this."

"You did great. Very charming. The vice-president should be so charming."

"Well, thank you so much." A stagehand came over to her, helped her off her chair and took her arm, escorting her off the set and leaving Doug to his commercial nap. As she walked off, she saw the Governor of Alabama waiting in the wings with a frozen expression. Distracted by his gaze, her feet got entangled with each other, and she fell flat on her face.

www.gossipmavens.com

Actress Denies Suicide Attempt on CNN

COMMENTS:

10:10 PM **Mr. Phipps**: *Never heard of her but she seems like a nice lady. Pretty face.*

10:12 PM **Stacy654:** *Lucy Who?*

10:14 PM **DerekBro:** *Right, she wasn't trying to kill herself. Probably changed her mind on the way down and saw dollar signs. Dumb bitch.*

10:15 PM **Wildean Wit:** *Doug Johnson died years ago, but still has his own show.*

10:17 PM **TawdryHausfrau:** *I saw her on Broadway, she was great. Better than the star, Lonnie Jones. Thought she had left showbiz or something.*

10:18 PM **RoscoePoovy:** *This is easily the most pathetic attempt at damage control I've ever heard. Of course she wanted to kill herself, but then realized it was going to be much more difficult than anticipated, so she makes up this story. I hate people.*

10:18 PM **Butchie:** *She looks like a lady who works at my Wal-Mart. I'd do her.*

10:29 PM **MediaWhore:** *Fat girls are OK if they're funny.*

10:20 PM **Libtard:** *Why is this newsworthy? People are dying every day, homes are being foreclosed, and some nobody falls off a boat and gets airtime. No wonder people hate America.*

10:22 PM **Starbanger:** *If nothing's happening with your career, this is as good a way to get attention as any.*

10:22 PM **PGHill:** *I missed the subtext.*

10:23 PM **NoDrBryson:** *Unbelievably ridiculous and stupid story. Another fabulous feather in CNN's cap. CNN stands for Crappy Nothing Nobodies. That was an hour of my life I'll never get back.*

10:24 PM **PESmith:** *What is this shit?*

10:24 PM **GreerDarius:** *LOVED LOVED LOVED her in "The Rag Trade." LOVED. And "You Can't Take It With You." She should be working all the time. LOVE her. Almost as much as Patti LuPone. Or Audra. Or Angela.*

10:24 **ZippySlauson:** *Agreed, She's great. But she should be on TV another way. She makes me laugh, though.. But not as much as Alex, my husband. He's hysterical. And he likes sushi.*

10:25 PM **Chris Topher:** *Just watch, she'll get a reality series. Each week, she'll have another accident, and let the laughs begin!*

10:25 PM **CynicalLady:** *In other news, a toothless stew bum from Detroit changed his shirt.*

7

On the floor of the *Doug Johnson Live* studio, stagehands helped Lucy to her feet. The Governor of Alabama, who had started walking towards the set, turned and gave her a sidelong glance that said, "No wonder this dame fell off a ship."

A stagehand said, "I'm Danielle. Are you sure you're OK?'

"Yes, I think so," said Lucy. "That was weird. What did I trip on?"

"Nothing," said Danielle. "You just fell. So the network would probably not be liable."

All anyone ever thinks about is being sued, Lucy thought. Still trembling from relief and exhaustion as much as falling, she entered the green room, sat on the black leather couch and fought back tears, her emotions close to screaming "Mayday!"

"Can I get you something?" asked Danielle, who didn't wait for an answer and opened the small refrigerator on the floor and got a bottled water. She handed it to Lucy. "You OK?"

"Yeah, yeah," said Lucy, taking the cap off the bottle and downing a gulp. "I'm just dead, and glad this is over. I just got home from the cruise a few days ago and I haven't slept, and I just want to go to the hotel and crash. Did you watch the interview?"

"Very entertaining, we were laughing. You look great on camera, very charming. It's pretty unbelievable, what happened to you. You probably need a vacation after that vacation."

"Yeah, right?" Lucy said, with a slight laugh. She took another drink. "Do I really look good on camera?"

"Yes, very pretty, nice smile."

"Thank you. I feel fat."

"Join the club," said Danielle. After a pause, she said, "OK, you rest here and when you're ready to leave, pick up that phone and someone will come and escort you out of the building."

"Thanks so much," said Lucy, ashamed at seeking approval from a stagehand. Danielle left the room, and Lucy opened her purse, fished out a tissue and wiped her eyes. Then she took out her phone and turned it on. She had messages.

"Honey, it's mom. I'm proud of you. The blue blouse was a good call. Call me."

"Lucy, Rick. You rocked. Call me."

"It's Jared. Call me tomorrow. I've got ideas. You looked great. Who did your makeup?"

"Hey babe, nice work, see you later."

There was no mistaking the last message, from Zack. They had talked for an hour the previous day, seeming like no time had passed since they had last spoken ten years ago. She was also surprised how much she still cared about him.

Zack's five-year marriage to a Waco girl, Tiffany, had fallen apart the previous year. The epitome of every trashy girl your mama warned you about, Tiffany was sweet at first until she got bored with Zack, failed to get pregnant and began having a highly indiscreet affair with a motorcycle riding, heavily tattooed bartender. When their marriage reached the latest in a series of last straws, Zack forced Tiffany into the car, drove her to her parents' house twenty miles away, and left her standing on the front lawn screaming like a possessed lawn jockey.

He filed for divorce, which is easier said than done in Texas. Local laws, made by lawmakers flush with religious piety, were designed to make divorce hellish. The divorce took months, and Zack's lawyer took his own sweet time proving that Tiffany was a common skank (not a legal term) who didn't deserve anything. He prevailed, but it got ugly and left Zack angry and disillusioned. Since then, he had been managing the store and spending his nights either bowling with buddies or alone, watching movies and sports on his flat screen HDTV, and drinking.

In the back of the chauffeured sedan on the way to the hotel, Lucy called Ida and relayed the experience of being on the show, omitting the trip onto the floor. She then hung up, leaned back, and looked out the window as the sights of Los Angeles whizzed by. She opened the window and breathed in the night air. It smelled that particular Los Angeles smell, like a car sputtering exhaust onto a freshly mowed lawn. She had only been here once before, and it smelled exactly the same as it had back then.

Seven years earlier, after Lucy's first Broadway musical *The Rag Trade* abruptly closed and she feared she would never work again, God seemed to say, "Don't worry, hon, I've got this," and she was surprisingly cast in a TV situation comedy pilot. The casting director said they originally wanted a sexy model type, as usual, but the network was so taken with her charm that they decided to rewrite the part for her.

Rewriting would be a good thing, because as Lucy read the script on the plane to Los Angeles, she thought it surely had to be a satire of a good sitcom. It wasn't. The plot centered on three shallow secretaries spouting manufactured "jokes" and smart-aleck comments that could only seem funny with a laugh track cranked up to 10. Since Lucy's character was a pill-popping sex bomb, she wondered how in the world they were going to recreate the part for her.

"Simple," said the director, Neil Towle, who she met at the first table reading of the script. "You'll play her as written, but because you're clearly not a sex bomb, it will be funnier. Like when you sit in the boss' lap, we're gonna have the chair break. Hilarious."

"Oh," said Lucy, insulted before she had read one line aloud. So she was to be the funny fat girl. Great. She took a deep breath. *OK, if they want a funny fat girl, I'll be the funniest one they've ever seen.*

The other actors had that TV surface charm wherein the men look like game show hosts and the women look like either models or Florence Henderson. Lucy felt like the only "real" looking person there. As the actors read through the script aloud, they laughed in all the right places, even when a line wasn't funny. Lucy wanted to scream, *You're kidding, right?* as the writers nodded in congratulations to each other on their genius at creating what was surely the next *Mary Tyler Moore.*

Lucy instantly saw why so much TV is trash: everyone is so afraid of losing their jobs that they don't say anything. The next day they were on the set blocking out the scenes, the actors doing their best to compete with banging hammers and moving cameras. As this was a TV pilot that had not been yet ordered as a series, Lucy thought they would be taking more time to explore the characters and situations, but they were plowing ahead like it was already a comedy classic, and if they just got it in the can everyone would become millionaires.

Neil was a nervous, loud man, a fox terrier on diet pills, barking direction to the actors. Lucy thought it the fakest acting she had ever seen. One of the other secretaries, a blonde name Maude, acted like the ultimate ditz brain, dingbatting her eyes for the cute boys. Maude had several lines where she said, "Oh, *really?* You've *got* to be *kidding!*" like her voice was electronically tweaked by a recording engineer, and that the music score would accent her line readings with a chorus of comedy trumpets blaring, "Waaah waaaah waaaaaaaahhh...."

Lucy's character, Wanda, forever flirted with her boss scheming different ways to get him into bed. Lucy tried to inject as much subtlety as she could, but Neil wanted her to overdo it, as if she were playing to either the last person in the balcony or the stupidest viewer in Alabama, a drooling mental patient with food caked on his pajamas staring at a day room TV.

At rehearsals, the gag of Lucy sitting on the boss' lap and breaking the chair was attempted by sawing off one of the legs, attaching it to a cord held by an off-camera grip, balancing it under the chair, and yanking the cord when Lucy sat down. When Lucy sat on his lap, the cord was yanked and both actors hit the floor with the force of a refrigerator thrown from a penthouse.

Gregory, the actor playing the boss, screamed, "OWWWW! MY LEG! HOW MUCH DO YOU WEIGH???"

"Calm down, Greg, we'll get a pillow," said Neil. Lucy lay on the floor, mortified. It was bad enough that her butt was being used as a sight gag, but worse because it hurt. Gloria, one of her secretarial co-stars, rushed to help her.

"Are you OK?"

"Yeah, thanks. I was afraid to say anything."

"I hear you," whispered Gloria. "Everyone is testy around here. You could go crazy figuring out the chain of command."

"Is this funny?"

"No more or less than the rest of this nonsense."

"I hear you," said Lucy.

After additional rehearsals, the gag worked. It was inane, but funny. Lucy also got over her resentment when she remembered how her idol, Lucille Ball, would do anything for a laugh. What if Miss Ball had refused to pretend that a hunk of cheese was a baby because the very idea was so stupid?

The day of the taping, Lucy vowed to perform it like it was Oscar Wilde, even though it wasn't even *Leave It To Beaver*. As the cast was introduced to the studio audience, the announcer said, "Please welcome a newcomer to Hollywood, fresh from her Broadway triumph, Miss Lucy Dixon!" The audience applauded wildly for the unknown actress. Studio audiences are so excited to be a part of a TV taping they will applaud a couch.

The taping proceeded with a lot of stopping and starting, the director and others huddling around the monitors. Lucy made it through with flying colors. But Maude, the flightiest secretary, flubbed her lines so often it seemed she had smoked pot before the taping, especially when she looked out the window and, instead of saying, "Thank goodness the fog has lifted," said, "Thank goodness the cog has flifted." This set off such a round of stifled hysteria among the cast that a break was called for everyone to regain their composure. It spoke volumes that the mistakes were funnier than the actual dialogue.

At the wrap party after the taping, she asked several people "in the know" whether or not they thought the show would be picked up for the fall season. The responses ranged from "Absolutely, " from Neil, to "Are you kidding?" from Simon, one of the cameramen. "But you didn't hear it from me," he eagerly added, ensuring job security in the unlikely event that it succeeded.

Lucy looked around the party and realized that she hadn't had one substantial conversation with any of them beyond shop talk. Lucy wanted and needed friends in her profession. But she was slowly grasping that these people are *not* your friends and, except in a few instances, never will be. They are your professional rivals and would be very happy to see you fail and get out of the way so that they might succeed. Despite the fact that your failure or success had nothing to do with theirs, they rooted for you as much as a fly roots for a swatter.

She wondered if anyone was rooting for her tonight after her *Doug Johnson Live* appearance, or if they just changed the channel mid-sentence. Riding back to the hotel, looking out the window and feeling the California night air on her face, she knew that she as far as people in her hometown were concerned, she had indeed made it and was a success. She was just on TV! But all she felt was burnout.

Arriving at the hotel, Lucy walked to the reception desk. "Dixon, Lucy," she said to the clerk, a crisp young man standing at attention who seemed to have been waiting just for her arrival. "Ah, yes, Miss Dixon. One moment, please."

Lucy looked around the elegant lobby. *At least they put me up somewhere nice.* To her right was a lounge with several people sitting at a bar with two flat screen TVs. She then turned to her left and, about six yards away, saw a nice looking man seated alone in a chair, a drink on the table next to him. He wore a pressed white shirt, khaki pants, and sneakers.

She turned back to the receptionist, who said, "I see you will be with us just tonight?" She nodded. She then turned and looked to her left. The man, sitting in the chair, had stood up and was looking at her. Momentarily wary, she looked back at him, then at the receptionist, and then, it hit her. Her heart beat against her chest like a policeman banging a fist on a fugitive's door. Her body felt ignited from within, flushing every available inch of skin. It was Zack.

He smiled and slowly walked towards her. She gasped. He stopped two feet away. "Hey, babe, told you I'd see you later."

"Oh my GOD. What the – " Zack smiled a huge smile, a smile that had not aged a bit in the twelve years since she had last seen it. Neither, it seemed, had he. Lucy was speechless. The receptionist said, "Ma'am, is there a problem?"

"What? Oh, no, thank you. No. Uh, what room?"

"719. The elevator is to your right. I, uh, hope you enjoy your stay with us." He eyed Zack suspiciously. Lucy then walked over to Zack, put her arms around him, and started crying.

"Aw, come on, babe. You done good on the TV show." Zack held her tightly and patted her on the back. Lucy held him, then pulled away and looked at him. "What the *hell* are you doing here?" She wiped her eyes.

"I came to see you," he said.

"But how did – "

"Your mama told me. Called her at the crack of dawn. Had to explain who I was, I think I woke her up. You had already left."

"You came out here just to see me?"

"Yep. Haven't taken no time off this year, figured this was as good an excuse as any. I watched you on the show tonight over there at the bar."

"But where are you staying?"

"Here. This dump ain't cheap, neither."

"I don't believe it. I *do not believe* it. You maniac." She hugged him again. Lucy then began to laugh, wiped her face some more, and said, "I need to go to the room. Have you eaten? I'm pooped, but starving."

"I done ate, but we can eat."

Lucy looked at the receptionist, who was schooled in discretion after having seen plenty of strange behavior from guests. "Do you have room service?"

"Yes, ma'am, but it's a limited menu. Our restaurant to your left is open until eleven with a full menu."

Zack reached for Lucy's suitcase, and they walked to the elevator. Lucy looked at him, an astonished smile on her face, and shook her head in disbelief.

"I reckoned, after we talked yesterday, it was high time we had a visit," Zack said. "I figured it would be OK, and if it wasn't, I'd just say hey and go back to Texas. What the hell."

As the elevator doors closed, Zack looked at her, leaned in and kissed her. She dropped her purse and kissed him back, the kind of kiss one had earned after a week of depression, vomiting, falling off a ship and international news coverage. She pulled away, reached up to his lips and wiped off lipstick traces, and said, "Let me just get settled. I feel like I've been shot out of a cannon."

"Tell you what. I'll meet you downstairs at the restaurant in a few, OK? I'm on 16. You still drink vodka and tonic?"

"Oh hell yeah, all right, give me fifteen minutes," she said.

In her room, Lucy looked at herself in the bathroom mirror. Every molecule in her body did the Mexican hat dance. She was on high alert, exhausted yet wide-awake, like a dozing fireman who had just heard an alarm. She checked her makeup, opened her suitcase, and pulled out a black blouse and a pair of jeans. She wanted to look as slim as possible. Zack was still stunning. She just felt stunned.

She arrived at the restaurant to find Zack seated with two drinks on the table. She sat down, looked at him, smiled, and said, "So, come here often?"

He laughed. "You know what I always loved about you? You wanted to do something, you just did it. Like movin' to New York only knowing one person. Or goin' on that cruise alone. And when we were talkin' yesterday, I kept thinkin', I wanna see her, now. Not later. Just do it. So I did."

"I'm glad you did, this is a riot. This must have cost a lot, at the last minute and everything."

"I don't care. I don't spend much these days. Tiffany wasted most of my money on stupid shit for the house. One time she ordered a damn neon palm tree, five feet tall, it was something like two grand. Damn thing buzzed so loud I just unplugged it and it sat in the corner till the dog knocked it over. She was always looking through catalogs and complaining we didn't have nice things. Like to drove me nuts. You know me, all I need is a couch and a TV. And she didn't have no taste, neither. Mama wouldn't shut up about how tacky our furniture was, and Mama's house looks like a funeral home. But the stuff Tiffany ordered? Shit, I ain't no decorator, but even I know you don't mix plaid and stripes. When I threw her out, I threw the furniture out. Now there's some homeless person with tacky shit."

She laughed. Zack seemed both the same and different, his face with traces of a sadness that it hadn't had in college. Inevitable, Lucy thought, since she probably had a similar look. She also thought, *wow, it was a lot easier when we were young and everything was ahead of us, before bitterness and regret set in.*

"Did you ever love her?" she asked, carefully.

He paused, looked towards the bar, then back. "Thought I did, but I mainly just thought she was hot. She liked to party too much. When the dust settled, we realized we were strangers who didn't have nuthin' to say. The sex went from great to boring to nothing. I thought it was my fault, but she was getting all the dick she needed at the bar. She wasn't smart like you, neither. One time she asked me what a coastline was. A coastline."

A waiter approached the table and said, "Would you like a menu?"

"Yes," said Lucy, and then, "Wait – do you just have something light, like a chicken Caesar?"

"Yes ma'am."

"I'll have that, with blue cheese on the side. Zack?'

"Nothing for me, thanks."

The waiter went away. Zack looked at her and said, "I had a crazy idea. You got to be back home tomorrow? Anything important?"

"Well, my flight leaves at ten. I'm supposed to be back at work on Monday. And mom needs to be looked after."

"What would you think about stayin' and spendin' the weekend? I never been here before, thought we could drive up the coast or somethin'. Maybe go to damn Disneyland."

Lucy thought, *let's see, Disneyland vs. Asheville.* "Why not? What a riot. Yeah. I'll have to call the airline, and mom, and see if the guys across the street can look in on her."

"You look real pretty."

She felt like crying again. "Stop it, I'm fat."

"You never did give yourself credit for nuthin'. So you done put on a coupla pounds. You ain't driving no dump truck yet."

"A what?"

"A dump truck. That's what we call this lady who comes into the store driving one of them motorized wheelchairs, she's too fat to walk. Her thighs are bigger than my waist."

No man she had ever met made her feel like Zack. The one man she had seriously dated in New York, Leo, constantly nagged her about her weight, and he looked like a mildly sexy mortician. At least, as a producer, he provided her with her first big New York break. Other than that, he was a rich, domineering shark with no chin.

Over her dinner, they caught up. It's always amazing how a certain two people never run out of things to say. But when she was finished, she could feel the curtain coming down.

As they walked back towards the elevators, she said, "I'll have to call everyone at, like, six tomorrow morning to make sure I can do this. Why don't I call you in the morning and then we can make plans?"

"Sure."

Lucy thought a second about bringing him to her room, but only a second as she knew that she needed rest, not more excitement, and wasn't sure whether revisiting their ancient passion was a great idea. But the sight of his body made a convincing case for a revisit.

The elevator opened on her floor and she stepped out, turned and looked at him, and said, "I still can't believe this. Let's regroup in the morning. You sleep well. I'll call you."

He leaned in and kissed her, holding the elevator doors open. She then pulled away, and said, "Damn. Tiffany was an idiot."

"You think?"

Back in her room, she took off her clothes, brushed her teeth, and collapsed onto the bed. She quickly fell into a deep sleep, and dreamed that she lived in a Malibu beach house between her famous movie star neighbors Katharine Hepburn and Cary Grant. Zack was the pool boy, wearing a red Speedo and skimming the surface for leaves and bugs. The *Fiddler On The Roof* cast album played in the background, and the dream abruptly switched to her first national tour of that show, with Zack driving the bus.

The next morning, she awoke at five forty-five am. She wiped her eyes and called her mother, who was surprisingly agreeable to being left alone all weekend, but then said, "Last night you got a call from some strange man with an accent. He said he was your doctor on the ship."

"WHAT?"

8

Thirteen years earlier, the very day she quit her singing telegram job and feared her New York life finished, she got a message.

"Lucy? Jared. Audition for a national tour of *Fiddler*. It's for Chava, one of the daughters. Tomorrow at Four Man Studios at three-twenty. Do your ballad and up-tempo. By the way, it's a year's contract. Call me."

The next day at the audition she belted "Matchmaker" like she had been performing it for years, which she had, and then sang "My Defenses Are Down" sultry enough to fog the windows. The director and three others huddled together at a table while she sang. The director then stopped her mid-ballad and said, "Thank you. That's all we need."

"Uh, OK." Her heart sank.

"You're hired."

"WHAT?" Her heart leapt.

"Congratulations."

"Just like that?" Her heart did the mambo.

"Just like that. You'll fit in with the other girls perfectly. Rehearsals begin in three weeks. You're a find and we're lucky to have you. Of course, you'll have to join Actor's Equity. We'll take care of that."

Recalling the moment in *The King and I* when Mrs. Anna says, "Your majesty, I don't know what to say," and the King of Siam says, "When one does not know what to say, it is a time to be silent," she just smiled.

Lucy's eleven-month tour of *Fiddler On The Roof* was, to her, heaven on wheels. Critics and audiences commented on her vocal prowess and how movingly she played Chava's serious scenes, when father Tevye disowned her for marrying a Russian outside of the Jewish faith. She was Episcopalian, so to play a Jewish girl she just started complaining.

The tour was a "bus and truck" tour, which is to Broadway what Velveeta is to cheese. The company traveled in buses, with the sets and costumes traveling in trucks. After a performance, the crew would strike the set, pack it in the trucks, and travel all night to the next city. The next morning the exhausted crew set up the sets and lighting in the venue, which could be anything from a fine theater to a high school basketball court. It was an ordeal and no one was paid enough for it. Lucy would have done it for free.

She loved getting up early (despite late night imbibing with the cast), getting on the bus, going to a different town, resting and then performing the show for a new audience. She was thrilled that the tour included Asheville, where her family and friends packed several rows. Cities across America are filled with people shaking their heads derisively at their children who left home, tried to succeed in show business, and didn't, so while basking in that hometown applause at the curtain call, Lucy wanted to scream, "See? See? See?" She was now that rare thing, a working actress, which given the number of hopefuls versus available jobs was akin to a house painter becoming Andy Warhol.

The tour went well, but typical glitches occurred. In one theater, the lighting board crashed mid-show and the remaining scenes were performed lit by the candles usually reserved for the "Sunrise, Sunset" wedding number. At another performance, both the actor playing the Fiddler and his understudy were sick and the show was performed without them, leading the cast to name the show *Nobody On The Roof*.

When the tour had four weeks left, Lucy realized she was about to segue from working to unemployed. She called Jared, reminding him to set up auditions, but also thought she needed her own project; that being proactive in one's career means the difference between working hard or hardly working. What that project could be, she had no clue. But late one night she saw a TV interview with Bette Midler, reminiscing about her early days in *Fiddler* on Broadway when she performed after the show at a gay bathhouse, setting off a chain reaction that made her a star. Lucy knew she needn't perform in a bathhouse – the audience would be paying more attention to the penises – but a nightclub somewhere would suffice.

The tour was to wind up with two weeks in Chicago and Lucy had heard about a gay nightclub there that had cabaret shows. She was nervous about phoning the club, but Janeane, the veteran actress playing her mother, Golde, said, "What have you got to lose? Honey, if I had waited for it to come to me I'd be a toll collector on the turnpike." So, while in Cleveland, she called.

"*Blue*, can I help you?" said Ronny, the manager.

"Could I speak to the manager, please?" said Lucy.

"You got him."

"Hi, this is Lucy Dixon, I'm an actress and singer and I'm on tour with *Fiddler On The Roof*, and we're coming to Chicago on the seventh. I was wondering if I could come in and sing for you, and maybe do one or two nights at your club."

"You're kidding. You're in town on the seventh?"

"That's right."

"Are you good?"

Lucy felt a twinge of self-doubt, but decided to go for it. "Well, I'm in a national tour, I can sing, I'm funny, and I love gay people."

Ronny laughed. "It's amazing that you called. We just had a cancellation. Can you do three weeks?"

Three weeks? She had just thought about doing one night. "I have the show every night, do you have late shows?" she said.

"We have an 11:30 show. Could you do 11:30 for three weeks?"

"We're only performing for two weeks, I'm free after that."

"Call me a few days before you get here. If it works out, we can start right away. It would be better than having karaoke every night. Do you have an accompanist?"

"No, I thought you might have one."

"We do, but he's in rehab. Call me. Lucy, right?"

"Right."

"OK, later."

Unbelievable. She had a simple idea that was about to possibly turn into a three-week engagement. She had no sheet music, no accompanist, and no act. Other than that, she was fine.

At the theater that night, she cornered the keyboard player, Tom. "I have an audition at this nightclub in Chicago and I have no music and no act, and they might hire me for three weeks. Help!"

Tom looked at her. "We've been on tour for ten months and we have barely had two conversations. Now you want my help. You're clearly insane. I love actors."

"Come on, Tom, that doesn't mean anything. I'm onstage and you're in the pit. We hardly see each other. Please? I'll pay you. How much?"

Tom thought a minute. "Just be nice to me. What songs were you thinking about?"

"I'll marry you."

"I'm gay."

"Oh, right, well, it's a gay club." Tom laughed. This chick had nerve. "I thought I could sing 'Matchmaker' since we have the music, but I'll go to a store here in Cleveland and find other music tomorrow. Can you play anything?"

"Don't pick Leonard Bernstein, I have to practice too much. And if you sing any Jerry Herman, the deal's off. I did two tours of *Hello, Dolly!* and *Mame* and by the end I wanted both those bitches to get hit by a truck. I never want to hear that shit again."

"No problem. Thanks, Tom. I'll remember you in my memoirs."

Lucy bought sheet music for songs she had sung and songs she had always wanted to sing. When Lucy and Tom arrived at *Blue* in Chicago, they were both struck with how the place resembled a New Orleans whorehouse. Red velvet chairs surrounded tiny tables with lamps, the lampshades a sickly yellow with gold fringe. The walls were covered in maroon velour fabric with framed pictures of cutout silhouettes of naked men and women, each lit by a tiny lamp overhead. A crystal chandelier hung in the center of the room, and the stage, with a baby grand piano to one side and a stool and microphone in front, was framed by a sparkly black curtain. As the afternoon sunlight streamed through the windows, Lucy could only hope it would look better in the dark.

A muscular bartender in a black tank top was setting up the bar, and when he saw them, said, "Are you Lucy?"

"That's me."

"Hey, I'm Ronny. Doing double duty. Why don't you guys go warm up or whatever? It's too quiet in here."

Tom sat at the piano and started tinkering. "Not bad, could use a tuning but we're OK," he said. "Want to do a scale or two?"

Lucy went onto the stage and starting doing her vocal scales as Tom played chords. Tom said, "Look at this joint, I feel like I should be wearing a visor and an armband."

"If I get the gig, you could wear that and I could dress like Mae West and sing about how my man done me wrong but I still got my diamonds. This place is so retro."

Ronny took a seat and said, "Anytime you're ready." Lucy cleared her throat as Tom launched into "Everything's Coming Up Roses." Lucy sang it like she had been playing it on

Broadway for a year and today was the closing performance in front of 2000 people. After she belted out the final notes, Ronny said, "Wow. You're hot stuff."

"Thank you," said Lucy. "I have a slow one prepared if you would - "

"Save it for the show. If you want the gig, it's yours."

"I'd love it, but we're only here for the next two weeks, and I would need a hotel or somewhere after that."

"We'll work something out, I'll get on it. Can you do some press tomorrow? Radio and phone interview for the paper?"

"Sure."

"Great. We'll have to move fast 'cause if you're opening Thursday, we will have to work to get a crowd in here and – "

"*Thursday?*"

"Is there a problem with Thursday? The opening we have is this Thursday through Sunday, then the same for the next two weeks with a Wednesday thrown in if you sell out."

"Uh, OK," Lucy said uneasily as she glanced at Tom, whose eyes looked like they would pop out and roll across the floor, as they both realized that they had three days to prepare a polished cabaret performance. Ronny said, "You guys can come here and rehearse whenever you want. We do a door deal – you get half, so if we're full that should work out to about $1600 each for four shows. I hope that's OK."

Since both Lucy and Tom were making less than that for an entire week, it seemed like they had just won the lottery. They looked at each other and then at Ronny and nodded yes, as nonchalant as possible without completely losing bladder control. They went over a few more details with Ronny and then left. Once on the sidewalk, Lucy looked at Tom like she was about to scream, and he said, "Wait until we're a block away." She did. Then, a block away, they both screamed.

For the next three days they lived for nothing but her upcoming *Blue* engagement. After they selected the songs they calculated added up to a forty-five minute performance plus encore, they rehearsed in the theater, at the club, on the phone and during intermission. Their dreaming psyches even compared notes in their sleep, and Tom helped Lucy come up with in-between song patter. Ronny created a title: *Lucy Dixon – Broadway to Chicago."*

"They should have said *Broadway to Chicago by way of Bum Fuck, America,* said Tom. He was enjoying playing something other than the *Fiddler* score that he had played it so many times he wanted the villagers of Anatevka to be massacred by the Russians, alongside the bleeding corpses of Mame and Dolly.

On Thursday, Lucy opened the newspaper to see a mention of her *Blue* debut, which impressed her fellow cast members, many of whom promised to attend. The *This Week In Chicago* website prominently featured her photo. She barely made it through that evening's performance, thinking only of her impending 11:30 pm cabaret doom. After the curtain calls, she threw off her costume and put on the sparkly black dress with fringe she had acquired the day before at a thrift shop. Tom was waiting at the stage door, having hailed a cab, and they sped to the club. Her heart was pounding faster than the taxi's drive shaft.

In the dressing room, she tried to create a little more makeup glamour than her earlier incarnation as a Russian Jew. Ronny stuck his head in the door.

"It's a good crowd, about three quarters full. Most of our regulars made it. As soon as the critic gets here, we can go."

"*Critic?*" Lucy's head spun around so fast it could have completed a full rotation worthy of *The Exorcist*. "I'm being *reviewed?*"

"We need a review in tomorrow's paper to get reservations for the rest of the run, don't worry, he's a big cabaret queen and once we get some cocktails in him, he'll be fine. You're going to kill."

"Or be killed," she said. When Ronny left, she said to Tom, "I can't believe there's a critic. We don't even know what works yet."

"Baptism by cabaret."

"Oh, who cares, it's my fault for picking up the phone and calling this dump."

At 11:38, Ronny came back into the dressing room and said, "He's here, let's go. Break a leg."

"Yikes," said Lucy. Tom embraced her and said, "Relax. It's a bunch of gay guys and you're a girl singing show tunes. It's like Sinatra in a roomful of Mafia."

Tom went out through the black curtain and sat at the piano as the house lights dimmed, the wall sconces staying faintly lit. Ronny's voice boomed, "Good evening, and welcome to *Blue*. Would you please welcome, direct from *Fiddler On The Roof* at the Geary, in her *Blue* debut, Lucy Dixon!" Tom played the intro from "Some People" from *Gypsy* as Lucy came out onstage to applause.

"Thank you for coming," Lucy said. "I could have just gone back to the hotel after my show was over, but I'd rather be right here." She then launched into "Some People," its lyrics entirely appropriate for a woman dying to get out of her rut and try something new. She sang the song like she was singing it without a microphone at Yankee Stadium and was determined that the last hot dog vendor in the top row cover his ears. When she finished, the applause, which had been polite on her entrance, was thunderous, the audience flabbergasted. *Where did this chick come from?*

"Thank you so much," she beamed, used to generous applause in piano bar settings but not this ovation. Maybe Chicago had hosted some crappy singers of late. As the applause died down, she said, "Oh, and by the way, I'm single." Several laughs and whoops came out of the dark. "But maybe this isn't the greatest crowd to advertise it." Big laughter. "But there's a song I sing every night in *Fiddler* that pretty much expresses how I feel about that." She then sang "Matchmaker" as a downtempo, sexy seduction, so slow and louche it stained the wallpaper. The applause at the end was as good as before. She was tearing up the joint, and she knew it.

She sailed through the next forty minutes like Streisand at the Bon Soir in 1962 Greenwich Village, the collective testicles of the audience firmly in her grip. Ronny noticed from the bar that Geoffrey Cross, the critic, was getting more hammered than usual and kept nodding off, but Ronny dared not stop serving him lest Geoffrey write something nasty about the establishment. As with many a second tier critic, Geoffrey loved to mercilessly trash a performance to show off his witty repartee, as if aspiring to be another spawn of Addison DeWitt in *All*

About Eve, but when he went down this road he just came off like so many bitter old hacks who wanted to be stars but ended up writing about them.

Since every performer wants every show to be all about them, Lucy was in hog heaven. She got laughs when she wanted and silence when she needed. One of her best-received bits was a monologue about her singing telegram career with details of mafia social club propositions and guns pointed at her head, followed by a medley of "Happy Birthday" in chicken, French maid and gorilla.

She closed with "I'll Be Seeing You," the old War World II song, making an audience too gay to have served in the military feel like old soldiers. As the pin spot on her face spiraled into darkness, the audience had a kiniption. Except for Geoffrey, who was about to fall off his chair from the four Long Island Iced Teas he had chugged. Ronny and a waiter went over and helped him to his feet and out the door into a cab, as Geoffrey slurred, "Sheesh fabulush."

A beaming Lucy bowed, waved, and went backstage. She looked in the mirror and mopped her face with a tissue. A performer who has just had a roomful of people go nuts for them feels strangely at peace alone in a dressing room. It gives one a few moments of quiet composure before the onslaught of fans bearing congratulations, which had by God better come. A performer is an addict who mainlines applause rather than heroin.

Tom came through the curtains. "You rock," he said, embracing her.

"No, you rock. I owe you forever," she said. "Who knew? Listen to that."

Tom said, "Hey, gay guys respond to a girl singer like rednecks at a wrestling match."

They had prepared an encore, so Tom grabbed a swig of water out of a bottle on the table, and went back onstage as the applause swelled. Lucy took one more breath, fixed a smile to her face, and went out to cheers and cries of "Brava."

She applauded the audience as well, and gestured towards Tom and said, "Please, a hand for Tom Mandrosian, everyone - cute, right?" Tom got up and did a quick bow, grateful for the attention after a year of banging out the same songs night after night in a succession of dank orchestra pits, and appreciative that Lucy had called him "cute" in a roomful of potentially available men. Lucy said, "Listen, a month ago I didn't know any of this was going to happen, but when I got the opportunity I went to Tom here, who plays for *Fiddler*, and I said, 'Help! I have a show and I got nothing!' And he agreed, and he's a saint, and a catch, and there's no way I could have done this without him, so thanks again, Tom."

Then she said, "I'd like to close with one of my favorite songs, which some of you may remember from my triumphant performance in the twelfth grade at Asheville High School in Asheville, North Carolina." She launched into "Everything's Coming Up Roses." At the climax, the audience went nuclear.

Later, in the dressing room, as Ronny and several of his friends gushed like pubescent boys meeting Batman, Lucy and Tom smiled and dispensed with pleasantries for about fifteen minutes until they both realized they were dead. They gathered their things, said goodbye to everyone and went through the curtains and past the bar, where a gathering of about fifteen people burst into applause as they exited. Lucy was so spent that all she could manage was wave like Queen Elizabeth from a passing carriage.

"I don't think we should change a thing, unless you get some flash of genius," said Tom. "You were born for this shit."

They sat in the hotel bar and went over every aspect of the performance, with Tom making suggestions that Lucy promised to sleep on. And sleep she did, the sleep of a month old cadaver, of a polar bear in the Yukon, of a 96 year old Jew in the Hebrew Home For The Aged. The next morning, Lucy picked up the paper in the lobby and went right to the weekend section.

"FIDDLER" STAR TURNS BLUE WHITE HOT
by GEOFFREY CROSS

Lucy sped-read through the review, wondering how the critic could have possibly written it in such an inebriated state. Perhaps he aspired to be another Eugene O'Neill, thinking drunkenness equals greatness.

Every cabaret fan within shouting distance should hightail it to Blue *to see the hitherto unknown Lucy Dixon, a singer and comic of smashing talents, superb voice and a seemingly endless range.*

It went on to describe highlights of the evening, with nothing but superlatives. Lucy couldn't believe it, until she got to a sentence near the end that she could, alas, completely believe.

Miss Dixon has the potential to be not only a major star, but also major cheesecake, if she would just lay off the cheesecake.

9

A major star. And major cheesecake. Five months later, Lucy remembered those prophetic words as she placed a plate of cheesecake on the restaurant table in front of her customer.

"Thank you," he said.

"Ya welcub," said Lucy.

The clanging noises of the restaurant reverberated like a helicopter landing on her head. It was bad enough being a waitress, and having a miserable cold didn't help. "And whud to drink?" sniffed Lucy at another table, trying not to let her nose drip on her customer.

"Uh, what you want, Harold? Coffee? HAROLD?" the bellicose, sixtysomething redhead nagged at her large, bald husband. He finally spoke with that New York accent that can cut through built up bacon grease: "Coa-fee."

"Me, too, with *real milk*," the redhead said, with a sinister edge implying trouble if the milk was not freshly squeezed from a nearby udder.

Lucy felt like she was suffocating under a diving helmet in an underwater Bermuda tourist attraction. At the coa-fee stand, she blew her nose for the ten thousandth time into a napkin and threw the wadded, soaked bolus into the trash. A pot of coffee was brewing and the nagging redhead would have to wait. Ralph, the crusty Italian bartender who seemed to have been standing in this same spot since before the building was built, eyed Lucy and shook his head.

"You should-a stayed-a home, Lucy. You sick."

"Ben couldn't get anyone to cover me. As long as I don't hack a loogie onto someone's plate, we're good. Table 14 wants a Mai Tai. I'll be back."

That she was sick added to her mortification that she was working here in the first place. After returning from Chicago with glowing reviews, the sweet smell of success and the promise of global superstardom, her career ran into a brick wall faster than a crash test dummy on crystal meth. She had no offers and only a few auditions, some of which were for zero-budget showcases of crappy plays in leaky downtown dumps. One of these was a musical written, composed, produced, directed, choreographed by and starring the same person. When that show opened, a review said, "Perhaps he could host the Multiple No-Talent Telethon."

Evidently, word of her stellar *Fiddler* and Chicago cabaret triumphs had not spread to the Manhattan theater cognoscenti. She was learning the oldest axiom of Broadway: *If It Doesn't Happen In New York, It Doesn't Happen*. Her only showbiz pleasure occurred a few evenings a week singing at Martell's. Some of her friends from *Fiddler* got new jobs right away, and Tom, her pianist, joined the orchestra of *Baby Face*, a long running musical. Lucy got nothing, and went from being the toast of the town to just being toast.

After five months of unemployment, she had no choice but to get a survival job and found it at this Times Square steakhouse, Chuckie's Steak City. Chuckie was a fictional character, like Ronald McDonald. However, the actor who played Chuckie in the commercials and repeated the catch phrase, "Come to Chuckie's and stuff yourself," came to regret ever taking the job because his face became so well known as Chuckie that he was unable to find other work. He filmed several final commercials before hurling himself in front of speeding subway train, and macabre jokes made the rounds all over town: "Come to Chuckie's and snuff yourself."

It was a restaurant catering to the tourist trade and to New Yorkers who wanted a cheap pre-theater dinner. The tables, chairs and booths were all weathered dark wood and the curtains red velvet. Gold encrusted mirrors were placed on every available wall space, so that patrons could watch each other. But no one was interested in watching, since the appearance of many of the customers could ruin one's appetite.

The dinner prix fixe included a steak, baked potato, self-service shrimp and salad bar, and all the beer, wine or sangria one could drink. The sangria was mixed at the bar by pouring cheap red jug wine over ice into a plastic pitcher, then adding ginger ale and 7-Up from the bar's spray gun and topping it off with slices of orange. The customers never knew the difference and routinely drank all the sangria they could drink, occasionally vomiting all the vomit they could vomit.

The restaurant employed an international cast of characters. The hostess was a statuesque Swedish platinum blonde named Katrina who routinely overdressed, as if she were attending the Oscars after work. She swept through the restaurant like a 1940s Hollywood star making grand gestures and calling people "dahling." She attracted even more attention with her husky voice, which was one of the vestiges of her former life as a man named Sven. Waiters would gossip about how she turned out to be such an attractive woman and whether or not she had gone full throttle and actually removed her throttle, but no one had the nerve to ask. Lucy thought she was a riot, the star of her own little show every night.

Many waiters were from South America or Thailand and the cooks from the Caribbean. The clatter of pots and dishes, the sizzle of steaks and the cacophony of languages and dialects made the kitchen sound like a third world train station. The grease on the floor added to the suspense that a waiter or busboy might slip in a slapstick pratfall, sending utensils flying in all directions and potentially stabbing someone in the thigh. A few nights ago, Lucy had slipped on a greasy spot while carrying a tray overcrowded with food and sent five steaks, five baked potatoes, and five broccoli spears flying to their deaths. Adding to the indignity, she fell flat on her fanny and bruised her coccyx. Oscar, a Jamaican cook with whom she had developed a personality conflict, cared only that he had to cook more food and screamed at her like she had just tossed his mama's body into a dumpster.

"Waitress? Hello?" said the redhead. "We asked for coaaaaafee."

"Yes, ma'am, it's coming, " sniffed the beleaguered Lucy, as she cleared empty glasses from the next table. Her ears felt like she was on a flight coming in for a crash landing. She wanted this stupid old bag to die a slow and graphic death right there at table 47. She wanted to stab her with a steak knife and then call the rest of the staff over to watch her slowly expire, her fat body bleeding and oozing on the –

"Jesus, how long could it take to get two cups of coffee?" snorted the redhead.

Lucy prided herself on being a nice person who could get along with anyone, but this perfect storm of exhaustion, humiliation and phlegm caused something from deep within her to snap. Suddenly, the nagging redhead assumed the persona of every person who had ever disrespected Lucy from kindergarten onward. She glared at the woman and blurted out, almost involuntarily, "It will take as long as it takes, lady. We're making some fresh coffee just for you, since this whole restaurant was built just to serve your fat ass, so just ...aaaah...."

She would have finished the sentence and then dramatically exited with a flourish, but she was overtaken by a series of huge sneezes. She dropped the tray of glasses back onto the table, grabbed a used cloth napkin, covered her nose and mouth and loudly sobbed and sneezed, as every customer turned to witness the pathetic spectacle.

From several yards away, Katrina saw that Lucy was in wretched high dudgeon and swooped down to help. "Poor dahling, you should be home. Please excuse her, she is sick and shouldn't be here."

"Well, she's not so sick that she doesn't have a mouth on her," said the redhead. "All we wanted was coffee and she had a cardiac arrest. That's the worst thing I've ever - "

Katrina, equally skilled in both customer service and sarcasm, quickly sashayed over to the bar, reached on a shelf, pulled down a jar of Instant Coffee Crystals, and put it on the table in front of the redhead. "Enjoy," she said.

She took Lucy by the arm, helped her up and said, "Sssh, it's all right dahling, let's get you out of here." The redhead stared at the jar as her husband slowly shook his head in disgust, just as he had done for thirty years with this gorgon.

Lucy changed into her street clothes and snorted, hacked and sniffed her way from the locker room up the stairs to the kitchen. Ben, the rotund manager who resembled a roll of cookie dough dressed as a lawyer, entered the kitchen. "So, you're sick," he said. Lucy nodded her head. "I heard you insulted a customer. The woman complained."

Lucy looked at Ben and said, "I'm sorry, but I was doing my best and I'm sick and it just slipped out and fire me if you want but I couldn't take it anymore and I should be in bed and…aaah…"

Her sentence was interrupted by another sneeze, and then she resumed the sobbing spree she had begun back at table 47. She wasn't crying because she was sick, she was crying because she was sick *and* working as a waitress when she was actually an extraordinarily talented actress and singer, dammit, forced to deal with nasty old redheads and hateful Jamaicans, slipping on greasy spots and injuring her private parts. While she knew these were luxury problems and at least she wasn't turning tricks in the meatpacking district or picking up hypodermic needles on a Vietnamese beach, she still felt like a sick, miserable failure. A prostitute, at least, made more money.

"Go home," said Ben. "Call tomorrow and let us know when you think you can come back. Feel better." That Ben was actually showing kindness was novel, since he hardly said a word to anyone that wasn't an order.

"Thag you," said Lucy, as she exited the kitchen and made her way to the front door, turning her face away from table 47 to avoid the redhead's deathly stare. She was about to indulge in another wave of self-pity when she noticed a corner table where a woman's hair had just caught on fire.

The woman's head was bent over the table to read the menu in the dim light, and the orange glass candle on the table was burning with way too much fury. The top of the woman's beehive had made unfortunate contact with the flickering flame, and she wasn't yet aware that she was soon to reenact Michael Jackson's Pepsi commercial.

Just as Lucy was about to run over to the woman to offer assistance, another waitress, the fiery Puerto Rican Norma Rivera, screamed, "Mira! Mira! Holy shit!" and ran to the woman and grabbed her hair. It was a wig. Norma yanked the flaming coiffure off the startled woman's head, threw it to the floor and doused the burning wig with a pitcher of coke, sending a crackling fizz into the air.

"I sorry lady, but jour hair was on fire, Jesu Christ," said Norma. The woman's hands immediately went to her head, struggling in vain to cover the white wig cap she was wearing. Any hopes of glamour she had for this evening had just drowned in a fiery heap.

Norma turned, caught Lucy's eye, and they stifled laughter. Norma rolled her eyes, and then the woman screamed like she had been stabbed with a screwdriver. The surrounding diners, already having witnessed Lucy's meltdown, were surprised to witness this latest drama. One man said, "I didn't know this place had a floor show."

Norma came up to Lucy, keeping her face away from the woman in the same way Lucy was hiding from the redhead. "How did you know that was a wig?" whispered Lucy, impressed with Norma's rapid response.

"My sister got one just like it, same color an' everythin', got it on 42nd Street. It's cheap and no wonder it lit up. I think the label inside even say, 'Flammable.'"

As Katrina swooped over to comfort the hopelessly embarrassed customer with a thousand "dahlings," Lucy stifled laughter amid her sniffles and made as hasty an exit as possible. What a night. First she had publicly humiliated a woman, and now she had watched a woman be publicly humiliated. It was not ladies night at Chuckie's.

She went outside into Times Square, which even to a jaded New Yorker feels like the most exciting place on Earth. Lucy felt no excitement tonight. She wasn't appearing in any of the surrounding Broadway theaters, so brightly lit with names other than hers. She was a waitress in a dump where people fell on their butts and spontaneously combusted.

Lucy knew that to someone back home raising one newborn while pregnant with another, her New York City life probably seemed the epitome of glamour, like Eva Gabor on a Park Avenue balcony. She knew that people always think the lives of young actors are filled with fashionable parties, freewheeling sexual exploits and close encounters with celebrities. They have no concept of the loneliness, fear and anxiety that accompany a fledgling acting career. On rare occasions, someone becomes a star right away. But for the majority, trying to succeed in showbiz is an endless succession of banging one's head against a brick wall, wiping off the blood, and then banging again in an incessant roundelay of sadomasochism.

To Lucy, everything seemed frozen in a state of despair. Even the mannequins in the department store windows looked depressed. She felt as if her dreams were going up in smoke along with that poor woman's hair, minus the entertainment value.

She eventually felt better, returning to work with a renewed determination to quit as soon as possible, but show business (and life) has its own timetable, and before she knew it she was nearing the end of four long years of working at Chuckie's Steak City.

One especially benumbed night Lucy schlepped about the restaurant, performing her tasks on autopilot with the burned out detachment of a stewardess well past retirement age who wants to open the emergency exit at 36,000 feet so the passengers will be sucked out of her life. Across the metal shelf that separated the rest of Chuckie's kitchen from the cooking area, Lucy handed Oscar the order on the ticket, robotically stating it aloud: "Two New Yorks, one medium, one well, one filet, rare. Are my other New Yorks ready?"

"In a damn minute, they workin', motherfucker," screamed Oscar. Lucy had long ago gotten used to Oscar's perpetual rage. At first she thought it was because he hated her, but then she realized that he hated *everybody*, his job, this restaurant, Jamaica, and Earth. She was just in his line of fire. She rolled her eyes and walked out into the bar area to order another round of cocktails for some annoyingly bacchanalian college kids.

She wasn't in show business; she was in the restaurant business. Her sole contact with showbiz came twice a year when she returned to *Blue* in Chicago, and singing several times a week at Martell's. Auditions, when they happened, yielded nothing other than statements like "You're the best actress we have seen, but we decided to go in another direction," or "Come back when you're older."

How old was "older?" Should she just hang on until she became the next Beatrice Arthur? Since she was now almost thirty, it meant at least ten more years until any breakthrough, and she knew her bleeding corpse would grace the pavement long before that, since she planned to hurl herself out of a skyscraper rather than be a career waitress.

That seemed to be in vogue of late. Several single women had recently made the trip from ledge to street. She had read an article about Amy Vanderbilt, the famous authority on etiquette and manners, who jumped out of a window and splattered on the Manhattan sidewalk. Lucy theorized that she might have finally snapped when a flower arrangement was too big to see the guests on the other side of the table. Lucy wondered, however, why Miss Vanderbilt had not had the proper etiquette to wrap herself in a Hefty bag before jumping, thus avoiding the unsightly mess.

Lucy feared a fate like Mona, the oldest waitress on the staff at fifty-six, unmarried, disappointed and childless, whose frozen smile had vainly tried to hide the creases of regret that encircled her mouth. Mona had sagged in all directions and her hair seemed styled by rodents. An actress who never "made it," she never got a proper job and career because she hoped she still had a chance. She still religiously read *Backstage*, hoping to find auditions for women her age, a rarity since most female roles were for the young and glamorous, the result of too many horned up male writers creating female characters they wanted to sleep with. Only a man would describe nuclear physicist as "brilliant and beautiful, like she poses for *Hustler* between research projects."

One day, Mona saw an ad for a part in a new Off-Broadway show:

JEANETTE, age 50-60, unmarried, disappointed, childless, a waitress at a Manhattan restaurant. Her frozen smile vainly tries to hide the creases of regret that encircle her mouth. She stopped caring about her figure years ago. This character must look her age – no actresses who have had work done, please. Prototype: Edith Bunker ("All In The Family.")

Mona got goose bumps. She wouldn't even have to act. She took the day off from Chuckie's and prepared herself for her first audition in six years. She arrived at the audition in a floral print dress and signed in. She looked around the plain white room, a nondescript waiting area with chairs, large dirty windows and a soda machine. Then she saw at least forty frumpy middle-aged women milling about the room, some attractive and some looking like they had just gotten out of bed. She had no idea that there could possibly be this many fiftysomething actresses still making the rounds, but most anyone who tries to be a professional actor never shakes the feeling that they, too, might get to walk the red carpet at the Oscars. It's a one in a million chance, but *I could be the one.*

Names were called and actresses walked into a separate room, coming out approximately fifteen seconds later. Most quickly grabbed their purses and left, as if fleeing the scene of a crime.

Mona looked at her headshot and resume in her lap. The picture was ten years old, and the resume was haphazardly stapled to the back of it. *It's insane what an actor goes through*, she thought. *Putting one's entire life on a sheet of paper and hoping that some unqualified stranger approves.* Her mind wandered to happier times, when she first arrived in New York from Missouri to enter show business, young and hopeful and full of -

"Mona Reese?"

Her mind snapped to attention and her heart yanked her out of the chair. She quickly brushed her dress with her hands, stood up straight, smiled, and walked into the room. Three men were seated at a long table.

"Hello," said Mona. She handed one of the men her resume. She stood in front of them, hands folded in front. One of the men looked at her and passed the resume to another man, who also looked at her. After not more than ten seconds, the third man said, "Thank you, Miss Reese, that will be all."

Mona smiled tightly and started to leave, then reconsidered and turned to the men and said, "Excuse me, but will I be reading?"

"We're looking for a specific type. Thank you very much."

Feeling like she had been hit in the face with a leg of lamb, she exited the room, grabbed her purse and hurried out. Her face flushed and she fought back tears. After years of not being the type to play a variety of roles, she now wasn't even the type to play herself.

That night, alone in the sixth floor walkup studio apartment she had occupied for twenty-seven years, Mona poured a glass of champagne and drank it. She had another, then another. Once the bottle was finished, she opened a window, stepped out onto the fire escape, stooped down under the waist high rail, gave a little push with her feet, and leapt out into the night air. She sailed through the sky for a few seconds before crash landing onto the top of a passing taxi, denting the roof and frightening the living daylights out of both driver and passenger. The irate passenger loudly cursed and demanded that there be no charge for the ride.

Twelve people attended Mona's memorial service, including Lucy, nine of them co-workers from Chuckie's. No family was present. She died as she had lived: alone.

Lucy was thinking of Mona, who ironically met the same fate as a suicidal actress in *Stage Door*, while waiting at the bar for eight cocktails. Ralph, the bartender, said, "Anything else? Lucy? You stand-a there like you somewhere else."

"Sorry," she said, "I was thinking about Mona."

"Ah, she crazy lady."

Lucy glared at Ralph and could only sigh. He would never understand that Mona suffered what many single women suffer: the feeling that they are missing out on just about everything. New York was full of them. In fact, one building Lucy considered moving into was so filled with spinsters that a young resident informed her, "Beware. If you move in here, you will never marry, never have sex again and go to a lot of opera, so you can experience the passion you won't get otherwise."

After a melancholy evening of annoying customers and substandard tips, Lucy decided she would go to Martell's after work, sing, and go home with the first man who propositioned her. Since a majority of the clientele was gay her chances were slim, but it had been known to happen and she desperately needed some attention, preferably male.

As she arrived at Martell's an hour later, the place was unusually hopping for a Tuesday night. The dark brown wood walls, stained glass window and L-shaped oak bar made her instantly feel cozy. The virtuoso pianist Chuck Alterman was banging a brass band out of those eighty-eight keys. The crowd was singing a raucous call and response "Trouble" from *The Music Man*. Chuck sang, "Oh, we got trouble!" and the crowd answered, *"Oh, we got trouble!"* "Right here in River City" *"Right here in River City!"* Lucy felt her own troubles quickly wash away, as if everyone was saying, *You think **you** have problems? Wait 'till you hear about freaking **River City**!*

Nothing made Lucy feel better than a room full of people singing show tunes. Politics, terrorism, tragedy and disease faded into insignificance when one was swept away by the Broadway songbook. As Chuck pounded out the final notes of the song, the audience burst into applause. Basie, the bartender, saw Lucy and promptly prepared her a vodka and tonic, which she downed in two gulps. "More! Mama's drinking tonight!" she said.

Basie signaled to Chuck that Lucy was in the room, and Chuck, knowing that Lucy was the best singer likely to show up tonight, said into the microphone at his piano, "Ladies and gentlemen, the lovely and talented Lucy Dixon has walked into the room." Half of the audience applauded and whooped, since as regulars they had watched Lucy perform here for years. "And if we behave ourselves, I bet we could coax her up here to sing, how about it, Lu?"

"I better do it before I get too hammered," Lucy shouted across the room, to laughs and applause. She strutted to the piano like Dolly Levi descending the stairs of the Harmonia Gardens Restaurant, and took a seat on the stool she had sat on so many times it had molded to her buttocks. At least there was one place in town she could be a star.

Chuck said, "How about 'Any Place?' I'm on an Arlen streak tonight."

"Sure, great," Lucy said.

They then launched into Harold Arlen's "Any Place I Hang My Hat Is Home," a standard immortalized by a young Barbra Streisand. Lucy sang the hell out of it, almost defiantly: "I'm going where a welcome mat is, no matter where that is, 'cause any place I hang my hat is HOOOME!" as if crying, *I still have a chance in this town, boys and girls!*

The audience responded like Lucy had just given the greatest performance in the history of show business dating back to Aeschylus. Once the applause died down, Lucy said, "Since Mr. Alterman here is in a Harold Arlen mood, how about a few songs from Oz?"

Chuck launched into "If I Only Had A Brain," to which Lucy had written satiric lyrics that made light of her struggles with her weight:

I would not feel quite so spastic, I might feel quite gymnastic

With suitors I'd be faced
All the men would give me money, in a bid to be my honey
If I only had a waist.

The funny, self-deprecating lyrics charmed everyone. At the end of the song, Lucy and Chuck segued into a yearning "Over The Rainbow," which almost caused the already ecstatic crowd to start shimmying on their bellies like reptiles.

After another ovation, Lucy walked through the crowd to the corner of the bar. In her usual seat sat a man who smiled at her. He was slightly attractive and slightly balding, resembling a high school chemistry teacher. He looked to be in his mid-thirties. He smiled and raised his glass to her. "You're great. I'm Leo. Want my seat?" He stood up and offered it to her.

"Why thank you, kind sir." Lucy sat down.

"Buy you a drink?" said Leo, just as Basie put a new cocktail in front of Lucy.

"I sing, so they're on the house, but thanks anyway," said Lucy.

"How come I've never seen you in a show or anything?" said Leo.

"Cause I've never *been* in a show or anything," said Lucy, yelling over the crowd, which had just begun wailing the theme from *Gilligan's Island*. "Actually, I did a year on the road with *Fiddler*, but that was a while ago. I do a Chicago cabaret a couple of times a year and I sing here. I'm still plugging away. What do you do?"

"I'm a producer," Leo said.

"A producer of what? Trouble?" She was just high enough to be playful.

"Shows. You know *Baby Face?* The revival of *Oliver?*"

"Oh my GOD," yelped Lucy, "Do you know Tom Mandrosian, in the pit?"

"Of course."

"He's my guy. He plays for me when I go to Chicago. He's one of my best friends. Tell him I said hi, would you?"

"Of course. You're incredibly talented. There's a part in the show I'm working on that you would be perfect for."

"Right, like I haven't heard *that* ten million times, next thing you'll be asking me to come up and see your casting couch."

"I wouldn't rule that out entirely," said Leo, smiling. Lucy looked at him, felt an instant mutual attraction, and realized she had cornered one of the only straight men in the room. Had she met him in another place she wouldn't have known what to say, but in this joint she was queen. Lucy put her hand behind Leo's neck, pulled his face to hers, and kissed him.

Two hours later, Lucy emerged from Leo's bathroom wrapped in a towel after showering. Leo lay in his huge bed, the sheets up to his waist. Even though she had a slight headache from the liquor and lovemaking, Leo had proved to be just the tonic she needed after all those vodka tonics. He was gentle, romantic and surprisingly had a great body. He had also given her a massage, which earned him extra credit.

The apartment was tastefully furnished and decorated yet somehow devoid of personality. Large canvases of abstract art covered the white walls, and the metallic furniture was covered with colorful pillows. "You either have great taste or – "

"Or I pay someone to have great taste for me, is more like it," said Leo. "I don't know what the hell to do. This was all done by this gal my partner recommended."

"It's very spare and clean," said Lucy, as she sat on the edge of the bed.

"It's OK. It's not really my personality, which would probably amount to *Star Wars* posters all over the place. But I'm not ten anymore. And I have to host readings here, and all that producer crap."

Sobering up, she looked at him, suddenly feeling the slightest twinge of Southern guilt, as if her mother was wagging her finger at her in disapproval from the closet.

"Leo, please don't think I'm a slut. This is the first time I've been with someone since the Eisenhower administration. I just didn't want to be alone tonight, and you're nice. Can I see you again?"

"Of course. I hope so. But I wasn't kidding about my show. There's a part you are right for. How old are you?"

"Thirty in a month."

"Perfect. It's the second female lead. Have you heard of *The Rag Trade*? We've got Lonnie Jones as the designer." Lucy felt so out of the theatrical loop that she hadn't heard of *Annie*, but she had definitely heard of Lonnie Jones, a star and notoriously difficult diva. "Oh, wow. She's supposed to be something."

"She's a nightmare, but her last show made back its investment in five months. Audiences eat her up, so it's worth the headache. But we've been having trouble casting her secretary. We need someone to counter her because in performance she acts like she's going to kill the audience if they don't pay attention. You seem vulnerable and likeable. I could tell the minute you opened your mouth. Are you interested?"

It had been so long since an actual theatrical professional had shown any interest that Lucy's eyes welled up with tears. She lay on the bed next to Leo and looked at him. "If you're not saying this just to get me to sleep with you, of course I'm interested."

"I already got you to sleep with me. If I weren't serious, I'd mumble something about how I have to get up and go to a meeting so you would leave. But I want you to stay tonight, if you will, and I'll make you breakfast tomorrow and then I can take you to meet the team. I can't guarantee anything since the director has final say, as well as Lonnie putting her two cents in, but they will listen to me. I put up half a million dollars for this dog show. Now, would you please get up, turn off the bathroom light, and then come back here?"

10

Eight years later, Leo was the farthest thing from Lucy's mind as she lay in bed in the Big Sur, California hotel. Over the crashing waves, so that she would not disturb other hotel guests, Lucy pushed her face into the pillow to muffle the cacophony of her second orgasm in a row, grabbing the sides of the mattress as if she might fly away, as Zack thrust a few final times before exploding inside her like an overheated hot glue gun. As he did, his drenched body slowly collapsed on top of her backside, and she could feel his heart banging out a house music track. His hands moved to hold hers, feeling her fingers, nails and cuticles. They both lay there, breathing heavily yet at the same time motionless, melted in the glory that is the union of two advanced mammals who know exactly what they're doing.

After what seemed like a few hours but was actually thirty seconds, Zack slowly slipped off and onto the bed, turning over on his back and staring at the ceiling fan. The late afternoon sun, parked over the Pacific, projected bright shafts of yellow orange on the wooden ceiling.

"Damn," he said.

She said nothing.

They lay in a bed in a hotel suite at Ten Trees, a cozy inn in Big Sur overlooking the rocky Pacific coast, surrounded by ten huge trees. Earlier that morning, they had checked out of the Los Angeles hotel after changing their airline reservations to a Sunday return, and sped away in Zack's rental car for a tour of LA. They opted to just drive around and see whatever they could see, since Zack had never seen any of it.

Lucy drove, having been here before, into Beverly Hills, the Hollywood Hills and the San Fernando Valley. She provided a rudimentary commentary about the surroundings, and Zack seemed perfectly content to listen and just look out the window. Occasionally he would remark, "Cool."

They ended up on Hollywood Boulevard, where Lucy photographed Zack standing on the Walk Of Fame above the star of Lucille Ball. When they saw Grauman's Chinese Theater, Zack said, "Ain't that where Lucy Ricardo stole John Wayne's footprints?" He surveyed the Boulevard tourist trap stores and said, "These stars on the sidewalk are cool, but the rest looks like an Indian reservation. Let's get out of here and drive up the coast."

After navigating what seemed like traffic on Academy Award Sunday after a terrorist attack, they finally headed up the Pacific Coast Highway. It was a gorgeous day, and the sunlight enhanced every surface for their viewing pleasure. As they drove along the winding road, the view became more and more spectacular, each cliff and jag thrusting forward like a chorus girl breaking into the front of the line for attention.

They pulled over several times on overlooks, getting out of the car and pausing to take it all in. Zack couldn't get over the staggering natural beauty of the place. "I should have brought Tiffany here and said, 'You wanna know what a coastline is, bitch? *This* is a coastline.'"

He pointed towards a gorgeous home perched on a cliff that seemed suspended in midair and said. "I could live there. Get yourself in one of them Spielberg movies and you could buy that thing."

"Oh, sure, why don't you call him? 'Hey, Steve? How about using Lucy? She'll work real hard.'"

He sat on a large rock. Lucy stood beside him and put her hand on his shoulder, and his hand rose to touch hers as they both looked out over the ocean. Waves crashed against the rocks at what seemed hurricane force, splashing drops of water on their faces. He felt at complete peace, here in the most stunning place he had ever seen with the only girl he had ever really loved. Texas seemed distant, insignificant and stupid. He wanted to leave it behind, never return, and move here and do road work so he could look at this view every day.

After they neared Big Sur around four, Zack suggested that they stop somewhere and eat. When he saw the sign for Ten Trees Inn, he knew. He pulled into the parking lot and they got out and walked into a spacious lobby that resembled a Colorado ski lodge. Zack said, "Wait right here."

Lucy sat on a large chair and thumbed through a decorating magazine on the coffee table, looking at the pictures of beautiful homes and wanting to live in each one for a week at a time, hosting some of those fashionable soirees she had dreamt of so long ago.

Zack returned from the front desk and said, "Come on." He led her down a hallway to the left of the front desk. To her right, behind the desk and a huge stone fireplace, she saw a large open-air restaurant with an overhead roof. But instead of heading into the restaurant, he led her down the hall to the end and stopped at a door, looked back at her, grinned, and produced a key like a magician flashing a coin.

He opened the door and pulled her into the room. It had dark wooden walls and a lazily rotating ceiling fan. A king size bed, with huge yellow pillows and red and orange gingham covers, dominated one wall. Double doors opened onto a balcony overlooking the rocky coast, and the afternoon sun spilled into the room, which screamed for a Conde Nast Traveler spread. Lucy was about to remark at how lovely it was, until Zack grabbed the back of her neck and kissed her, setting off a chain reaction that led to their present sopping wet state.

Zack got out of bed grunting like a corpse with arthritis, having spent considerable energy for the last hour getting reacquainted with Lucy. He went to the open double doors and looked out onto the ocean. He cut a dashing tableau, his naked silhouette outlined in orange and red. Lucy thought that he looked a lot like Romeo in Franco Zefferelli's film *Romeo And Juliet*, which she watched in high school and became so flushed with erotic overkill she almost lost her virginity on the spot.

Lucy thought, *I just got nailed by that. Hooray for me.* For the first time in three years she felt like a human woman alive on the planet. She knew that this had probably been a mistake, but such is life and mistakes are bound to happen. Them's the breaks.

She got up and stood next to him, looking out at the horizon. The sun was seconds from setting, the sky and clouds smeared with changing lines of gold, orange, yellow, deep blue and purple, as if an impatient artist was rapidly painting to keep up with the final crescendo of a symphony.

She put her arm around him. Zack, looking at the sun, said, "Three...two...one...ta dah" as the sun disappeared with a flash and said, "Goodnight, folks." They stared at the stunning sky. The air temperature blanketed their bodies in a warm, dry breeze.

Lucy said, "I feel like we're in a James Bond movie."

"Then you gotta have some Bond girl name, like Pussy Dixon."

"That works."

"Look where we are," said Zack, awash in both post-coital bliss and incredulity at his surroundings. "Can you imagine seeing this night after night?"

"Easily. What I'd really like is a kitchen right here, with the counter facing this way, so I could watch the sun set every night while I cooked."

"There are some nice sunsets in Texas, don't get me wrong, but this beats them all to hell."

"Thanks, Zack."

"Huh?"

"Thanks for coming here to see me and rescuing me in a strange land."

"No problem."

"Can we stay here tonight?"

"Of course. I bought the room till tomorrow. You hungry?"

"Starving. Let's eat. I need to shower. Oh, yeah, our suitcases."

"I'll get them." He moved to the bed, grabbed his jeans, and jumped into them. Just the sight of him jumping into his jeans was hot.

After he left, Lucy went to the bathroom, turned on the shower, and stepped in. It was one of those elegant showers with jets on the sides as well as overhead. Steam filled the bathroom. She let the water roll over her, washing off the entire week, which began with her falling into the ocean on a moonlit night in the Caribbean and ended with her first sex in four years in a sun filled room on the California coast. Talk about whiplash. She recalled one of her lines in *The Importance Of Being Earnest:* "A life crowded with incident, I see; though perhaps somewhat too exciting for a young girl."

Thirty minutes later they sat at a table at the open-air restaurant at the railing overlooking the rocks below. Candlelit lanterns illuminated every table, and patrons engaged in sotto-voce repartee mixed with smooth jazz from a live trio in the corner that created an atmosphere of elegant civility. Lucy was impressed with the cordiality of the hostess, who seemed to embody the whole concept of gracious customer relations. The polite pleasantries of a total stranger somehow made one feel more valued as a human being.

The bottle of Chardonnay and salads had been served. Zack picked at his salad. "I need to get out more. Just sittin' on my ass in Waco ain't doing me no good. This is pretty damn great."

"I'll say," said Lucy, as the chewed a mouthful of salad and looked out over the ocean. The deep blue and purple sky had almost made the transition to darkness. She looked at one particular star and, for some reason, felt melancholy. She paused, took a breath, wiped her mouth with her napkin and looked at Zack. "Can I ask you something?"

"Yeah."

"What are you doing here?"

"Eatin.'"

"You know what I mean."

"Uh, no."

"Why did you come see me?"

"I told you, I just wanted to see you."

"I know, but did ... did you want to start this - us - up again? You and me? After all this time?"

Zack knew this was coming, but he still stumbled through his answer like Frodo Baggins tripping over underwater corpses. "I don't know. Yeah. No. I'll tell you what's the truth. There ain't been one day in twelve years I didn't think about you for a coupla seconds. Even when I was with Tiffany, I thought about what it would have been like if it had been you. I just talked to you the other day and thought, I gotta see her. I never go nowhere and I don't do nuthin.' I reckoned if you weren't cool with it we would just have a drink and I'd go back home. But here's the deal. I didn't know if I would want to get naked with you or not, but one look at your face and I thought, woof. Gal's still got it and I still feel it."

"Thank you," she said. He was the only man who had ever made her feel sexy. And he was her friend. She loved him as much as any friend she had ever had. Anything else was negotiable.

"So I'll go back to Waco, and you'll go back to Asheville or New York or wherever, and I reckon we'll see."

"OK."

"See, our problem always was, we was from two different worlds. It would be sad if it wasn't so damn cliché it's funny. It's damn literary, like you was royalty or some rich person in *Downton Abbey* and I was a servant or some shit." He laughed. Despite his country talk, Zack was smart as a whip.

"I am *far* from royalty," she said. "Look, I just asked because this whole week has been such a mind warp." She looked at him, then out into the dark, and her lip trembled and a tear fell down her cheek. She was on emotional overload, not knowing whether to jump head first into the rocks below or just finish her salad.

"A week ago I was minding my own business, alone on a ship, then….aah! It's too much. I'm going home on Sunday and back to the stupid grocery store on Monday. I'm tired of being resentful every day. I want my life back."

"Let's say I can wave a magic wand and give you everything you want. What is it?"

"Well, um, I'd like to be a working actress again, and I'd like a husband or, failing that, a suitable main squeeze, and I'd like to not have to take care of mom anymore, and, not worry about money, and…"

Tears suddenly fell down her cheeks. She realized that it had been ages since she even considered this question. She just had assumed her dreams had dried up a long time ago and that she would remain at home with her ailing mom, flipping through channels at night and drowning in guacamole.

"Oh, please, I want to be a star, everyone in show business wants that, who am I kidding?" she said, laughing through tears. "If they say they don't, they're lying."

"Well, you're famous now."

"Oh, yeah, famous for being a total klutz," she snorted. "That's great fame. Sheesh."

Zack remembered something someone said in a meeting he had attended: *If you want to be famous, you're condemned to a life of disappointment. Nothing is ever enough.* "OK, just don't think about it now, and enjoy the night. Just don't think for a while. Think about how great it would be to be here all the time."

"You really like it here, don't you?"

"Are you kidding? This is damn paradise." He took her hand. "If what's happened in the last week has shown you anything, it's gotta be that you just never know what's next. So don't worry about it. You'll see."

She wiped her eyes with her napkin, took a deep breath, and said, "OK, awkward moment of reflection over. Next! And *scene*." She clapped her hands together like a clapboard to end the scene, picked up her fork and dug into the salad.

"Listen, I gotta tell you something. Just so you know," said Zack, his eyes darting away uneasily.

"What?"

"Um, I did some jail time. Back before I got rid of Tiffany."

Lucy froze with the forkful of salad in mid air, as if time had stopped, and looked at him. "You were in jail? Why?"

"'Cause, um, one night Tiffany came home drunk, and we had a fight, and I couldn't take it anymore and I got mad at something she said and I slugged her. I hit her harder than I thought. I shouldn't have done it, but I did. Anyway, long story short, she pressed charges and I did four months. When I came home, she was all nice and acting like it never happened, but I knew it was over."

"What did she say? That made you so mad?"

"Um…she told me I would never be man enough for her and some other emasculating crap, and I just hauled off and slugged her. To tell you the truth, she deserved it. She had been banging the biker and lying about it. But I felt awful, having been assaulted myself, you know, so that's why I decided not to fight it and just do the time. But I do have a domestic abuse rap hanging over me, which is one reason I've stayed at the hardware store. At least our family owns it."

Lucy realized that his natural sweetness would probably always be soured by the unwelcome memories of various traumas, forever lurking in the background waiting to strike. She put her hand on his face and said, "It's OK. I understand. What was jail like?"

"Boring as shit. OK, I just wanted to tell you I have temper problems sometime. Maybe I oughta see somebody about it or something." He exhaled, leaned back, rapped his hands on the table a few times, and picked up his fork.

"I hear you. Just don't slug me."

"Never." He smiled a sheepish smile, and said, "OK, let's talk about something else, please."

The rest of the meal was spent talking about places she had been and places Zack wanted to go. He hadn't traveled much out of Texas, and neither had been out of the United States. They talked about movies, the news, and college memories. They sat for two and a half hours and went through two bottles of Chardonnay. Zack knew he shouldn't be drinking, but he was anyway.

That night, they slept. Lucy slept better than she had in weeks, the sleep of a marathon runner at the thirty-mile finish line. Zack slept about the same as he always did. He was blessed with the gift of being able to just conk out, instead of lying awake all night parsing through his problems, like Lucy often did. She knew there was absolutely nothing she could do about a particular problem at three thirty AM in the dark, but that didn't make it any easier.

The next morning, after a breakfast on the patio, they drove up to San Francisco. When they arrived, the city welcomed them with open arms and a jazzy soundtrack, courtesy of the rental car's satellite radio. They drove around Fisherman's Wharf, across the Golden Gate Bridge and back, downtown, Chinatown, and the Castro, where they had a late lunch. Lucy loved the city, as did Zack, who was fascinated by the large populations of homeless people, gay people, and pigeons. He had never seen so many pigeons. Pigeons, and gays, avoid Waco.

At about nine pm, they began the drive back to Los Angeles to stay at the airport hotel for their early flights the next morning. Taking the interstate instead of the coastal route, their ride back was quiet, with the occasional comment about the lack of scenery and repetition of business establishments. Zack said,

"Look at this. It could be anywhere in America - Olive Garden, McDonald's, Exxon, Gulf, Olive Garden. McDonald's, Exxon, Gulf. It's all the same. Small businesses are dying. The only reason our store is still alive is 'cause the Wal-Mart is on the other side of town."

Then, suddenly, Lucy's cell phone rang, having been silent for the entire day. "Hello?"

"Lucy, Jared. Is this a bad time?"

"No, hi, I'm just – we're just – driving back to LA. What's going on?" He never called her on a weekend, much less Saturday night.

"Oh, great, you're still in California?"

"Yeah, an old friend is with me, we've been tourists."

"When are you going home?"

"Tomorrow."

"You can't leave yet. You have an audition at Paramount on Monday."

"WHAT???"

Her voice was so loud that the startled Zack almost drove off the highway and through the windows of Olive Garden, McDonald's, Exxon and Gulf.

11

pg 43

WINTER OF OUR DISCONTENT

Republic Pictures, DIR: August Huff, DP: Salwomir Zsigmond

INT. VEGAS CASINO, NIGHT

The casino is bright, bustling and crowded, the clanging of machines providing constant background noise. JOANNE strolls through the casino, martini in hand, with CHARLIE, looking at the tables and slot machines filled with people of all ages. They look tired and unfocused, their minds not on gambling. Camera stays on them from the front and slowly pulls back as they look to their sides. JOANNE is slightly drunk and slurs her words a bit. CHARLIE appears antsy and nervous.

JOANNE

See that one, over there, in the motorized wheelchair with the oxygen tank, smoking? She just doesn't give a damn anymore. A few years ago, she probably said, "Hell with it, I'm going to eat until I'm as big as a house, and then I'm gonna get a brand new house, 'cause this is America, and I can." Some might say she's miserable, I think she's probably free. *Free at last.*

CHARLIE

How can someone get that fat?

JOANNE

I don't give a damn anymore, either. I'm just going to eat until I'm morbidly obese, in a scooter on oxygen, just like her. I want to be her.

CHARLIE

I didn't marry a fat woman. I'll leave you…

JOANNE

If that's what it takes, Charlie.

JOANNE turns to look at CHARLIE with contempt. Camera stops tracking and slowly moves in close.

JOANNE (con't)

You know, I'm getting really tired of pretending I don't hate you.

CHARLIE

(tight smile) Joanne, please, don't make me kill you right here.

JOANNE

Go ahead. There are security cameras everywhere. I'll be dead and free of you, but you'll go to prison and rot in solitary. I won't be alive to see it, but I don't care, do you hear me? (Her voice rising) I... DON'T ...CARE.

CHARLIE grabs her wrist and liquid spills out of the martini glass. GAMBLERS and DEALERS turn to look at her.

"And...RESET, check the gate, keep rolling," said August, the director. Lucy, playing Joanne, and Billy, the actor playing Charlie, relaxed.

"That was really good, I thought you hated me, with that look in your eyes," said Billy.

"Was it OK?" said Lucy. "This is hard, with all this commotion. It would be so much easier if we were alone in a room."

"Ambience, baby. Is it just me, or does this dialogue suck?"

"A friend of mine said, 'I just learn the lines and pray to God.' So that's what I'm doing." Actually, she thought the dialogue, and the characters, had a *Who's Afraid Of Virginia Woolf?* quality that she completely understood, having performed it in college. She knew instinctively how to look at her husband and despise him.

August emerged from behind the monitor and approached them. He was a hyperactive Brit prone to profane outbursts, but he had won a screenwriting Oscar and was considered an auteur, so everyone put up with his antics. He said, "I cut because some bitch over there was looking right into the lens as you passed her. This is the problem when everyone in background isn't bloody union. We'll go again, just do what you're doing. Remember, everyone around you is festive, but you are ready to kill each other, don't be too obvious, it's deep within. Don't show me too much, the camera is right on you and sees everything. Lucy, when you say 'I don't care' at the end, you can even make the ending louder, like 'I....don't....CARE!!!!' You know, like a crescendo, like you're going up an octave."

"Got it," said Lucy, grateful that August occasionally directed in musical idioms. "What if I actually sang it?"

"Perfect, try it. Let's go."

She took a deep breath. She could not believe she was standing here, in this real Las Vegas casino shooting this authentic location scene for a major motion picture at two AM on a Tuesday. Just two weeks ago she had been summoned to Paramount Studios for an audition when she thought she was on her way back to Asheville, her mom, the grocery store, and an early grave. August Huff, director and writer of the film, entitled *Winter Of Our Discontent*, happened to be watching her *Doug Johnson Live* appearance in his hotel room between conference calls, and thought her vulnerable personality perfect for the role of Joanne. It was a key role and the actress originally cast was fired because, in August's words, she was a mercenary, predatory, rapacious swamp sow.

After she had put Zack on the plane to Texas on Sunday, Lucy auditioned on Monday, read the script like she was born to play it and was hired on the spot, following the unlikely pattern of her life – long periods of nothing interrupted by sudden serendipitous events that seemed to magically occur. She had no clue what the rest of the movie was about, as she was only given her scenes, but they made sense – she was a disappointed housewife with drinking and eating problems who hated her life. Other than the housewife part, it wasn't a stretch.

August was thrilled to find an authentic looking actress who had not yet had liposuction or a facelift. Lucy, to him, was real thing, every lonely woman at the shopping mall staring longingly at the jewelry counter while several annoying kids nipped at her heels. Not only that, she was an unknown giving a great performance, and August knew that if the film was a hit, so would she be. She had already shot two scenes, performed them brilliantly, and had twelve to go. He was thrilled with his genius and out of left field casting choice. Other directors would never have had the brilliance to cast Lucy Dixon. They would have cast Jennifer Aniston and tried to persuade us that she was a real person with actual problems.

"OK, everyone, take two, places, please," said Trevor, the assistant director, through a megaphone. Lucy had never been in a movie, but her theater and TV experience had taught her simply following directions, hitting her mark and saying the words with conviction was probably enough. Lucy and Billy moved several feet back to where they had begun the scene. August, having told the background extras to *NEVER LOOK INTO THE BLEEDING CAMERA OR I'LL FIRE YOUR NON-UNION ASSES* returned to the monitor.

"Background action," said Trevor, into the megaphone. The actors playing dealers and gamblers resumed acting like dealers and gamblers, with appropriate improvisational mumbling. "And ACTION," said August. The camera focused on Lucy and Billy.

> JOANNE
>
> See that one, over there, in the motorized wheelchair with the oxygen tank, smoking? She just doesn't give a -- phhhhhbbbt. I'm sorry. Oops.

"RESET. What happened?" said August.

"Sorry, just a mild stroke," said Lucy, giggling nervously. "My mouth just stopped working. I'm OK."

"See that little nervous laugh you just did? Use that. You're drunk and ready to kill him, and if you don't laugh, you will kill him," said August. "OK, let's go again."

"Quiet please. Background action," said Neil.

"And ACTION,' said August.

> JOANNE
>
> See that one, over there, in the motorized wheelchair with the oxygen tank, smoking? She just doesn't give a damn anymore. A few years ago, she probably said, "Hell with it, I'm going to eat until I'm as big as a house, and then I'm gonna get a brand new house, 'cause this is America, and I can." Some might say she's miserable, I think she's probably free. Free at last.

CHARLIE

How can someone get that fat?

JOANNE

I don't give a damn anymore, either. I'm just going to eat until I'm morbidly obese, in a scooter on oxygen. I want to be her.

CHARLIE

I didn't marry a fat woman. I'll leave you..

JOANNE

That's the idea, if that's what it takes.

JOANNE turns to look at CHARLIE with contempt. Camera stops tracking and slowly moves in close.

JOANNE (con't)

You know, I'm getting really tired of pretending I don't hate you.

She giggles nervously.

CHARLIE

(tight smile) Please, don't make me kill you right here.

JOANNE

(giggling again) Go ahead. There are security cameras everywhere. I'll be dead and free of you, but you'll go to prison. I won't be alive to see it, but I don't care, do you hear me? (Her voice rising) I... DON'T ...CARE.

CHARLIE grabs her wrist and liquid spills out of the martini glass. GAMBLERS and DEALERS turn to look at her, suspiciously.

CHARLIE
This is a casino, dear. They have security. If you cause a scene, they'll arrest you.

JOANNE
I truly do not give a damn. Let them. At least in jail I'll have some peace.

A SECURITY GUARD approaches them.

GUARD
Is there a problem?

CHARLIE
No, sir, we're fine, she's just –

JOANNE
Yeah, there's a problem, my husband is a jerk, that's the problem, Officer. Arrest this man. He's a JERK.

GUARD
OK, ma'am, let's go.

CHARLIE
I'll take her back to the room, sir, she's had too many –

JOANNE
I've had too many of YOU is what I've had. Hey, everybody, I'm gonna get as fat as that bitch over there so my husband will leave me!

GUARD takes JOANNE by the arm and leads her away. CHARLIE stands there helplessly as the crowd looks on, a few of them mumbling to each other.

"And CUT," said August. "Perfect. Print it. Bravo, Billy, well done, Lucy. You're brilliant. You reek of the staggering emptiness of suburban middle age."

"I do? Oh, my," said Lucy.

August said, "I do believe that's a wrap for tonight, talent. Tomorrow we have to wrap the pool scene before eleven or the rental on this bloody hotel doubles, so see you in about six hours, everyone."

EXT. HOTEL POOL, DAY

Sunshine pours onto the pool deck, alive with activity – swimming, sunbathing, people having cocktails. The mood is festive and noisy. Camera pans across, ending on JOANNE and CHARLIE seated on lounges, JOANNE in swimwear and protected by a large sun hat and sunglasses, CHARLIE in a swimsuit and T-shirt, seated facing JOANNE with his feet on the ground. JOANNE is clearly in distress.

CHARLIE

If you just … you turn into another person when you drink that much.

JOANNE

I don't … think I'm another person entirely, I just say what I'm –

CHARLIE
Do you really hate me? Do you? Because I love you.

JOANNE looks at CHARLIE, says nothing, removes her glasses and looks at him.
CHARLIE (con't)
I just wish you hadn't gone away. When you drink, you go away.

JOANNE'S eyes well up with tears. She is clearly having a hard time with what she should say. CHARLIE reaches over and takes her hand, and then she starts crying.

"And CUT! DAMMIT!" screamed August, as a beach ball landed in Lucy's lap just as she began emoting for the camera. 'IF YOU'RE GOING TO THROW THE BLEEDING BALL, THROW IT BEHIND THE PRINCIPALS, FOR GOD'S SAKE! Are you OK, Lucy?"

"Yeah, I'm fine, I was just getting in the mood, and that sort of killed it."

"Trevor! Do something about these idiots! And I only want the extras with good bodies up in the front! The audience DOESN'T WANT TO SEE FAT PEOPLE at the pool! This is Vegas, they see enough of them on the street!" screamed August, as he walked away. Trevor proceeded to corral the fat people to the rear.

"Then he should put me in the back," said Lucy.

"You're the star of the scene. He has to let you stay here," said Billy. "Wait, that came out wrong."

Lucy suddenly found this hilarious, and burst into laughter. Billy smiled and started laughing as well. "Wait, I didn't..."

"I know, I know," laughed Lucy. "How hilarious would that be, we do the scene in the back because I'm fat?"

"Stop laughing, you have to cry," giggled Charlie.

August returned from yelling at Trevor, and the fat extras, to find his two principals laughing. "And what's this, then?"

"I'm sorry, we just got tickled," said Lucy. "We'll be fine."

"All right, everyone, let's go again. The fucking clock is ticking."

"You ought to watch the language, there are kids over there," said Trevor.

"They're being paid and they can deal with it, this is show business, not bleeding day camp," barked August.

This outburst made Lucy and Billy laugh even harder, and they desperately tried to stifle it.

"All right, you may find this funny, but I GUARANTEE you it's not, Lucy. Now let's do this again, this has to be done just right or it's bad soap opera. It's a very delicate balance. I want to see real pain, not acted bullshit. So far, both of you are acting like you're on *Days Of Our Fucking Lives*. Now let's have some honesty, dammit. Let's go again. Ready? And ACTION."

> CHARLIE
>
> If you just ... you turn into another person when you drink that much.
>
> JOANNE
>
> I don't ... think I'm another person entirely, I just say what I'm –
>
> CHARLIE
>
> Do you really hate me? Do you? Because I love you.
>
> JOANNE looks at CHARLIE, says nothing, removes her glasses and looks at him.
>
> CHARLIE (con't)
>
> I just wish you hadn't gone away. When you drink, you go away.

Lucy looked at Billy, began tearing up, and then burst into laughter yet again. It was clear that she had the helpless giggles, with only several hours of sleep before she had to report to the set two hours ago.

"CUT! DAMMIT Lucy, what's so funny?"

"I'm sorry, August, I just ... Aaah! You called it *bleeding day camp*."

"Oh yeah? You can't stop? How about I replace you with one of those cows in the background? That will get you to stop. Or how about I send you the bill when we go overtime? Shouldn't be more than several thousand bleeding dollars, not to mention the bloody equipment rental. How about we just forget the whole bleeding picture so you two can have a laugh fest and then you can go back to bloody Alabama or whatever hole it is you come from and take care of your mum? Would you like that? How about you go back to the bleeding cruise ship and fall off the deck again? Might get you some more attention."

Lucy looked at August, and her smile vanished faster than a sand sculpture in a windstorm. She looked, and felt, like she had just been slapped. Her eyes filled with tears.

"And ACTION," yelled August. "ACTION! LET'S GO, ACTION!!!"

>
> CHARLIE
> If you just ... you turn into another person when you drink that much.
> JOANNE
> I don't ... think I'm another person entirely, I just say what I'm –
> CHARLIE
> Do you really hate me? Do you? Because I love you.
>
> JOANNE looks at CHARLIE, says nothing, removes her glasses and looks at him.
>
> CHARLIE (con't)
> I just wish you hadn't gone away. When you drink, you go away.
>
> JOANNE'S eyes well up with tears. She is clearly having a hard time with what she should say. CHARLIE reaches over and takes her hand, and then she starts crying.

                    JOANNE

I'm...I'm...so tired of it. So tired. I just can't seem to ... dredge up the sincerity anymore. I just want to end it.

                    CHARLIE

Why?

                    JOANNE

(she looks at him, hard) Charlie, that I have to explain anything to you at all should tell you everything you need to know. We're done, baby. We're done. Just let me go. Please.

JOANNE sobs, and CHARLIE looks helpless. A WAITER approaches them.

                    WAITER

Bar service?

                    JOANNE

I'll have –

                    CHARLIE

No, no thank you. We're fine. We're just ... fine.

                    JOANNE

Right. We're fine. Right.

"And CUT," screamed August. "Beautiful, perfect, Lucy. Bravo."

Several crewmembers applauded. Lucy wiped her face with her hand.

She was realizing that August was someone who would do whatever it took to get the emotion out of the actor, be it compliments, insults or threats of violence. All August had to do was to remind her what she could be doing instead of this, and she instantly became a basket case.

"OK, hold that, darling, we're going to do it two more times for additional coverage. Stay with it, Lucy. Ready? And ACTION!"

Lucy and Billy performed the scene two more times, each time better than the last, since her crying jag had started and she was weeping like a spinster deserted at a train station. After August called a wrap for the scene, he embraced her.

"Sorry if I was rough, but it was a rough scene and it wasn't happening and I had to do something. You're going to get nominated for a bleeding Oscar for this if you keep this up."

"Please," said Lucy, wiping her eyes. "I don't know what I'm doing."

"You have an authentic quality that you can't fake, believe me. You seem jolly on the surface but miserable beneath. Your forced smile masks the agony. You are a classic American archetype – the woman who thought she would find fulfillment in husband and children and got none of it. The original desperate housewife."

"Oh, dear. Well, thank you, I guess."

"You just keep doing what you're doing, darling, and if I yell at you again, and I will, it's all for art." He kissed her on the forehead and walked away. "That's a wrap for this location, everyone. Onward to Denver."

The next day Lucy flew to Denver, where she spent ten days and shot most of her remaining scenes, usually domestic scenes of forced smiles masking the agony. They were shot out of order, and she never knew what mood she was supposed to be in until she got to the set. Movies have little or no rehearsal, something she wasn't accustomed to. You are just expected to show up and give a fully formed performance, like performing open-heart surgery without going to medical school.

August had more than a few screaming fits, sometimes directed at her. But she tried to be grateful and do as she was told. After all, she was only cast in this picture because of a TV appearance talking about her ridiculous experience on the ship, not because she was in demand as a screen goddess. It was either this or watch soap operas with mom.

Her final scenes, one of which involved sixteen takes of fending off unwanted advances by her ex-husband, requiring her to scream for a day and a half, were filmed at a soundstage in Hollywood after the company wrapped up in Denver. August hollered so much she thought he was going to attack her himself, and then would hug and kiss her at the end of the scene and proclaim her brilliant. She could only imagine the horror of his kinky private life.

The last acting job she had had was nearly four years ago doing a classic stage comedy, and now she was doing this deadly serious domestic tragedy, yet another British director's take on the emptiness of American suburbia. After this, she couldn't wait to be in a musical, preferably a stupid one like *Dames At Sea*. She was thrilled to be working again, but so emotionally spent she felt like staring at the TV for a solid week watching nothing but endless *Lucy* episodes.

But it was here in Hollywood she truly felt that she was in a real movie, showing up at the Paramount lot and walking through the same gates as had Marlene Dietrich, Cecil B. DeMille and Popeye. In an odd way she felt like she was finally living her MGM dream, but with screaming and crying instead of tap dancing. She had not seen the other scenes with other actors so she still didn't really know what the movie was about. She just wanted to come out of it with her dignity intact.

At the conclusion of her final scene, August said, "Ladies and gentlemen, that's a wrap for Miss Lucy Dixon, star of tomorrow!" The cast and crew applauded and a beaming Lucy embraced August and said, "Thank you, thank you for rescuing me. I thought I was finished."

"Darling, you're just getting started," said August.

The next evening, she landed at the Asheville airport. After she collected her bags, she was momentarily surprised to see no limousine waiting to whisk her home, until she realized, *oh, right, I'm home.*

"Taxi?"

12

Lucy and Dr. Perooj Bejravi, known as Perry, looked out over the gorgeous Asheville scenic vista. "I never get tired of these mountains. Whenever I feel worried about something, I just take a drive up here and look around. It's so gorgeous, don't you think?" said Lucy.

"This makes Morocco look like a box of cat litter," said Perry.

Lucy laughed. They have cat littler in Casablanca? Of course, they must.

They were parked at a rest area on the Blue Ridge Parkway, about ten miles outside of downtown, overlooking the ridge to the valley below and the mountain range in the distance, a pastoral velvet of green, blue and purple. Lucy thought that this was as good a spot as any for him to see the natural beauty of her home state. It also kept them away from her mother.

"It's funny," said Lucy. "Being back here makes me realize how beautiful it is, and when I was a kid I couldn't wait to leave it."

"It is the opposite for me," said Perry. "When I was young, I loved my country. It is now I want to leave. This is indeed very beautiful. My country doesn't have this much green. Most of America like this?" asked Perry.

"Oh, no. The U.S. is everything. Some of Pennsylvania is like this. The Southwest is desert, like your country I would imagine. The Midwest is flat. I was just on the California coast recently. Mountains on one side, cliffs and ocean on the other. Very dramatic. I wish you could see it."

"So do I," he said, "maybe next time." He flashed his smile, that dazzling smile that gave her chills, like four giggling eunuchs had just teased her skin with a hundred feathers. He was, without question, the strangest, most exotically beautiful man on the face of the Earth, and he was sitting here in her Toyota. She was alternately talkative and tongue-tied, like she had a just popped a Vivarin into a mouthful of rubber cement.

When she had returned home ten days ago, her mother told her of the doctor's message. He had watched her on *Doug Johnson Live* on the ship, which mortified her, since she thought there was no way he would witness her mention the "very handsome doctor." He also said that he was interested in "her offer."

"What offer? What did you offer him?" asked Ida.

"He said he had never seen America, and I told him he was welcome to come here and I would show him our part of the country, mother, I didn't think in a million years he would actually do it."

"You invited a strange Arab to my house?"

"He's not a *strange Arab*, he's a very nice doctor, from Casablanca, and he said he had a few weeks before he was going back to Morocco and, I said, come see me."

"*Come see me?* You just invite strange men to fly into town at the drop of a hat? What if he's a terrorist? He saw you on TV, what if he thinks you're rich and wants to kidnap you and make me pay? I don't have any money."

"For heaven's sake, there are some nice Arabs."

"Oh, yeah? Who?"

"If he was a terrorist he wouldn't be a doctor on a ship."

"You never know, Lucretia. Don't you read…"

"I am not going to have this stupid conversation."

"What if he comes?"

"What if he does? He would be the most interesting thing to walk into this house in like, ever. I'll just email him back and see what he says."

"You should never have gone on that cruise. You fall into the ocean and make a fool of yourself, then you're on TV apologizing to the country, then you're in California with your old boyfriend, then you're in a movie where they made you cry all the time, now you're inviting Arabs into the house. What next? A neighborhood orgy? Have you thought about your job?"

"If I ever see that godawful store again, mother, I'll stab myself. I'm quitting. I told you, I'm going back to New York. We've been over this. As soon as my tenant's sublease is up, I'm going. Jared says there have been calls for me, and I'm going back while I have some heat. Otherwise, it will be all over. Now please, give me the message."

Reluctantly, Ida reached into her purse and gave the note with Dr. Bejravi's details to Lucy, who then hightailed it to her laptop and emailed him. She had insisted that her mother install wireless Internet service, for three years Lucy's only link to her other world. Ida didn't understand any of it, saying, "This whole Internet business has just passed me right by."

Dear Dr. Bejravi –

I was so surprised to hear from you. It has all been quite the adventure. My mother said that you were interested in coming to visit. My door is always open, so please let me know when you think you might be coming, and for how long.

Sincerely, Lucy Dixon

She later regretted saying, "my door is always open," because it implied that *she* was always open. But two days later came the reply:

Miss Dixon –

How do you do? I have arranged to visit relatives in Brooklyn, New York, with an extra trip to Washington, DC. I must be in New York on 23 September, but I leave the Seafarer *on 21 September. Should you be available, I would like to come to your city for a day on my way to New York. You could show me the "real America," as you say. I will of course make hotel arrangements through the* Seafarer. *Please advise me as to your availability. I remain*

Yours, Dr. Perroj Bejravi

PS – Please call me Perry, as does everyone in the West.

The very wordage in his email gave her shivers, like he was blowing into her ear while examining her vulva. "I remain..." *I remain???* Who writes like that in America? Nobody since Edith Wharton.

They exchanged more emails and made plans for him to visit in eight days, which filled her with both excitement and dread, like she was awaiting the results of a pregnancy test. What did she think she was doing? Their entire acquaintance had been a few minutes in the ship's medical center while she was a wet mess. Did he have intentions, or just an urge to see grass? Lucy thought of calling Zack for advice, but then thought better of asking a man she had just slept with whether or not she should sleep with another.

Her sister Joan weighed in on the phone: "My God, girl, your dance card is on fire. First Zack, now this. You should fall off ships more often."

"I don't know what to think. Why do you think he's coming?"

"Honey, when a guy gets on a plane to come see a girl, it ain't for cooking lessons. Hey, if he's the knockout you say he is, I'd jump at it. You'll probably never see him again, unless you get a gig in Marrakech or wherever. I have a better idea – send him to me. I've had it up to here with hyperactive teenagers and a doped up husband. I'd love for Ali Baba to bang the bejeesus out of me for a few days."

Lucy had always been slightly jealous of Joan, the cute one who always got the boys, and Joan knew it. When Lucy had returned to her dad's funeral while working on Broadway, Joan looked at Lucy and said, "How the tables have turned."

"What do you mean?"

"When we were kids, I got all the attention. Now it's you. Now I'm the one who is envious."

Lucy wanted to say, *don't flatter yourself, honey, I didn't envy you that much.* But she didn't. Joan was stuck in a loveless marriage to a prescription med addict who occasionally would sleepwalk into the yard and urinate on the house next door, and with delinquent teenage boys who were prone to things like shattering windows, wrecking cars and snorting cocaine in a 7-11 parking lot. Joan had it rougher than Lucy.

When Perry arrived at the Asheville airport from Miami at noon, Lucy was waiting. He was impossible to miss, clad in a tight long sleeved black T-shirt and black jeans that hugged every curve of his torso, with his long black hair hitting his shoulders. He oozed international glamour, while the other passengers looked like they worked in a cafeteria.

"Miss Dixon," he said, as he shook her hand.

"Lucy, please."

After they exchanged nervous pleasantries, she drove him to his hotel. She had no idea why the *Seafarer* agents had booked him into the Foggy Mountain Court on Tunnel Road, a fifth-rate motel that doubled as a flophouse for afternoon assignations at an hourly rate. She invited him to stay at her home, but he declined. She thought it just as well. Her mother would freak out at the thought of a strange Moroccan sleeping down the hall.

Lucy waited in the lobby while he got settled in his room, and then he emerged to "drive around and just look," as they had decided on the drive from the airport. Lucy insisted that he come to her house for dinner that night, and he accepted. Ida was able to cook again, and Lucy would assist her in preparing a classic Southern meal of fried chicken, fried okra, black-eyed peas and greens.

"Let's go outside," said Perry.

They got out of the car and walked to the edge of the rest area, looking at the vista. Lucy tried grabbing at whatever conversational straw she could, like her speech button was set on shuffle. "There are a lot of legends about these mountains. Some say witches lived here many years ago. Nice weather today, right? We have a craft fair every year downtown, and square dancing and country music. The people who live here are mostly nice people. Good quality of life. Is Casablanca like the movie? Are you hungry?"

"I would imagine, like a lot of the people in my country, they work, raise their families, see friends, and that's it," said Perry.

"Yeah, I guess so," said Lucy.

"And you do not have the call to prayer five times a day."

"Oh, you just can't hear it, but there's plenty of praying around here, believe me."

Perry had a precise, stiff way of speaking that she guessed was probably the result of learning English as a second language, as well as a career of speaking medical jargon. Where Zack spoke like a cowboy, Perry spoke like a Middle Eastern diplomat being interviewed on *60 Minutes*.

Perry looked at the gorgeous mountain vista, took a deep breath and stretched his arms out, as if to embrace the scenery. He saw a rickety cabin perched on the side of one hill and immediately wanted to move in to it, become a hermit and not speak to anyone for a year. The thought of returning to Casablanca and its heat, dust, overpopulation, noise, poverty and oppression made him nauseous, like he had just eaten spoiled Moroccan Chicken Mezgueldi. For a brief moment, this place made his homeland seem like a burning cesspit. He turned and looked at Lucy. She was different from Moroccan women. There was something fresh and open about her.

There was a long pause. Lucy could feel the nervous electricity between them. She looked at him. Here was the second man in a row who had flown in to visit her, for reasons not entirely clear. Had she suddenly become irresistible? She was *very* confused, but decided to just ask, as she had with Zack.

"Tell me something, why did you come? Here?"

He looked at her with black satin eyes that drilled a hole through her body, down her alimentary canal directly to her coccyx. "I will tell you. First, you invited me, and I have not been invited to America by anyone on the ship before, ever. Second, I arranged to visit my cousin Hajab in New York, and you were on the way, and I thought, why not? I saw you on TV and you were very charming. Tomorrow I will fly to New York. Perhaps we will see each other again, perhaps not, but I am grateful that you have given me this opportunity to see a little of your country."

She felt better, relaxed a bit, and imagined what a kiss from those lips would be like. She thought a second, and then, remembering her acting training to be "in the moment," decided she might as well go for it. What the hell? She reached up and touched his face and said, "Well, thanks for coming. This is unusual, and – "

He looked at her, moved in, and planted an Arabian whopper on her lips.

Bedouins erected an oasis in her mouth. Camels made orgasmic camel noises. Arab women shed their hijabs and danced naked in the town square, openly defying Muslim authority. Cobras hissed and threatened passers-by who would threaten her pleasure. Omar Sharif had unprotected sex with Barbra Streisand.

As she pulled away she was overcome with an avalanche of insecurity. Bereft of male attention for years, she was suddenly Miss Universe.

"Woah," she said.

Perry looked at her. "I am grateful you made the first move, I was not sure," he said, brushing his hair back with his hand. No doubt about it, he was one hot steaming plate of tahini.

"Um...I ... I'm sorry, I just ... don't understand why you are attracted to me. I mean, forgive me... "

Perry's eyes were disco lasers aimed dangerously at her pupils. "You're a very beautiful woman. Don't ask questions." He took the back of her neck in his hand and kissed her again, and she was in a Persian market filled with music, spices and screaming barkers, tourists bargaining for cheap rugs, belly dancers shimmying and clinking wind chimes.

She reached around his waist and held it, a cement wall with a flesh coating. She kissed him, and he kissed her, or both, for the foreseeable future. Her nerves did a confused square dance, do-si-doing and changing partners and promenading.

After what seemed like the longest kiss since James Stewart and Kim Novak in *Vertigo*, she pulled away. Her nerves stopped dancing and applauded the square dance caller. Her mind cleared. At last, she knew what to say.

"Perry, can I say something? I'm, um, how do I say this?"

"Just say it."

"OK, well, OK, um, how do I? Um, I can't sleep with you. Not yet. I've been through too much, and the fact that you're here is kind of freaking me out. Can we just, um, call this our first date?"

"Why not?" he said, flashing that transcontinental smile. "If something happens in the future, we will see. I am glad to be here with you. It is enough."

"Cool. That's great." She took a deep breath. *Good. That's over with. Should I have said it? He's really gorgeous and I want – oh, shut up. I can't go sleeping with every guy who shows an interest, no matter how boring the last three years have been. I'm a good Southern girl. On paper, at least.*

"Anyway, you're the world's greatest kisser. I just need to wait for anything else."

"I do too."

"You do?" She couldn't imagine a man wanting to wait for anything involving sex.

"Yes. I must clear up things with my wife."

"Your...?" Her nerves, waiting for their next square dance call, collapsed onto the floor.

"Yes."

"You're *married?*"

Perry held up his hand, in a gesture of reassurance. "It was arranged by our parents, and we never loved each other. We learned to get along well enough. She is a teacher. We have a son who is thirteen. You would love him; everyone does. But I tired of living with her in this fiction, so I went out to sea. Now that our son is old enough, I want to end it and set both of us free."

Lucy looked at him as if perusing a strange sculpture in an avant-garde art museum. "Wow. An arranged marriage."

"They do not have that here, I assume."

"Oh, God, no. It's hard enough on people who actually like each other. How did you – how old?" She was suddenly fascinated with this ancient custom foisted on the modern world, and Perry abruptly morphed from a hot Arabian fantasy into a three dimensional human being with an actual backstory.

"Our parents were very traditional. When children are of age they are expected to be married whether they like it or not. I waited until I was twenty-three. I was in love with a young Saudi girl my parents did not approve of. She was a modern girl who ignored her religion and her family's wishes and did what she wanted. She loved to dance, get drunk, and make love. She wanted to be a lawyer. And one day her father cut off her head."

Lucy gasped, but said nothing.

"For honor, you see." Perry looked out into the valley, his expression turning sad and wistful. "Most Moroccan men are not like that, but her father and mine were both religious fanatics. They would have been perfectly happy as Taliban in Afghanistan. My father expected me to be like him, and I refused, but I was afraid. He made my mother's life a living hell, and I was happy when he died."

Lucy, again, had no response.

"My father said my girlfriend was a whore who got what she deserved. I did not say anything, but I never forgave him. It was not long after that I was married to the daughter of his business associate. We met the day of the ceremony."

"Was that weird?"

"We thought it was the end of the world. It was not, but we never felt comfortable around each other. We only made love when our parents would not shut up about grandchildren. She was not a virgin and afraid that I would beat her when I found out, as many men do. I did not care. I just wanted to stay with her long enough to one day be able to get out. We have never had much to say to one another. This conversation is more interesting than my marriage."

She looked at him, and his revelations made him even more stunning. She wanted to massage his world-weary bones in essential oils.

"I make enough money to send back home and care for my family. Most of the men on the ship are in the same situation. They are home for four months and out at sea for eight. It seems to work. I am not sure what my future holds. I will be in Morocco for four months and then I have another contract with the *Seafarer*. Someday I may leave Morocco. I would..." His voice trailed off.

"You would what?"

Perry paused, and then said, "I would like to leave it and never speak of it again."

He looked into the distance. Lucy then tried to lighten the mood. "I'd love to go there some day. I've never been out of this country. Morocco is really conservative, right?"

"They say it is one of the most liberal Arab countries, but that is like saying Saddam Hussein had a great personality."

Lucy laughed.

"Someday maybe I will have a real marriage," he said.
"And you?"
"Me? Who? Oh. What about me?"
"Were you ever married?"

"No, no. Not me. I was sort of married to my work before I came back here to care for mom. It might have happened once with someone, if we hadn't lived in two different worlds."

"Of course."

"I seem to meet men who are unavailable. Either they live in a different city or just act like they do. Hey, you know what? Let me take you somewhere really cool."

"Why not?" He smiled and moved towards the car, but first leaned in and pecked her on the mouth. *Woof.* She felt relaxed, happy, and attractive.

An hour later they were visiting the Biltmore House, the largest private mansion in America, long the property of the Vanderbilt family. Perry was impressed by this ostentatious show of American wealth, but he noted that it had nothing on the ludicrous opulence of the Middle Eastern palaces.

"I have never needed such money. How many rooms can I be in at once? What do I need with a bowling alley?" he said.

"Oh, I'll take the money, but I'd buy several homes. I just saw one on the California coast I would buy in a second. And a nice New York penthouse, of course, where I could host fashionable soirees. You could come to one."

"What is soirees?"

"Parties."

"Why not?"

He seemed so nonchalant about everything, as if nothing mattered but what was happening right now. She thought she could learn from this, since she spent most waking hours regretting the past or dreading the future. Just being here, right now, with the gorgeous doctor, seemed enough, yet the endless loop in her head of her mother's suspicions couldn't help bubbling to the surface – *what does he want with me?*

Later, when they arrived at her house, Ida was waiting at the door. When she saw Perry, she lit up like an electric Santa Claus lawn ornament and said, "Oh, my." Ida had set the dining room table for company and the candlelit room was homey and inviting.

"I am very grateful for you for hosting me," said Perry, taking Ida's hand. "This is a new experience for me. A dream come true. I have felt today that I am beginning to see the real America."

"You ought to take him and show him a trailer park over in Weaverville with some of them snaggle-toothed folks, that ought to do it," laughed Ida. Perry's presence seemed to wake Ida from a long sleep. He was not only the most interesting man who had been in the house lately; he was the only one. Ida clearly found him as stunning as Lucy did and he made Ida suddenly wish she was a young available Arab woman, a feeling she hadn't had in, well, ever.

Over dinner, Perry entertained them with stories of his exotic childhood in a traditional Moroccan home, his career, and how Morocco suffers from a shortage of doctors since so few can afford medical school. Perry's superior intelligence and specialty in cancer studies catapulted him to the first rank, but the chaotic and crowded hospitals made practicing medicine a chore, which was one of the reasons he started working on ships. The working conditions and pay at sea were better than at home. "On a ship, I see one patient at a time. At home, I see five."

The ladies were transfixed, and he continued. "I seem to be in a place where I want to throw everything in my past away and start over again. Life in Morocco feels like someone is hitting me over the head with a – how do you say? What you dig a hole in the ground with."

"A shovel," said Lucy.

"Yes, a shovel. It is so quiet and beautiful here."

"It can get boring," said Ida.

"I will take boring," said Perry, smiling.

"Well, my life feels like a complete bore next to yours, that's for sure," said Ida. She also thought, *we really do have it better here in America.*

Lucy said, "I just remembered, I wanted to ask you this – what were people on the ship saying about me after I left?"

Perry sheepishly smiled. "Are you sure you want to hear it?"

"Uh, yeah."

He paused and said, "Most people thought you were probably some crazy lady who had a bad marriage or something. It gave some crewmembers another excuse to speak ill of Americans, who have a reputation on ships as the most difficult guests. There were all kinds of stories, and most of them didn't have anything to do with your reality. I had met you, so I told anyone the truth who asked me."

"Thank you so much," Lucy said. "I figured as much. What else would they think?" She laughed and momentarily excused herself. When she was gone, Ida looked at Perry.

"Doctor, can I ask you a question?"

"Certainly."

"What are your intentions with my daughter?"

Perry smiled. "They are honorable, I assure you. She asked me to come. I'm here. Tomorrow I will be gone. That's it. Perhaps I will see her again, perhaps not. But she is very nice, and I wanted to accept her invitation. I wanted to see some of America."

Ida smiled and nodded, and was torn between fantasizing about an exotic wedding for Lucy with a Middle Eastern flair that would impress the neighbors or worrying that Perry would whisk Lucy away into white slavery. At the end of the evening, after Ida said good night, Lucy drove Perry back to his motel. It had been a long, nervous and fascinating day, and she found that she was exhausted from the sheer novelty of it. Perry gave her a kiss before he retired to his room, just a quick one that left no time for a Moroccan bandir drum to start playing in her head.

"Sweetie, that man is either the biggest con-artist in the world or a real catch," said Ida, the next morning. "Lord have mercy, he looks like a movie star."

"I know."

"I just can't figure out what he's doing here."

"Me neither."

"He's a strange man from a strange country where they cut off people's heads. And he wants to leave his country. Maybe he wants to move in here and make us sleep in the basement. You be careful, now."

"Oh, please, I don't see how it could go anywhere. He lives either in Morocco or on a ship, and it will be Judgment Day before I go on a ship again."

"Well, honey, you're not going to meet a man sitting in this kitchen."

"Wait a minute – I actually meet a man who *flies into town* to see me, and now you're all suspicious and warning me about him. Make up your mind. Anyway, I'm going back to New York, and what happens will happen. Stop trying to get me married off."

"I'm your mother."

"I'm aware," she said. She kissed Ida and then went to the car, drove to Perry's motel and picked him up to go to the airport. "Someone was having a party in the next room," he said. "They were up very late. There was banging on the wall. I think that motel is for people of a certain underclass."

"You mean trash," she said. "I don't know why in the world they put you in this dump."

"The company is not interested in giving me a luxury vacation."

"Well, that's another side of America you got to hear."

Perry was even more fascinated with this interesting American woman, unlike any he had met. She was smart, funny, and personable. He was used to women who literally hid behind a veil of state sanctioned modesty. With Lucy, it was there for all to see. How refreshing.

At the airport, Lucy made sure he was properly checked in. He looked at her and blinked those eyelashes that looked personally styled by Max Factor himself, and said, "Thank you very much, Lucy. I will not forget your kindness. You have my email, so please keep in touch. Until next time."

He then leaned in and kissed her, and she heard the Islamic call to prayer played by Lawrence Welk of Arabia, who galloped past them while chasing robbers and repeating, "A-one and a-two…." Then a Moroccan dog barked.

Woof.

13

The crowded Casablanca market was almost too much for Lucy, as the sights, sounds and smells made her ears ring, her head hurt and her lungs fill with saffron seasoned exhaust. Broiling sun scorched the skin like lasers from an alien ship. Everything was a swirl of brown, black, gold, beige, yellow, red and purple. Endless kiosks selling unidentifiable food, trinkets, clothes, hookahs, electronics, jewels, fruits, cigarettes, magazines, DVDs, rugs, glass, spices, dogs, cats, brassieres, headdresses, hamsters, chickens, and snakes competed for space on the dusty street with the pedestrians, who seemed to have no sense of personal space, crashing into one another like drunken sailors on shore leave.

This went on for blocks and blocks, and Morocco seemed an endless cacophony of cheap commerce and suspicious characters, a bizarre bazaar. The men, mostly dressed in white or gray linen, had thin eyes that darted back and forth and looked like they might be taking hostages any minute, even though they were just regular folks. The women were either dressed like modern Westerners or covered head to toe in black, which to an unseasoned traveler like Lucy made even the meekest of housewives look like a revolutionary. It was hot, stifling and noisy, like a llama sitting on your face in a Tanjier disco.

It was easy to see how her friend Nancy could have termed Morocco an "intimidating and unpleasant shit hole." It was indeed a big mess, filled with collapsing buildings and sewage, more chaotic and trashy than even the poorest U.S. city. Lucy noticed the American, Scandinavian, British and German tourists – the hapless white folks - being harassed and pulled this way and that, unaware that local hawkers don't take no for an answer. But she felt safe holding onto Perry, who projected an intimidating air of *mess with us and I'll break your neck.*

Perry was able to haggle with merchants in his native tongue over the prices of things. There was not all that much she wanted, but she did buy an exotic handbag for Ida, some rare spices unavailable in America, and a Casablanca refrigerator magnet. Had Perry not been negotiating she would have definitely been ripped off. Everyone got ripped off.

She simply could not believe she was here. *Could…not…believe it.* She had retuned to New York, kissing the floor of her apartment with tears of joy and expecting a gradual transition back into city life and work. Two weeks later she got a call from Jared.

"Want to go to Casablanca?"

"What? Casablanca where? Who?"

"My dear, you have been given your first movie offer."

"A *what?*"

"It's an *offer*. They are *giving* you the part. People have seen the dailies from August's film and the buzz on you is great, and the director of this movie saw a couple of your scenes and thought you were right for this part. It's a lot like the other one – a beleaguered housewife – but you know Hollywood."

"Jared, I don't know Hollywood. I've made one movie by the skin of my teeth."

'Once they see you as one thing, that's all they see. Anyway, he's a good director and a lot less sadistic than August. You're playing a tourist who gets abducted in Morocco and falls for her kidnapper because he's so hot. It's some sort of mystery comedy caper, like *The Man Who Knew Too Much* meets the Stockholm syndrome, or some bullshit. The offer is 150 grand, plus air, hotel and per diem for three weeks work in Morocco, starting in two weeks. Is your passport in order? They're sending the script over today by messenger, but if I were you I'd grab it."

One hundred fifty thousand dollars for three weeks of work? That was nearly quadruple her salary for August's film. She hung up the phone and sat down. In two months she had gone from misery and obscurity to mulling an offer to make a movie in *Casablanca. You have got to be freaking kidding! Hello, doctor, here I come!*

Of course, the first thing she did was email Perry to tell him that – surprise! – she was about to show up in his hometown. Perry replied within six hours.

My dear Lucy –

What a surprise that you are coming to Morocco, and so quickly. Of course we can meet. As soon as you know the particulars of your stay, please let me know, and we will. I remain –

Yours, Perry

Then she called Ida, who said, "Be sure to tell the Doctor I said hey. But be careful, dear. His relatives might be kidnappers."

"No, mom, that's my co-star. A guy kidnaps me in the movie."

Was it fate? Had the heavens conspired to magically and oh so conveniently throw her back into the arms of her Arab prince? Some say that coincidence is simply God's way of saying hello. This seemed like God's way of beating down the bedroom door, shaking her awake, slapping her face and screaming, "Get dressed, bitch!"

She had arrived in Morocco five days earlier and had already filmed two scenes, despite major disorientation and jet lag. Fortunately her tourist character felt the same way, like she was emerging bleary-eyed after days of floating in an isolation tank. The movie was a complicated comedy caper written by someone who apparently wanted to further the stereotype that most Arabs are terrorists, but in this case funny, good-looking, lovable terrorists. Her part was small but crucial, and the character of her kidnapper turned out to be a sympathetic guy who was only participating in crime due to peer pressure. Like her previous movie, she had no idea what was actually going on, but except for the required screaming her part was basically comic, and for this she was grateful.

Today was her second Morocco date with Perry, a day of sightseeing and dinner with a native, and despite the noise and dust she was fascinated. *How do people live like this?* It was her first trip outside of the U.S. and her middle class suburban upbringing was Versailles compared to this. This was chaos, everything piled on top of everything else, with no border between a five star hotel and a slum.

The restaurant Perry chose was so far off the beaten track she thought she was the only Westerner who had ever heard of it. Since the menu was in Arabic, Berber and French she let Perry order. Dish after dish appeared – hot and cold salads, bread, soups, couscous with lamb and vegetables, all seasoned with strange spices she had never tasted. Dessert was deep-fried dough dipped into a hot honey pot and sprinkled with sesame seeds, with a huge plate of exotic fruits. It was the most unique meal she had ever had.

"I'm in awe," she said. "This is another world. I love it."

"I thought you might," said Perry. "This is an impressive restaurant to foreigners, but to locals it's just a regular place."

"I vow to never eat at an Olive Garden again."

"A what?"

"Typical boring American restaurant, never mind," she said. "Thanks for taking me around today. I never would have seen all this."

"Were you frightened?"

"A little. I probably wouldn't have left the safety of the hotel if not for you. I just can't believe I'm here."

Perry thought a moment, took a breath, and decided, *OK, now.* He reached over, took her hand with both of his, and looked into her eyes. "I want to tell you something."

Lucy, in the midst of chewing, said a garbled, "What?"

"I think I am in love with you."

Lucy almost choked on her honey dough thingy, struggling to avoid spitting it in all directions and simultaneously remain ladylike. She held up her free hand to Perry and finished swallowing, took a drink of water, put down the glass and looked at him, mouth agape. She tried to speak but no words came out, as if she had involuntarily hit the mute button on her vocal cords. She took a deep breath, and actually vocalized a sound check: "Testing, one, two, three, testing, OK, I can talk."

Perry was still smiling.

"You're *what?*" she finally managed.

"I think I am – "

"I heard you," she interrupted. "How could you possibly – "

Perry smiled. He had never seen a woman so endearing. "Do you have any idea how beautiful you are? I don't think so."

Lucy felt the temperature in their hands rise to the level of the Casablanca pavement and pulled her hand away, lest it get singed. "Oh, my God. Really. How is this possible?"

"Lucy, I told my wife that it's over. She was upset, but she understood. The Moroccan government has a modern family code so we can divorce under irreconcilable differences with no proof. Six months from now, I will be single. Then I can marry you."

She gasped. No man had ever mentioned marriage to her, even as a goof. Now, in the unlikeliest of places, her proposal cherry had at last been popped. She looked at Perry as her heart started tap dancing on the concrete floor. "W-what? Are you kidding? Marry me?"

His smile stretched all the way out in the street. "So…what do you think?"

She struggled to speak. "I think…I…why?"

Perry's eyes were more mesmerizing than ever before, and she found herself helplessly falling into them without a net. He was one intense dude. "I have thought about nothing but you since I saw you. You are the woman for me. I know it. You are honest, fun, without nonsense, smart, not to mention very beautiful. You can still have my child. Why not?"

"Why *not?* Because I barely know you is why not," she sputtered, as she wiped her mouth with the cloth napkin. "Not only that, you're *here* and I'm – "

"You're here," he said. "Something bigger than both of us brought us together here. I prayed that this would happen, and it has. It was meant to be."

"Wait, you're going all snake charmer on me. Hold on. You want to *marry* me?"

"I do. I love you. I am certain."

Lucy dabbed her mouth with her napkin, took a sip of coffee, paused, looked at Perry, and burst out laughing. Giggles turned to guffaws, which turned into howls. She laughed so loud that the noisy restaurant started quieting down, until her laughter was the only sound in the place and every patron and waiter was looking at her. A passing dog stopped to witness the commotion.

Lucy buried her face in her napkin and stifled her gasps, as the volume in the restaurant gradually returned to normal. When she removed the napkin she looked at Perry, who was smiling so broadly he could have lit the street. "What's so funny?" he said. "This is not the reaction I expected."

"You're kidding, right?" she managed to say after she regained her composure.

"No."

"This is a joke."

"I assure you, it isn't."

"Perry." She took a deep breath and then blurted out a stream of talk. "I'm flattered. You have no idea how much I'm flattered. Really. I like you and I think you're fascinating and interesting and gorgeous and don't think I haven't had a few thoughts myself. But my God, this is the fourth time we have laid eyes on each other. The *last* thing I'm thinking about right now is marriage. I'm finally getting some work after a long time, things are happening, and I don't want to get married now. I can't. I'm only beginning to process what has happened to my life in the last months. And you live here, and – "

"You're a beautiful woman."

"Who you barely know," she said, suddenly slightly nauseous. Ida had warned her, and she had inherited more than a tiny bit of her mother's nature, like it or not. She didn't know what to think. The most she expected from this brief visit was a short affair, if that. Now it had developed into an international romance novel.

Perry reached for her hand. She did not take it. "I did not think you would respond this way," he said.

She struggled to find the words. "Perry. Where I come from, no one asks someone to marry them after four meetings, unless the woman is some poor girl who gets pregnant and her parents force her into it. In my world it takes a long period of dating, maybe living together, maybe even a little sex. So forgive me if I'm more than a little suspicious."

"Suspicious of what?"

"You're from a really weird foreign country that makes me feel upside down. There are people with no legs begging in front of my hotel. You want to *marry me?*" She thought, *I always figured that the man who asked me to marry him would be named Steve, or Joe, not* Perroj, *it's just too random.* "Forgive me if I suspect some ulterior motive. What could you possibly want with me?"

"I understand. Just think about it, please."

"Oh, I'll think about it, I'll think a *lot*," she said. Her mood abruptly turned more sour than hummus in the hot desert sun. She wanted to immediately go back to back to working on the movie, which was what she was here for. Sure, it was an incredible coincidence that she was here in Morocco with him after such a short time, and maybe the stars had indeed collided to bring them together and – *oh, please, give me a break. What stars?*

"Actually, no, I don't have to think about it. I'd like to go back to my hotel, please. Let's just drop this. This is weird."

"Of course."

Perry paid the check. After they left the restaurant, they walked along the river looking for a taxi. Pedestrians, cars, animals and kiosks crowded the grungy street, a clanging and crowded night market. Lucy was confused and a bit frightened to be in this strange land with this strange man. All of these foreigners were suddenly threatening, not interesting and exotic. Finally, Perry broke the silence.

"Lucy, look at me."

She stopped walking and then turned to look at him. *Those eyes,* yet again, ad infinitum. He put his hands on her shoulders and stared at her.

"Lucy. I am very sorry if I shocked you. Very sorry. You must never, ever think that I would have any motive, as you say. Never. I am an honorable man. I think I fell in love with you when you were on the hospital gurney in the ship, with your hair such a mess. In my country, courtship is very fast. I apologize. If we never see each other again, it is your decision. But please don't think I would in any way take advantage of you. If you want to date for years, we can do that. If you want to say goodbye tonight, we can do that. But please don't."

Lucy felt like crying, but she decided to save it for the cameras. Finally, she said, "Perry, I just don't get how you could want to marry me after –"

Perry grabbed the sides of her head with his hands, and stared though her eyes to the back of her head. "Because you don't understand how *any* man would want to marry you. You don't think you are beautiful. Please, stop it. Every time I have complimented you, you don't believe it. The world knows you are beautiful. I want to make you feel beautiful."

With that, he pulled her face to his, and planted a kiss on her that vaporized everything on the street. She tried to resist for a few seconds, but resistance was futile. Nothing else existed. Traffic went silent. The river stopped flowing. Birds in mid-flight crashed to the ground.

Perry was the greatest kisser in the pantheon of all-time legendary kissers, and Lucy was helpless. Every hormone in her body did the cha-cha, the rumba and the raqs sharqi. Lucy melted, then solidified, then regained her composure and pulled away.

Law-zee mercy.

"Wow. Uh, take me back to my hotel, please," she said. She was on another planet, where gravity is an afterthought.

"May I call you tomorrow?" said Perry.

"Yeah, sure," slurred Lucy, not knowing if she should head for the hills or strip naked and spread her legs on the street.

Perry hailed a cab and barked orders to the driver. Arabic was the strangest language Lucy had ever heard, a garbled mix of consonants and grunts. The cab driver drove like he was maneuvering an amusement park bumper car, dodging pedestrians who didn't seem to care if they got hit or not. Perry and Lucy said nothing about their evening along the way, but Perry pointed out several local sites. Lucy could only respond with, "Mmm-hmm."

When the cab pulled up to the hotel, Perry quickly got out and rushed around to open the door for Lucy. Say what you will, the guy was a gentleman. He took her hand and helped her out of the cab, which was a good thing since she thought her legs might buckle under her. They stood there while the cab waited. Perry looked at her, grinned, and kissed her on the cheek.

"I will call you tomorrow. Sleep well."

Lucy looked at him, smiled a weak smile and nodded, but feared that if she said anything she would be speaking in tongues like an evangelist in a tent revival. She turned and wobbled up the stairs to the hotel entrance, dodging a beggar with no legs on the sidewalk.

Perry stood and watched, making sure that she got in safely, and got back in the cab. He felt furious with himself, misjudging the situation and possibly forever shutting this window of opportunity. He was so desperate for change that he had moved too fast, frightened this poor American girl and possibly ruined any future with her. He gave orders to the driver and the cab sped away in a cloud of dust.

Perry arrived home to the usual evening tableau of his wife reading alone on the couch and his son watching TV. He told his wife he had been doing research at the hospital, which he didn't expect her to believe since he was technically on vacation, but he didn't care. He and his wife had even less than usual to say to each other these days; their conversations commonly involved the welfare of their son, and otherwise stuck to surface pleasantries usually reserved for strangers in elevators. By any criterion his wife was lovely, with long black hair and the sharp, ruddy features of most Arab women. But from the wedding day onward she had been cold, distant and resentful, her hatred of her father gradually morphing into hatred of Perry. Any disagreement became a rebuke from her abusive father. Perry felt pity for her, as none of this had been her idea any more than it was his.

His pleasant home, tastefully yet sparingly decorated with traditional artifacts and paintings, suddenly felt like his grave. In the kitchen he poured a glass of wine, sat alone at the kitchen table, closed his eyes, took a deep breath, and thought.

One way or another he would end this marriage, set both of them free and move on, even if it was back to the middle of the ocean. He said a silent prayer that his other dreams and ambitions would succeed, and if they didn't, to simply accept what came his way even if he despised most of it. He then vowed that, if he were to see Lucy again, he would proceed with extreme caution. She was right: he barely knew her. She just seemed available.

In her bathroom at the hotel, Lucy stared at herself in the mirror. She took account. Yes, she had a pretty face, except for the double chin. Yes, her body was adequate, except for the fat. Not great, but not hideous. But this strange knockout wants to *marry me? What the hell? How did I get here? This isn't in the script! I had no man, now I have two!*

This is all because I fell off that damn ship. If I had just stayed in my cabin nothing would have happened, and ... oh, right, and I wouldn't be doing any movies and I'd still be in Asheville and eating chips and slouching towards oblivion. Is that what life offers? Either total misery or confusion and fear? These are the options?

She got into the bed, set the alarm for her nine o'clock wakeup call, and took a sleeping pill. She gradually drifted off to sleep and dreamed that she was a concubine reclining on a couch in a Persian market, lounging on a sofa, scantily clad, bedecked with jewels, fanned and fed fruit by eunuchs. Then Perry purchased her and took her away.

14

In the filthy, roasting, brick-walled cell that served as the location for Lucy's abduction, a sweltering hellscape where the living envy the dead, she was standing pressed against the wall by Mohammad, her captor. Cast for his looks, since an attractive kidnapper is more audience friendly than an ugly one, his sweaty, bare torso showcased camera-ready biceps, deltoids and abdominals, as he held her hands over her head and stared at her with a predatory expression that made the Forty Thieves seem like the Muppets.

"And, reset," said Marvin Olias, the director. "OK, Lucy, when he pushes your hands against the wall, push back a little more, and then when he leans in to kiss you, turn your head away faster, and then, Mohammad, go back a bit, give her that little smile, your expression is too scary, OK? You want to kiss her, not hurt her. I just want a little more tension. Then, Lucy, it should be obvious that when he kisses you, you resist at first but then you're helpless, and you should start to relax. Wait - maybe it would be funny if you then grabbed his face, and turned him around, and pushed *him* against the wall. That would change the whole dynamic. Want to try that?"

"OK," said Mohammad.

"Got it," said Lucy.

"Why didn't we think of that before? That's great," said Bruce, the screenwriter.

"Because I'm a genius and you're not," said Marvin.

"Goes without saying."

That kind of sarcastic banter between the director and his crew had been going on for the entire shoot, which made the atmosphere on the set light and fun, the opposite of Lucy's previous cinematic experience. A good thing, since shooting in Morocco tested everyone's patience. Locally hired background extras stared directly into the camera, ruining shots. Sets fell apart in the middle of scenes. Animals refused to take direction, one camel in particular copping insufferable movie star attitude. The 110-degree heat required the makeup crew to work overtime, lest everyone look like they had done sit-ups in a pizza oven.

"And, *action*," said Marvin. The camera closed in on the actors, who acted out the scene with Marvin's adjustments. It was easy for Lucy to draw from her own life experience for the scene. She just recreated the moment when Perry had kissed her on the street after he asked her to marry her, when she had no choice but to succumb. She found it ridiculously coincidental that she was basically acting the same scene on film, only two weeks after it had actually happened. Maybe it was her destiny to be attacked by a series of hot Arabs.

It was also helpful that Perry added tension by standing at the back of the set, watching.

After Lucy's fear-based meltdown with Perry two weeks earlier, she decided *what the hell – I'm here, he's here, why not?* and continued to see him when she wasn't filming one of her thirteen scenes, occasionally bringing him on location as her escort. Despite her uneasiness with his newfound feelings, she couldn't deny that she was attracted to him in a strange way she had never been attracted to anyone, even Zack. She thought it probably a bad idea to continue to see him, but the heart has its own agenda that makes terrible ideas seem acceptable. She decided that she might as well seize the opportunity to at least use him to escort her around Casablanca. He seemed to have the time. Today was her final scene and tomorrow she would be going home, with plenty of time to consider the ramifications of her bizarre yet undeniably exciting Moroccan adventure.

The first time she brought Perry to the set, gossip spread like a tsunami. She was the only actor who seemed to have hooked up with a local. The women on the set, and some of the men, found themselves staring at him, sometimes missing a cue. Marvin even offered him a walk-on part, which Perry respectfully declined. Laura, an actress who played a fellow tourist, took Lucy aside and said, "Woah, girl, you work fast. Who the hell is *that*? You win the prize for Best Souvenir."

Lucy found herself explaining, more than once, the story of how she had met Perry on the ship and how they had "stayed in touch." She didn't tell anyone of his proposal until, late one night in the hotel bar after a few cocktails, she confided in Laura, with whom she had developed a friendly camaraderie.

Bad decision. In two days, everyone knew. All it took was for Laura to say the conspiratorial. "You didn't hear this from me, but..." and the information that no one heard from anyone was heard by everyone. A grip on the set even said to Lucy, right before she was about to film a scene, "I hear you guys are getting married. Congrats," causing a flustered Lucy to flub her lines several times. That night, back at the hotel, she read an embarrassed and apologetic Laura the riot act.

But her time with Perry had been interesting, to say the least. She rode a camel, which was surprisingly comfortable despite smelling like a bonfire of dead dogs. In addition to the Central Market, they visited the Notre Dame de Lourdes cathedral, the seaport with its overpowering smells of fish and sewage, a mosque where Lucy was required to cover herself in the traditional hijab, and the Habbous district with its many souks selling everything imaginable. So much was for sale she thought she could have bought a baby if she wanted to. All the time she thought, *this is fascinating, and no way could I live here. Not even with the hottest man in town.*

And one day, at lunch, Perry surprised her by bringing along his thirteen- year-old son, who instead of an Arab name was called Luke, spelled "Luc" in French. Perry explained that he had named him after Luke Skywalker, since Perry was a huge *Star Wars* fan and to him the name symbolized heroism. Lucy remembered that Leo, the producer, was also a *Star Wars* fan, and wondered if every man in the world was secretly an adolescent science fiction geek who masturbated to a poster of Jane Fonda in *Barbarella*.

Luc was such a gorgeous boy that Lucy found herself uncomfortably attracted to a thirteen-year-old, which added yet another layer of dizziness to the mind warp she was experiencing. He did not speak English, so they had as interesting a conversation as possible with Perry translating. At one point, after Lucy told Luc about the movie and her career, Luc asked a question that caused Perry to shoot Luc a stare of disapproval.

"What did he say?"

After a moment, Perry smiled sheepishly and said, "He wants to know if you are my girlfriend."

"Oh, no, we're just friends, I met your father on the ship," she hastily replied. The look on the kid's face said there was no way he believed it. He knew his parents did not like each other. He had the same piercing eyes as his father, whose own eyes were now attempting to reduce Luc to a boiling pool. "He is a smart boy, I told you, sometimes too smart," said Perry.

Lucy thought, this kid is *nobody's* freaking fool.

"And that's a wrap for Miss Lucy Dixon," said Marvin, after eight takes of the scene gave him what he wanted. "Well done!" The crew broke into applause, and Lucy hugged Mohammad, Marvin and several other crewmembers. Then she looked back and saw Perry, who was also smiling, his smile shining more brilliantly than the others. She went over to him.

"Nice work," he said.

"I need a shower. How about I go to my trailer and get cleaned up, and we can go back to the hotel?"

"Perfect."

Before she walked off the set, Marvin approached her. "Let's have a drink at the hotel tonight before you leave, how about it?"

"Great, would love to."

"You did a terrific job, Lucy. You have a natural quality on film that you can't teach. And you're really funny. I think this movie is going to work, and you're a major part of it."

"Thank you, Marvin, I had a great time."

"Looks like it," said Marvin, looking back at Perry.

"Please, I'll explain later," she said, and walked to her trailer. Perry nodded politely at the director and followed her.

After Lucy cleaned up, a car took them to the hotel. On the way, Perry said, "I would like to come up for a moment, if it is OK with you. I would like to give you something."

Lucy thought, *what the hell is he going to give me? The guy wants to marry me, what if he gives me a ring? I should say no. Say no.*

"OK, sure," she said.

They went up to her hotel room. Lucy said, "I'm sorry for the mess. I've sort of piled everything everywhere. I haven't had much time to –"

Before she knew it, Perry was kissing her yet again, and Lawrence Welk Of Arabia returned for an encore, this time with an added Ghaytah woodwind section and the Champagne Lady singing Arabic. She dropped her purse on the floor, and Perry began to unbutton her blouse. *Oh, my God, I have to stop this, now.*

She resisted by undoing his belt, reaching for his shirttails and pulling his shirt up over his torso, revealing his naked chest, a smooth, caramel colored, perfectly formed physique that made an Olympic swimmer look like Fred Mertz.

And again, before she knew it, they were both naked, his mouth exploring parts of her body that had not even been explored by soap. Her libido, not her common sense, was at the wheel.

They said little or nothing during their lovemaking, just making a series of random grunts in an alien language that not even Perry spoke. She just couldn't stop kissing him, and still could not believe that he was next to her in bed. At one point, the devil on her shoulder said, "What's this guy doing with you?" She flicked the devil away with a snap of the middle finger, thinking, *get out of here, dipshit.*

Perry was so soft that Lucy thought he must bathe in a Palmolive jacuzzi. He held her closer than anyone had held her, even Zack, and his body melted into hers like they were merging. Her orgasm, and his, happened simultaneously, the long-awaited climax to everything that had happened in the last three weeks or even the last three years.

As she lay, panting, her heart beat so fast that she reached for Perry's hand, took it, and put it on her chest.

"If you have to call a doctor, this is why."

"I am a doctor," he said. "Are you all right?"

"You tell me."

Perry put his ear to her chest, listened, and said, "Just breathe. In and out."

She obeyed, and her heart rate began to slow down, though it would still probably qualify as cardiac dysrhythmia.

"For what it's worth, I knew this was going to happen," she said.

"Me too."

"You did? Oh, nuts, I thought it was up to me. I'm the girl."

"It was. But I knew."

He kissed her, and then sprung out of the bed and picked up his pants.

"You're leaving? Oh, God, how typical. Men are all alike."

"No, I told you, I have something for you." He reached into one of his pants pockets and pulled out something wrapped in a muslin cloth. He looked as good from the back as the front. He then bounced back onto the bed. His movements had always been smooth and catlike, like a James Bond villain; now he seemed like a puppy wagging his tail to go outside.

"I want you to have this, Lucy. It was my grandmother's, a beautiful lady from India called Aris Aswinkumar. Don't be afraid, it's not an engagement ring. My grandmother was a wealthy woman who had a lot of jewelry. This was one of the things my wife didn't want. I hope you like it. It's very old, and it might be valuable. Please."

Lucy looked at him. "You had an Indian grandmother?"

"Who married a Moroccan, who had a daughter who married an Iranian. I'm a – what's the word for a dog of mixed ancestry?"

"A mutt."

"Yes. That's me." He smiled, the most stellar result of inbreeding in history.

From the cloth, he pulled out a gold ring with what looked like an emerald stone encircled with rubies. The stones reflected in the light, sending flashes of brilliance that burned her retinas. It was one of the most exquisitely beautiful things she had ever seen, as if it had been looted from an ancient palace.

"Let me see if it fits you," he said, and put the ring on her right ring finger. It fit. "Good. It's yours. You can wear it or not, but I hope it will help you to remember our time together."

Lucy looked at the ring, and had to admit it was stunning. "You know what? I shouldn't accept this, but what the hell, I'll take it. It's so pretty. Thank you, Perry."

"I love you."

"Please don't say that."

"I am sorry if I frighten you, but I do. You excite me. I haven't felt excitement like this in years, perhaps ever."

"But – but - how the hell are we going to do this? You live here, and I live in New York, and in three months you're going back on the ship, and we need to spend more time together, and – "

"We will see. There is no way to know. What if I came to see you in New York? It's only a flight away. I can come."

"Yes, indeed, you can. All right, what the hell. Come see me."

"I will. We will email, all right?"

"All right, yeah."

"Now, I am going to leave. You have to meet the director downstairs. I will not forget our time together, Lucy. I hope you will not."

"Believe me, I won't. "

He kissed her. Then again, and again. She couldn't move, lying in the bed like a quadriplegic on Ambien. He could have thrown her against the wall and she would have been helpless. Then he got up off the bed and began putting on his clothes, moving like an athlete, frisky and fast. When he was dressed, he moved towards the door, opened it, turned and looked at her, blew her a kiss, smiled that dazzling smile and then, like a silent film star making a dramatic exit as the iris closed and the screen went black, was gone.

Every pore of her body vibrated in its own individual aftershock. She lay in the bed, and random thoughts bombarded her brain like protons crashing into neutrons.

OK. What just happened? Is he supernatural, and has put me under some ancient spell? Nobody wanted me, now everyone wants me. No men for four years, now two in two months? I can't move. I have to move. I have to meet Marvin. Move. Get up. Get UP. Uhnnnnggggggh.

She dressed, adjusted her makeup in the bathroom mirror so she didn't have that "sex face," adjusted her pert smile and raised her chin to look as composed as possible, and then went downstairs to the hotel bar, which on a location becomes headquarters where everyone meets and tries to establish temporary camaraderie away from home. She saw Marvin.

"Do you have vodka and tonic?" she asked the bartender.

Marvin said, "I'll get it. A vodka and tonic for the lady, and a Courvoisier for me."

"Thank you so much," she said.

"Are you OK? You look funny."

"I'm fine."

"You have a sex face."

"Stop it. I'm fine."

"Where is your friend?"

"He went home. He brought me back to the hotel, then left."

"I just saw him walk through the lobby not ten minutes ago."

"As I said, he left."

"Uh *huh*. None of my business."

"Marvin, I met him on the ship. He was the doctor who looked after me. We struck up a frie – um, we struck up something, kept in touch, blah blah blah. Kind of amazing that I ended up here, where he lives."

"Again, none of my business, but the word is that you're engaged."

Lucy took a breath, trying to appear unfazed by the uncontrollable power of blabbing tongues. "Please, we're not, we just sort of dated. He's nice."

"And very striking. He could do film if he wanted."

"Well, he's a doctor, not an actor, and I probably won't see him any time soon. I'm going home and he lives here." She rushed to change the subject. "Anyway, thanks for this. It was great."

"You have a very unique quality, Lucy. Don't take this the wrong way, but you make a hefty woman look great onscreen. You look like a real person other women can identify with. The camera loves you. Do you have good representation?"

"Yeah, he's OK, he's the only agent I've ever had. He's good when someone wants me and bad when they don't."

"Most agents are useless. I hope he's pursuing other films for you. You could be big if you are handled correctly."

Lucy almost burst into tears at that comment. "Marvin, you have no idea how long I've been waiting to hear that again. I heard it a long time ago, and it's the only thing that kept me going. I've had some pretty lean years, and all this stuff lately has been a total fluke."

"This whole freaking business is a fluke. Life is a fluke."

"But thank you very much."

"I knew it when I saw the scenes from *Winter Of Our Discontent*. If I'm not completely wrong, you're going to get a lot of attention from that. Maybe an Oscar nomination, if the movie does well."

"Stop it. No way. Are you nuts?"

"You are great in that picture, and it's going to come out sooner rather than later. August edits very fast. I bet it hits the festival circuit in a few months. August always wants his films to appear as prestige projects."

"That's insane, we just finished it."

"Mark my words. You'll see. Anyway, I'm going to try to finish this thing as soon as I can, but I'd like you to do my next movie, whatever it is. If there isn't a part for you, I'll write one in. You game?"

Lucy, flabbergasted, couldn't possibly say no. "Of course, I'd be honored."

She spent the rest of the night chatting with Marvin and the other crewmembers that stopped by, and then excused herself around one AM, exhausted. In her room, she threw everything into her suitcase, folding be damned. She slept a fitful sleep, tossing and turning more than usual.

On the plane on the way back to New York, in first class yet again, she sifted through the events of the last months. After deciding she had no idea what to make of any of it other than incredible coincidence, luck or the Grand Plan of Allah, she decided to watch a movie, and surfed through the movie channels and stopped on an Egyptian movie about a prince who seduces an American woman. He looked like Perry with a haircut, and she couldn't take it. She switched it off after ten minutes and watched *The Hangover, Part 2*.

15

"He wants to *marry you?* What the Sam Hill? " said Zack, on the phone with Lucy.

"I know it's unbelievable, but there you have it."

"But – but he *can't* marry you."

"Why not?"

"Because I want to."

Lucy nearly swallowed the phone. She had been home in New York for two months, and had only called Zack to tell him about the movies and Morocco. They hadn't spoken since they were in California, and Lucy just wanted to catch up. After a while, she told him about Perry, thinking that as one of her oldest friends he might give her some advice. But *this?*

"You *what?*"

"I wanna marry you, Lucy. You're the only girl for me, always have been. I knew it in college and I knew it in California."

"Why didn't you say something there?"

"'Cause you were so crazy with everything that had happened. But I love you, Lucy. Will you marry me?"

Jesus, Mary and Joseph on a popsicle stick.

Lucy blurted out the words like a rap singer. "Zack, darling, I love you too, but I can't. I'm getting work. I've got buzz, and the last thing I'm going to do right now is settle down. I'd be a lousy wife. The most you would get from me is occasional sex and a few good meals. I'm not marrying Perry; he's in Morocco and has a kid and it would never work. And I can't marry you. We have to move on."

Zack was silent, then said, "OK. I just thought I'd ask. I'm going nuts here. I hate my life." Zack didn't sound exactly like himself. He sounded like he was calling from the bottom of a fifth of Jack Daniels. "What if I moved to New York? I could get some job somewhere. You could do what you do," he said.

"No. All the things about New York that bother most people don't bother me. You would go crazy. I'm a stage girl, Zack. It's in my bones, not yours."

"I could try."

"No. You couldn't. Listen, I have to run, I have a meeting, but I'll call you soon, OK?" Lucy wanted to hang up the phone immediately, blow a long distance kiss to Zack and never talk again. She didn't have a meeting. She just had to hang the hell up.

"Bye, sweetie," she said, and hung the hell up.

Little twirling stars and chirping birds circled her head, like she had just been hit by a cartoon frying pan. She was speechless and yet had to talk to somebody, immediately, who knew this territory. She picked up the phone and dialed. "Can you meet me for a drink this week? I need to unload."

"How about tonight, after my show? Meet me at Joe Allen at eleven-thirty," said famous star and notoriously difficult diva Lonnie Jones, who was enjoying a long run in a hit musical, ironically titled *Please Marry Me.* Lucy could only shake her head in disbelief that they had become buddies, since their initial meeting had been a disaster.

After Lucy was cast in Leo's Broadway musical *The Rag Trade* eight years earlier, she excitedly began rehearsals and developed a great relationship with most of the company. But Lonnie Jones, the star, more than lived up to her reputation as "difficult." The slender, egomaniacal, blonde bobbed Jones was ill equipped for an ensemble piece where she was the star but not the center of attention. Other characters, including Lucy's "Velma," had almost as many featured moments, and Jones didn't like it one bit. She fought daily with the authors to make the show more about her, even suggesting that they spice up the plot by making her character a closet lesbian, a ludicrous proposal since the story centered around her conflict about leaving her big city fashion industry job for life in the country with her boyfriend.

Lucy found out, a couple of weeks into rehearsals, that Jones was trying to get her fired. One day, as Lucy sat in the rehearsal hall memorizing her lines, she overheard the following exchange in a nearby office:

Jones: *Get rid of her. She's a cow. She even makes the scenery look small.*

Mel Harper (director): *You're just mad because she's getting more laughs than you, but she wouldn't if you would start giving a performance.*

Jones: *Dammit, Mel, who's the star of this clambake?*

Mel: *You are, Lonnie, but you are not, repeat not, irreplaceable. No amount of money is worth putting up with your shit day after blessed day.*

Jones: *But —*

Mel: *Now hear this: Lucy is going to be great. You say your lines and sing your songs, or I'm going to fire your emaciated ass and leak a story to Page Six of the Post about how nasty you are. You'll get publicity that might ruin your career. I swear to Christ on the cross I'll do it. Got that?*

"I don't know to do, Leo," said Lucy, over a drink at Martell's that evening. "She hates me."

"She hates everybody. She's a total twat, I told you. There's a sign in her vagina that says, 'You are here.'"

Lucy spit out her drink. "Stop!"

"Her next show should just open in her vagina. There's plenty of space for standing room only."

"Aaah! Stop!"

"She's the vortex, sucking the life out of every -"

"Then why did you hire her?"

"Because she sells tickets. She's OK, but you're stealing the show."

"Stop it."

"You're a star, Lucy. Wait 'till the reviews come out, you'll see. I knew what I was doing when I saw you that night over there at the piano. Just do your job and don't worry about that hag."

Lucy took that to heart and stopped worrying about Jones, until one night at a preview performance when the author, Benson, gave Lucy a rewritten line but neglected to inform Jones of the change. When Lucy said it in the show, it got the biggest laugh of the night. Jones glared at Lucy onstage and ad-libbed a nasty comeback that got a dead silence from the audience. At intermission, Jones pulled Lucy aside.

"Dammit, Dixon, don't go *changing your lines*! Just because you're giving a lousy performance you don't need to make things up! I'll get Equity on your ass so fast you'll get *hemorrhoids!*"

"But…Benson rewrote it, didn't he tell you?"

"Yeah, right."

"I swear. Ask him."

Jones turned redder than Mexican hot sauce and stormed off, no doubt to rip Benson a new rectum. But a few minutes before the second act started, Benson and Jones appeared at Lucy's dressing room door.

"Lucy, Lonnie has something to say," said Benson.

Jones looked like she had been slapped with a mammoth wet noodle. Benson rolled his eyes to the ceiling and shook his head. Then, with great effort, she spoke.

"Miss Dixon, I want to apologize. I was not aware that your line had been changed. Benson here, um, apologized to me for not informing me. I did not …" she stopped. There was an uncomfortable pause that seemed to stretch out into the next week.

"Go on, Lonnie," said Benson.

"Um, I did not ... I did not mean what I said before. You are ...you're *awful*. No, wait; you ...are very good in this show. You..." Jones was eating so many crows that feathers protruded out of the sides of her mouth.

"That's okay, Lonnie. Apology not necessary."

"No, but it is. I can ... be a real bitch and I am *sorry* about that," said Jones.

Lucy laughed. "Thank you, it's okay, really. Let's just do our jobs, OK?"

"Right," said Jones, breathing deeply. "Okay." She turned and walked out the door. Benson gave Lucy a thumbs up signal, and Lucy smiled, knowing that this apology was more difficult for Jones than singing on a dumpster in the back of a grocery store to an audience of inattentive rednecks.

From that point on, Jones started giving a better performance. Benson must have threatened to kill her, or worse, create bad publicity. By the end of the preview period the audience response was much better. Jones became even cordial to Lucy, which basically meant she stopped grunting, actually said hello and attempted mild conversation.

Opening night of *The Rag Trade* was a smash, or seemed like one. When Lucy took her curtain call, it was the happiest moment of her life. She had always wanted to star on Broadway, and now she was. She saw her parents' faces streaming with overjoyed parental tears from the fifth row on the aisle.

When the curtain came down, everyone hugged everyone, jumping up and down and squealing. At moments like these, actors act like first graders who have just been given a lollipop and a snow day. Even Jones was beaming and hugging cast members whose names she still didn't know. She then came up to Lucy and put her hands on Lucy's shoulders.

"*Congratulations*. You did it."

"Thanks, Lonnie."

"No, girl, a star is born. Everyone knows it, especially *me*, which is probably why I was such a *bitch*. I remember my first show where everyone was talking about me like I was a star. Well, the same thing is going to happen to you, and I'll just have to *step aside*."

Lucy was momentarily speechless. "I don't know what to say."

"When one does not know what to say, it is best to be silent," said Jones. "Quick, what's that from?"

"*The King And I*."

"Well *done*. OK, I'm off. Get-together in my dressing room in about thirty. You come?"

"Sure." Lucy had to be with her parents, but decided to bring them along. She was astonished at Lonnie's sudden friendliness, and wanted to take advantage of it. Maybe Lonnie was in therapy, on medication, or both.

"My Lord, you were wonderful," screamed Ida in Lucy's dressing room.

"Did you like the show, mom?"

"Oh, it was real cute. Didn't you think so, Frank?"

"It had its moments, but you were great, Lucretia," said Frank. "What a thrill to see Lonnie Jones in person. What's she like?"

"She's a trip. You'll get to meet her in a minute."

"Really?" Frank's expression became that of a sixties schoolgirl about to meet The Beatles. "Do I look all right?"

"Very handsome, dad, love the tie," said Lucy. "How about this, right? Broadway."

"*So* exciting, thought I was gonna poop in my pants," said Ida.

After Lucy changed, they went downstairs to Jones' dressing room suite, where a sizable entourage had gathered. Flowers were everywhere, appropriate gifts for a star's opening. Soon, Jones emerged from her private room in a stunning floor-length red satin gown that hugged her figure. She looked every inch the star, with her short blond hair teased into a perfectly organized mess. She exchanged air kisses with everyone, to a chorus of *fabulouses, marvelouses* and so on. Eventually, she saw Lucy and came over.

"Well *done*," said Jones.

"Lonnie, these are my parents, Ida and Frank," said Lucy.

"How do you do, Miss Jones?" said Frank, kissing her hand like she was royalty.

"You have a *very* talented daughter, congratulations."

"Oh, well, she was born talking and never stopped," said Ida.

"Mother."

"Well, so nice to meet you. Refreshments over there. I have to make the rounds. See you at the party?"

"You bet," said Lucy, who marveled at how effortlessly Jones played this superficial game of backstage hoo-hah with hangers-on who wanted to be around someone famous. She doubted she would ever have the stomach for it.

At the party in the grand ballroom of the Hilton, she realized how strong her stomach was. Person after person complimented her, coo-cooed to her parents, and told her she was the next big thing. Lucy smiled to the point of severe cheek pain.

The tables were decorated with centerpieces of twisted fabric strategically lit from below. The lights were so low that the vision impaired would be in trouble, making the banquet hall feel like a candlelit Roman cistern. After everyone had finished their sit down dinner, the first reviews were being circulated. Several small newspapers offered raves, but the first one Lucy saw of was the most important review in the theater, *The New York Times*:

FASHION, LIKE SAUSAGE, SHOULDN'T BE SHOWN BEING MADE

By HILTON COLLINS

Jogging and step aerobics notwithstanding, there are still tired businessmen in the world. But are they tired enough for "The Rag Trade," the new musical that opened last night at the Lunt Fontanne?

The show wants to be an edgy expose of the fashion industry, a sort of uptown, big city "Pajama Game," but it is afflicted with a terminal case of attitude. Where "Game" made you care about the simple, rural factory workers struggling to get a seven-and-a-half cent raise, this show makes you glad that you don't see the clothes you're wearing being made by such annoying people. No wonder we import fabrics from other countries.

It's not the fault of the performers, although the usually dependable Lonnie Jones should be forbidden by court order from belting her numbers loudly enough to break Macy's windows ten blocks away.

Uh, oh, Lucy thought.

Where this show errs is in the hackneyed book and score, where the composer and lyricist seem to use a rhyming dictionary with borrowed melodies from better musicals, and in the arch and superior attitude of the characters, few of whom are likeable, save for a few moments with the secretary, Velma, played winningly and warmly by newcomer Lucy Dixon.

Whew, Lucy thought. *I'm unscathed. So far.*

The rest of the review worked overtime finding clever wordplay to trash the show, such as:

"The Rag Trade" is, alas, directed squarely at the tourist trade.

This snarky jab, especially, made Lucy want to scream: a snooty New York critic implying that the target audience was a bunch of yokels just too stupid to realize they were watching garbage. *What's wrong with a show that appeals to tourists?* she thought. *After all, they keep a show going after all the New Yorkers have seen it.* Lucy wondered if this critic saw the same show that was getting nightly standing ovations. Was everyone delusional? Had they all taken leave of their senses and put on a show that was not even good enough for county fairs?

She sped-read through the rest of the review to see if it said anything else about her, and then she found it:

Although the winning, portly Miss Dixon shows great promise, the show around her shows little, and she should start looking for a better vehicle to showcase her talents.

"PORTLY!" cried Lucy. "Oh, my God." Lucy slammed the newspaper on the table and leaned back in her chair. "He said I was portly."

"What's portly?" said Ida.

"It's fat, Ida, for Heaven's sake," said Frank.

"Well, honey, you're not exactly thin," said Ida. Frank grabbed Ida's arm and squeezed it, which after thirty-five years of marriage she understood to mean *shut the hell up*.

Lucy fumed. "The newspaper of record just said I was fat."

"What else?" said Frank.

"He hated it. He reviewed the show with the same nasty attitude he accused the show of having."

"Ah, I see you read it, "said Leo, suddenly appearing next to Lucy. "Collins is a prick. We knew he would have problems with the show, because it doesn't expose the dark underbelly of humanity. He probably spends his weekends in some sex club downtown, so he wants every show to be decadent. If it's not German cabaret, forget it."

Lucy alarmingly sat upright with a bolt, grabbed Leo's wrist, and said, "Uh, Leo, these are my parents, Frank and Ida. This is Leo Krause, one of the producers."

Leo snapped to attention like a palace guard yanked by a rubber band held by the Queen, and his face turned a deep shade of magenta. Lucy had never seen him blush. "I'm so sorry. Hello, Leo Bloom here. Lucy is great, isn't she?"

"Yes," glared Ida.

Lucy stifled a laugh. In his shock, Leo had just gotten his own name wrong and substituted the name of the Gene Wilder/Matthew Broderick character in *The Producers*.

"Well, so, uh, nice to meet you. Don't worry, Lucy, the Post and the News are raves. We'll see what the other critics say, but as long as we can get 'money quotes' for the ads, we're fine. At least Collins liked you."

"He said I was fat."

"Fu – " Leo started to curse, but instantly reeled it in. "Never mind him, everyone knows you're great. It's very nice to meet you folks, I'm sure you're proud of Lucy." Leo then vanished so fast he almost left a puff of smoke.

"Well, he has a mouth on him. Such sex talk," said Ida.

"Sorry about that, mom. He's a great guy." Lucy dared not use this moment to admit that she and Leo were involved in some sex talk of their own.

For the rest of the evening Lucy put on a happy face. Frank and Ida couldn't help but see the disappointment under their daughter's smile. Lucy decided to read no more reviews, lest she encounter other judgments in print about her figure.

The next day, her parents flew home. Lucy performed the next night's performance in a way that seemed to say, "Screw all of you, I have a great body, so eat me." Lonnie Jones, however, began phoning in her performances more and more as time went on. Many reviews were not as kind as she thought should be to a star of her magnitude, and she rapidly lost interest. After the show ran three months, she broke her contract.

Jones had an out clause whereby she could leave with two weeks notice for a film or TV offer. Miraculously, an offer came through, but gossip flew that Jones' agents had engineered the offer deliberately so she could get out of a show where people weren't nightly crawling across broken glass to kiss the hem of her garment.

The *Times* review had been so negative that the New York theater cognoscenti stayed away, thinking it the first and last word in theater criticism. Despite the positive reaction of the audiences, the snobs of New York had been told that they must hate it, so they did, even without seeing it. New Yorkers, despite their pretensions of superior intelligence and sophistication, can be just as gullible as the most uninformed voter swayed by a propaganda-spewing politician. Once the news broke that Jones was leaving, ticket sales ground to a halt, and the closing notice was posted one week after Jones left.

So, Lucy's dreams of a long Broadway run abruptly came to an end. She performed her last performance as if her life depended on it, which it did. This was what she was born to do, giving a great performance in a great part, and she was happier than she had ever been. She had a few moments where she considered more stable career choices, like selling toilet tissue, but soon came to her senses.

One week later, she was cast in *The Front Office* and flew to Los Angeles. She then shot the pilot and returned home, flush with success, waiting for the show to be picked up by the network. It wasn't.

After a vacation weekend at a friend's summer home on Fire Island where she got sunburned, drunk and made out with the Speedo clad pool boy, she returned to Manhattan to look for another job in showbiz. She looked for nearly two years.

16

For months, Lucy auditioned until she felt she could audition no more, and then she auditioned some more. She auditioned for a commercial where she sang what was probably the only song ever written about tampons. She usually lost the part to a more glamorous girl, even on the radio. She was too tall, too short, too fat, too thin, too young, too old, or too "too."

She auditioned for a television show as a delivery woman. The casting director told Jared, "She seemed gay." Later, she auditioned for the part of an actual lesbian. The casting director said, "She's not gay enough."

She was too gay. She was not gay enough.

Her savings and unemployment insurance kept her alive for ten months. When she wasn't auditioning, she sang at Martell's, hung out with friends, took classes, practiced cooking, tried to lose weight and tried not to lose her mind. She sang at weddings with a band of unemployed Broadway musicians.

Having done both weddings and singing telegrams, she thought if she went any lower in showbiz she would be singing in the subway.

Occasionally, feelings of failure enveloped her like San Francisco fog, a clammy spirit that kept her in bed until mid-afternoon, staring at the ceiling, unable to even toss and turn. She had always assumed success was going to happen. For the *Fiddler* tour, *The Rag Trade* and the *Front Office* pilot, it happened. But after nine months of nothing, she couldn't help but think that *maybe I was just meant to get a taste of it, enough to make me bat shit crazy.*

She feared that she had actually grown to *hate* her life, which frightened her more than the threat of bankruptcy. She hit bottom when Amanda informed her that she was pregnant, marrying her boyfriend and giving up the apartment. Not only was Lucy jobless, she was soon to be homeless, and spent several nights paralyzed with fear, curled up under the sheets like a fetus with scoliosis.

Her net worth down to $1800, she made a tearful call to Frank and promised that she would get a survival job if he could just front her some money for an apartment. Her dad listened patiently and, after a short fatherly lecture, agreed. Her mother picked up the phone in the bedroom.

"Honey, we just want you to be happy, but come home."

"If I come home, I'll hang myself in the closet."

"Stop that right now, Lucretia. How morbid. What would the neighbors think if they knew I found you hanging in the - "

"Ida," said Frank, "Hang up. I'm talking to Lucretia."

"Oh, so it's none of my business? She always had you wrapped around her finger."

"Ida, hang up the damn phone." *Click.*

"Your mother is queen of the worry warts."

"I know, dad."

"I'll send you a check tomorrow. Consider it a delayed opening night present. You picked a tough career."

"It picked me. What else can I do?"

"You can cook."

Sometimes desperation breeds opportunity. "That's a thought. Thanks, dad."

"Promise me, Lucretia. Don't be afraid, keep trying and work hard. You're too old to be crying to daddy."

"I promise."

First, she had to find a safe, affordable apartment in a decent neighborhood. Finding a Manhattan apartment that is safe, affordable and in a decent neighborhood is like finding a virgin on the New Jersey shore. Everything in her price range was either a dump, in a terrible neighborhood, or a dump in a terrible neighborhood. Eventually she went to Actor's Equity and perused the apartment listings on a bulletin board, since the network of unemployed performers usually unearths something out of the traditional loop. She saw one that looked promising, and called.

"Hi, I'm calling about your apartment listed at Equity?"

"Huh? Oh, right," said a groggy woman. "It's my condo. Would you sign a two year lease?"

"Sure."

"OK, meet me at 150 West 47th, 10A at four. The doorman will let you in."

Lucy showed up at the address and took the tiny elevator to the tenth floor, nervously knocking on the door. When the door opened, she gasped. A thin woman in black sweat pants and sweatshirt, with slightly disheveled blond mop of hair and no makeup, did the same. Lonnie Jones screamed, "Oh, my GOD." She grabbed Lucy and put her arms around her. "What are you *doing* here?"

The flabbergasted Lucy was momentarily mute but finally spat out, "Uh, I need an apartment is what I'm doing here." She smiled and laughed a half-laugh, somewhere between surprise and horror.

"This is *too much*, of all *people*. Come on in," said Lonnie. "My *God*, if the world was any smaller we'd all fall off."

After Lucy got over the shock that Jones was her potential landlord, she looked around. It was a large studio with a tiny kitchen and bathroom, a nice view of the street and lots of sunlight. The furniture was modern and tasteful.

"The couch folds out," said Lonnie. "I did what I could when I first had this back in the day. My father bought this for me. If you want it, it's yours. I would so rather rent this dump to someone I know. How's *life?*"

"I'll take it," said Lucy.

Then she sat and talked to Lonnie, their first conversation where Lonnie seemed like an actual human and not a diva from on high. After she abruptly left *Rag Trade*, Lonnie had flown to Hollywood and filmed her own TV pilot. From her description, it sounded even more idiotic than *The Front Office*.

"And those network clowns didn't pick it up. 'We're going after a younger demographic,' they said. Evidently, the only people who watch TV are horny teenage boys. At least I got a nice chunk of change. I've been looking for another show here, but there aren't enough new shows for all us leading ladies who litter the district. I was an idiot to leave *Rag Trade,* truthfully. I've had more than a few sleepless nights about that. I've been singing with symphony orchestras all year, in all these Podunk towns. It pays the bills, and Midwestern people are *nice,* my God, they treat me like I'm the Queen. You want to feel like a star? Do Broadway and then go do something in fucking *Nebraska.* They can't believe you even *came.* But it's been hard. I dug my own grave. I've had a crappy reputation as a bitch, and I *was.* I've been in therapy working on it. Between you and me, of course. One thing my therapist said is to do things myself and not go through assistants, to interact with people, which is why I'm here."

Lucy listened in amazement to Lonnie, astonished that her onetime nemesis was pouring out her heart. Lonnie was rich and famous and still had to hustle for work, still subject to the same disappointments and rejections of any actor. But Lonnie was tougher than a lady wrestler or a gun-toting redneck driving a Harley Davidson.

"By the way, I haven't even asked you about *you.* I'm yapping like a maniac. Tell me, *tell* me."

Lucy related her life since they had last met, leaving out the suicidal crying jags. Lonnie was encouraging. "You're just going through a dry spell. It happens. Look at me. Everybody knows you're great."

"Then why hasn't anyone hired me?"

"Because they *haven't.* To try to figure out why will guarantee you admission to an asylum. Why didn't I win an

Oscar for *The Magician?* Because I *didn't*. You just have to plug on. Look, I've been lucky, had success and come from a rich family. My dad made a *fortune* in textiles before it all went overseas. But my career could have tanked and I could be married to some idiot stockbroker like I meet all the time in the Hamptons. They're *hideous,* yammering on about credit default swaps and derivatives until I want to *scream* at the top of my lungs. How are you fixed for money?"

"Not good. I haven't had to get a survival job, but I'm going to have to. I love cooking, so I thought I might try some catering places, or maybe try to be a personal chef. But I don't know how to go about that."

"You're kidding. Are you good?"

"Sure. Anything so I don't have to waitress. If I have to listen to one more New Jersey lady scream for coffee, I'll die."

"Then come work for me. I share the same girl with Sting and Itzak Perlman, and she's quitting in a month because she's pregnant. She does two nights a week for each of us. You would have to guarantee us a few months, though. Finding someone decent is hard. The personal chef business is loaded with openings, and nobody knows it."

Lucy struggled for the next 30 seconds to remove her jaw from the floor. Not only did she have an apartment, she had a job offer from a woman who had once tried to get her fired. "Sure, Lonnie, but I've never done it."

"If you can cook, what's to learn? I'm on the road half the time, anyway. What kind of stuff do you make?"

"How about macadamia nut crusted mahi-mahi with a Kaluah, lime and ginger sauce, with some Moroccan cous-cous and steamed asparagus?"

"God, I'll have that *right this minute. Fabulous.* I'll pay you the same thing I paid Svetlana. The three of us are a good team because we only need a couple of meals a week. The rest of the time we go out or something."

So began the new and unexpected phase of Lucy's career. She paid Lonnie the first month's rent, moved in and became a personal chef to the stars, putting her acting career on hold to get back on her financial feet. It was surprisingly enjoyable. Her employers were affable, chatting with her in their kitchens while she whipped up one mouth-watering concoction after another. Sting even provided her with lots of gossip about his days with The Police, which made her feel like Barbara Walters. She was discreet and never acknowledged the stream of men that came in and out of Lonnie's apartment. She grew to like Lonnie and wanted her to settle down with someone, but Lonnie was crazy.

She held this position for eleven months until she saved a financial nest egg, and then bit the bullet and started auditioning again. One of her auditions was for a Broadway revival of George S. Kaufman and Moss Hart's classic comedy *You Can't Take It With You*. This time, at long last, she got the part.

Lonnie cried, "Congratulations and good for you, sweetie, but *now* what the hell am I going to eat? Fucking McDonald's?"

Tonight, five years later at Joe Allen's after Lonnie's show, Lonnie laughed reminiscing. "I actually ate at McDonald's recently. I loved it, but I felt dirty."

Lucy laughed and regaled Lonnie with the tales of her cruise ship debacle, California, her movies and her twin marriage proposals. She showed Lonnie the emerald ring from Perry on her finger. Lonnie gasped, as riveted as a frat boy in Bangkok watching a stripper shoot ping-pong balls from her vagina.

"Wow, girl. When you kiss them, they *stay kissed*," said Lonnie.

"Evidently."

"Do you actually *want* to marry either of these guys?"

"Here's the deal. Zack a small-town Texan, and I would jump off the Chrysler Building before I moved to Texas. But back in school, he was my first."

"Oh, dear, so there's *that*. And the doctor?"

"Perry is a mysterious Moroccan who is *completely irresistible*. When I'm around him I feel like I'm under some spell. I can't figure out why he wants to marry me. It makes no sense. Why do I meet these men who are either unavailable or from another planet?"

"Honey, welcome to *my* life. I can't tell if men like me for me or because I'm famous and I'll be their trophy. Not only is it hard being a woman, it's *killer* being a rich and famous woman. Men *hate* that, especially if the woman makes more money. It's the way they're wired. Men just want you to perpetually coo about how wonderful they are: 'Oh, you're the best, you're the baddest, the earth moved thirteen times…' - which makes any sane woman gag."

"Yeah, right?"

"If you were forced to marry one of these guys, who would you choose? Gun to your head."

Lucy thought, and then said, "Gosh. Zack was the first guy in history who made me feel pretty, but it's *history*. We had a fling in California, but I was lonely and exhausted and he just appeared. I felt he was trying to pick up where we left off. I've moved on, and he hasn't."

"Texas does that to people."

"But you should see Perry. He looks like the Prince of Persia. My own mother wants to nail him. I don't mean to sound shallow, but he walks into a room and you can hear people thinking, 'who's *that?*'"

"What's wrong with shallow?" said Lonnie. "You're going to be a public figure, with two movies coming out. A glamour guy might be just the thing."

"He's a Muslim. I'm Episcopalian, sort of. Not that that matters, but…"

"Would he make you wear one of those head things, those fucking *shawls*, or whatever? Would you have to dress like a ninja?"

"Ha! No."

"Then have him here, and see."

Four days later, Lucy received an email from Republic Pictures inviting her to a screening of *Winter Of Our Discontent*, shown at the Venice Film Festival in Italy, three weeks hence. Wow. August *really did* work fast. It was a "rough cut," meaning that it was not completed, but evidently the powers that be decided to show it to the masses to get reactions.

Who should be my escort, I wonder?

She emailed Perry.

Want to come to Italy? My movie is opening in three weeks. It's a festival. We could meet in Venice and you could come to the premiere with me. You need a tuxedo. Xoxo Lucy

Within four hours, she received a reply.

My dear Lucy –

Just tell me when and where, I will come. I have a tuxedo. I remain – what is xoxo? Perry

The next day, a press agent from Republic called her to inquire if she already had a dress to wear, and if not, would she be interested in being fitted by Malan Tatou to wear one of his couture creations, with the caveat that she would mention his name to reporters on the red carpet?

Who am I all of a sudden, Catherine Zeta-Jones? Are you kidding?

Designer Malan Tatou was a slender dandy who sported an accent of indeterminate origin, as if born in the middle of the ocean and raised by Vikings. At his studio, he and his assistants fluttered about Lucy like moths around a porch light, fitting her for one gown more staggering than the next, until he screamed, "RED!"

"Sorry?" said a startled Lucy.

"Ah don't know why ah have been doing all these purples and blues, you must wear red! You are beautiful big girl, you will be fire hydrant! Don't move!" He scurried into another room.

"I'm not moving," said Lucy, standing in her underwear. *A fire hydrant?*

Tatou retuned with a dress of silk, taffeta and bugle beads that was, indeed, *red*. Not like a hydrant; like a caboose that glowed from within, as if in Disneyland's Main Street electrical parade.

Lucy had been used to wearing dark, slimming colors and a dress this *red* was intimidating. She struggled into it. It was too tight, of course, at which point Tatou simply began strategically cutting to let it out. When he was finished, she looked at herself. Yep, a caboose.

"You like?"

"Gosh, I don't know," said Lucy, trying not to be impolite. It was indeed a gorgeous gown that hugged her bust and flowed out from the waist with a slight trail, but she was afraid –

"You think it make you look fat? You will not. Trust me. *This* is the dress. I will take in here and let out here, and will add bustier. You will look like princess."

"It's just so…"

"So what?" said Tatou, daring Lucy to criticize his couturier genius.

"Red," said Lucy. "Is red in season?"

"Always," snapped Tatou. "Red gown always makes papers. Is daring and you will be talk of town. Come back tomorrow."

Lucy was afraid that she might be overdressed for a screening of an unfinished movie, but Audra, the press agent, assured her that this was an international film festival and everyone treated it like a rehearsal for the Oscars. Even the janitors wore tuxedoes.

When she returned the next afternoon, she was stunned. Tatou was, indeed, a genius. The dress was redder than a five-alarm fire, but it fit her perfectly, and the addition of a brocade bustier in a slightly darker shade was the icing on the cake.

"Wow," she said.

"You say my name on red carpet, I not gonna have you look like prostitute. You will make Angelina Jolie want to kill herself. You do hair like this." Tatou fussed with her hair and approximated a styling. "I will call Giorgio, in Venice, to do hair. I give you jewelry."

Tatou exited and then entered again in a flash, like the cartoon Road Runner. He returned with a two-stranded diamond necklace, and put it around her neck.

"Is by Harry Merrick, loaned for Meryl Streep, but she pooh-pooh it. You like? You lose it, it cost you $24,000."

Lucy couldn't believe she was standing in a roughly thirty-five thousand-dollar outfit, and the shoes and earrings hadn't even been selected. But she had to admit that the overall effect was smashing. "I'll take it," she said.

For the next two weeks she floated along on the biggest high she had ever experienced. She was about to attend her first premiere in a designer dress on the arm of a designer man. She sang a few nights at Martell's with the aura of a long gone star returning in triumph. The entire New York show business community was aware that her cruise calamity had generated two movies and Oscar buzz, due to an item in the *Post* placed strategically by Audra, and some were quite envious, planning their own headline-grabbing antics to jump-start flailing careers.

Four days before she was to fly to Venice, she had a meeting with Audra covering talking points to give to reporters. Lucy said she would work with Rick to come up with quotable lines. As this was her first red carpet experience, she didn't want to say too much, the wrong thing, or a combination thereof.

Suddenly her cell phone rang. "Excuse me. Hello?"

"Hey, babe." It was Zack.

Lucy shuddered at the inconvenience. Audra saw her mood abruptly change. "Hey, I can't talk right now, I'm in a meeting."

"You going home after?"

"Uh, yeah, I'll call you then." She hung up. "Sorry, where were we?"

"Anything wrong?"

"Uh, no. Old boyfriend. Never mind."

"I feel your pain."

After the meeting, Lucy walked to her apartment. Near the entrance, she saw something in the corner of her eye. She turned to look, and her heart banged out a *wham*, like she had seen a ghost, but it wasn't a ghost. It was leaning against a car.

"Hey, babe."

"What the - "

"Hope this ain't a bad time."

Lucy did her best to camouflage her shock, took a deep breath and walked towards Zack. When she got close to him, it was unsettling. He looked like he hadn't bathed, shaved or changed clothes in several days, like he had hitched a ride on the floor of a freight train. He carried a worn backpack.

While she had been shocked and happy to see him in Los Angeles, this time she was shocked and annoyed. She needed this now like she needed quadruplets.

"What are you doing here?"

"Ain't you glad to see me?" Zack leaned in to kiss her, but she pulled away, as if he smelled of spoiled armadillo meat. She shook her head moved her hands in the air, physically searching for the proper words.

"Zack, you can't just keep *showing up* without a phone call. You're moving into stalker territory. What if I hadn't been here?"

"Then I woulda gone back to Texas."

"How did you get my address? I never told you."

"Your mama."

Good old mom. Next thing you know she'll be giving my address to total strangers after the movie comes out. "Hi, I loved your daughter in that movie and I'd love to meet her." "Sure, here's her address and phone, just show up, I'm sure you're a nice person and she'd love to take you to dinner!"

"Zack, I'm going to Italy in three days. I can't visit right now. I'm really busy."

Zack looked stricken, like she had just informed him she was about to abort their baby. His lower lip trembled and he stared at the concrete. Lucy had no choice. "Look, come on up, let's talk." He followed her into the building like a lost puppy.

Zack sat on the couch, staring at the floor, while Lucy went to the kitchen. "Do you want something? I have juice and soda."

"Vodka?"

"I'm out. And I haven't been drinking much lately, anyway. I'm trying to lose weight. Liquor makes me puffy. You look awful."

Zack was surprised at Lucy's sour demeanor, like she had spent the night in a pickle barrel. "Well, I reckon this is what happens when you go Hollywood," he said, resentfully.

"What are you talking about?"

"I guess old friends don't mean nothing to you no more."

"Zack, that is totally unfair and you know it. How do you expect me to react when you just *show up?*"

"You sure seemed glad to see me in LA."

"I was, and that was convenient. This isn't."

"And now you're too busy for old strays like me."

"I'm too busy for *anybody,* and you're not an *old stray,* what's with the dramatics? Are you drunk? Where are you staying?"

"I thought I'd stay here, with you."

Of course. Now what?

"You need a shower. What's going on? You don't seem like you. Talk to me."

Zack took a couple of breaths, his hands nervously patting his knees.

"OK. I'm...yeah, I've been drinking. A lot. I ain't thought about nothing but you since California. I can't sleep. Every day I walk into that damn hardware store I want to nuke it. Yesterday I couldn't stand it no more and I called the airline. I had to see you. I want you to marry me." His gaze moved from the floor up to her. He looked like a homeless man about to beg for change.

Overcome with concern for her old friend, Lucy sat on the couch next to him, choosing her words carefully. "Zack, no. I love you and I always will, but I'm not going to marry you, not now, not ever. What we did in California was wonderful, but you caught me at a weak moment and – "

"A *weak moment?* That's *it?*" Zack sputtered, flush with anger. "You just think I'm some grapefruit you can squeeze the juice out of and forget? None of that meant *nothing* to you?"

Lucy was startled by this outburst and the sudden role reversal. It was usually a spurned woman who jacked up the melodrama, not the man.

"I didn't mean it like that. I was happy to see you and we had a great time. But you have your life and I have - "

Zack abruptly stood up and started pacing, his words spitting out like soda from a shaken bottle. "I got *no life,* Lucy. I got no reason to get up in the morning. All I got is that stupid store and my family that drives me nuts. There's nobody like you, never has been. If you don't marry me, I don't know what I'll - "

"You'll move on is what you'll do. You'll – "

"And do *what?*" he screamed. "The same crap I'm doing? I don't even listen to people no more, I'm stuck in my head, and that's a dangerous neighborhood."

Other than calling for takeout delivery of electroshock therapy, Lucy didn't know what to do. This was a Zack she had never seen. This wasn't the good old boy who never let anything bother him. She recalled the same look on his face she had seen that day in acting class, when he confessed his barnyard horror. And, to her shock, it was the first time in her life she was frightened of him.

She took a breath, and said, "What can I do?"

"Marry me." The look on his face was not the stuff of proposals. It was the stuff of threats.

Lucy stood up and looked at him, and put her hand on his face. She wanted to somehow wash away his pain, but was as helpless as a lost child at the bottom of a well.

"No."

Suddenly, Zack grabbed her shoulders and screamed into her face, "No? You can't marry that fuckin' Arab! What are you, crazy? You know what those people are like! You gotta marry me, goddammit!"

"I'm not – "

Zack abruptly slapped her on her left cheek, ending her sentence. She let out a little yelp, put her hand to her face and looked at him in horror. Her face stung. No one, in her entire life, had ever slapped her. Zack withdrew his hand and glowered at it in disgust, as if it were radioactive.

"Zack, what has *happened* to you?"

Unable to say anything, he grabbed his backpack from the floor. "I gotta get out of here," he sputtered.

"And go where?"

He stood up, walked towards the door, and looked at her with the look of someone about to jump off a bridge. "You have a good time wherever you're going," he said. "Don't worry about me. I'm real sorry, Lucy." He opened the door, walked out, closed the door, and was gone.

In fifteen minutes she had whiplashed from excited and confident to petrified. Lucy sat on the couch and burst into tears.

Wow, girl. When you kiss them, they stay kissed.

17

"Miss Dixon, over here!" *Flash.* "Lucy! Over here, please!" *Flash, flash, pop, flash.* "Over here, Lucretia!" *Flash flash flashflashflashflashflash.* Lucy was astonished that some Italian paparazzi even knew her name, much less her given name, but blinded by the flashbulbs and jostled by the cacophony of the red carpet, she didn't have time to ask. But she had to admit that *Lucretia* sounded better with an Italian accent. *Lu-cre-ti-a!*

"Who's the man, Lucy? Is that your boyfriend? Over here!"

Holy crap. Flash. Flash. Over here, please! Flash.

"Are you believing this?" she said to Perry, through her frozen smile.

"No, it is like a movie."

"It *is* a movie," Lucy said.

Having already done five red carpet interviews and saying, "fabulous," "thrilling" and "thank you" so many times she thought the next time she spoke it would be accompanied by vomit, Lucy was still amazed. No matter how schooled you are by press and marketing people, no matter how many times a designer instructs you how to maneuver your gown, nothing prepares you for your first time on a red carpet in front of the world press. It's like trying to casually stroll through a nuclear explosion singing "Edelweiss." And from all over the world they were – Europe, Madagascar, the Delaware Water Gap, you name it.

Lucy's mind briefly flashed back to her previous red carpet experience four years earlier at the Tony Awards. That night, as she sat in Radio City Music Hall and listened to her name read as a nominee, she felt like she had just run a marathon but had to stop a foot from the finish line and wait until the judges allowed her to finish. She thought she might collapse if she weren't already sitting. It was the biggest night of her life as a critically acclaimed nominee in a Broadway hit, on a nationally televised show, about to perhaps be awarded Broadway's Oscar. Her mind reflected back to her days back in Asheville religiously watching the show with her theater buddies, that ragtag bunch of misfits who wait for the Tonys with the same fever most jocks wait for the Super Bowl.

Rick, her escort, was seated next to her and apparently oblivious enough to choose that moment to pick his nose, seen on camera for a few seconds by the viewers at home. Lucy smiled as she subtly kicked him, and his moist finger quickly disappeared between his legs and soiled his tuxedo.

She didn't win the Tony, and life went downhill from there. The show closed, her father died, Ida had the stroke, and she moved back home to be a nursemaid. Now, as she was standing on the red carpet in Venice with Perry at her side, she thought, *Wow. All that, and somehow I ended up here. And it's all a fluke.*

Lucy had warned Perry that the world media would photograph him and that there was a chance his wife might see the pictures on the Internet. Perry said, "I am here to escort you, and that is what I will do. Don't worry. It is your show."

Lucy looked like a million dollars – more accurately, about $40,000. An Italian associate of Tatou's showed up at her hotel room to help her get dressed and styled, and was also in custody of her ridiculously expensive necklace. Giorgio of Venice did her hair, a simple styling that made her face seem thinner. She felt like one of Cinderella's more glamorous stepsisters.

Perry proved he possessed sartorial elegance in addition to medical skills, emerging from his room wearing a black tuxedo, black silk vest and black shirt. Instead of a tie he wore a dark green pendant at his neck, another jewel that belonged to his grandmother. His jet-black hair grazed his shoulders. Lucy realized that, except in the cruise ship's medical center, she had never seen him wear anything but black. He looked like the world's chicest cat burglar.

TV correspondents were camera ready, with perky smiles and chirpy voices. Lucy had seen it for years on shows like *Entertainment Tonight*. Now, she stood ready to be interviewed by an attractive, and surgically enhanced, woman from that very show.

Audra, the press agent, resplendent in a silver gown and holding a clipboard, escorted Lucy and Perry to their mark in front of the camera. "This is Lucy Dixon, who plays Joanne, this is her film debut and her first premiere, and there's already Oscar buzz," she barked to the interviewer, who clearly had no idea who Lucy was. "Got it. Are we rolling?" the interviewer said to the cameraman, who nodded.

"So, Lucy Dixon, welcome to Venice, and I understand this is your first premiere?"

"Yes, this is really something," said Lucy, struggling to speak over the hullabaloo of the crowd. The bright camera floodlights nearly gave her cataracts. "My first time in Venice, too; it's such a beautiful city."

"So, Lucy, what was it like working with August Huff, your director?"

"I learned a lot, he pushed me, definitely, but he seemed happy with my work, so we'll see. I haven't seen the movie yet so the jury's still out."

"I understand there's Oscar buzz about your performance."

"Well, if that's the case, I'm grateful that people have lowered their standards," laughed Lucy, using one of Rick's self-deprecating lines.

"And who's the handsome gentleman with you?"

"Oh, this is my friend, Perry," said Lucy, turning to see Perry standing about a foot behind her.

"Are you excited about tonight, Perry?"

Perry leaned into the microphone and said, "This is Lucy's night and I am very excited for her." He then pulled back to behind Lucy, his body language saying, *that's all, folks*. The *Entertainment Tonight* interviewer found herself staring at him for a few uncomfortable seconds. "Well...um, thank you Lucy, enjoy your big night."

"Thank you so much," beamed Lucy, who then took Perry's arm and moved down the press line escorted by Audra. Another camera crew promptly snapped to attention. Audra said a few words to the interviewer, and the lights flared on again.

"Lucy Dixon, Simon Wells, BBC. So, how does it feel, your first premiere?"

"It's wonderful, Simon. I didn't think it would be this big a deal."

"So Lucy, is it true that August Huff cast you after he saw your appearance on CNN talking about your experience falling off a ship?"

Lucy was prepared for this, yet surprised at the interviewer's bluntness. But this was the BBC, and British journalists were notorious for going for the gossip faster than a pledge in a sorority. "Well, you'll have to ask him that. I had to audition for it."

"But I understand he asked you to audition after seeing you on that show."

"Who knows? He also knew my work from the theater. Hey, if falling off a ship and talking about it got me here, I should do it more often." Lucy laughed, feeling her forced smile was about to break her jaw.

"Some say you used your suicide attempt to get attention."

Lucy was instantly annoyed. *It wasn't suicide, you limey jerk.* Yet she gamely laughed, and said, "It was just my natural clumsiness. I'm just a klutz, and I'm amazed I haven't fallen on my face right here. This dress is a hazard." She laughed again, stifling her impulse to shove Simon's microphone down his throat. Rick had told her this might happen, and all she could do was to laugh her way through it. To argue with an aggressive reporter is to lose, but to smile and laugh it off it is to win. She wanted to say nothing and run away, but didn't want to seem like a Republican Tea Party Senate candidate fleeing from the Liberal Media.

"Is this gentleman your fiancée?"

Lucy took Perry's arm and knew that she had to get away from this insufferable nudge, pronto. "He's here to make sure I don't fall on my face, which is likely at this point. Thank you so much."

Perry pulled her away from the interviewer, who looked cheated, as if Lucy had snowballed him on the scoop of his career. Perry whispered, "He was rude, wasn't he?"

"That's what we call being 'in your face.'"

"Are you OK?"

"I feel like if I smile any more I'll need a facelift."

"Are you enjoying yourself?"

Perry was so chivalrous Lucy could picture him rescuing her from a burning castle and then galloping away together on a horse. "It's unnerving, but hell yeah, this is a scream. Are you kidding?"

Audra barged into their conversation and said, "That guy was a dick, sorry about that. We've done enough on camera stuff anyway, want to just go in?"

"Sure," said Lucy.

"*Love* the dress, Tatou really delivered. You look great."

"Thanks."

Lucy and Perry inched their way past the phalanx of reporters and photographers. There were no more interviews, just more smiles and flashes. Perry never actually smiled; he just grinned like a North African Cheshire cat, retaining his mysterious air. Lucy knew that many reporters were wondering, *who's that, some Bollywood star?* Perry was the one who looked like a celebrity. Next to him, she felt like a South Carolina homecoming contestant.

In the theater, Lucy and Perry sat on the tenth row among the chi-chi audience. August took the stage and spoke. He said that the movie was almost finished and did not yet have the titles or music score, but it was very close to what the final cut would look like. He made a few more remarks and left the stage to applause and the lights dimmed. *This better be good,* she thought. *This crowd didn't get all dolled up for nothing.*

Lucy and Perry settled in to watch the movie. The one title that managed to be edited into the presentation said, *Winter Of Our Discontent – A Film by August Huff.* Lucy thought that it might as well have said, as had so many esoteric foreign films, "Un film de August Huff."

As the movie unreeled, it became clear that it was indeed a *film,* not a *movie. Spiderman* is a movie. This was a *film,* like Ingmar Bergman at his most depressingly Swedish, with lots of close-ups and pregnant pauses. All it needed was Liv Ullmann tearfully staring at a vase. It was the dark story of a suburban family in crisis, centering on the husband's infidelity, the wife's religious fanaticism, and the teenagers' drug use and promiscuity. Even the dog had issues. Lucy's role was small but key as an alcoholic with marital problems. The first time Lucy appeared onscreen, she was alarmed at how she looked, shuffling around the house in her bathrobe with a severe hangover. She had to admit it looked authentic, but for her first film role she would have preferred a little glamour.

She also thought the performances were phenomenal. It was almost as if the actors were real people and the camera, often hand-held, just happened to be there. An intimate scene between the husband and wife was so up close and personal the audience almost felt it was none of their business. One of Lucy's scenes, where she stood in front of her bathroom mirror wearing only a bra and panties, looking at herself in the mirror with utter contempt, was even embarrassing. But it said more about her character than any dialogue could have.

Lucy hoped for a few laughs, and there were, indeed, few. This bunch of characters needed a month at a spa in Maui. Her domestic attack scene was particularly harrowing, as the husband attempted to force himself on her in the kitchen and she fended him off with various utensils and appliances. She thought that if Ida ever saw it she might have another stroke.

Thankfully, the film ended as hopefully as possible considering the grim lives of the characters, and for the most part it was moving, though one would be hard pressed to call it *entertaining*. It reminded Lucy of other down-elevator-to-hell films that might cause a viewer to say to their date, "Next time *I* get to pick the movie." She thought it might find an audience with the art house crowd, but die the death in shopping mall cineplexes. The *Harry Potter* audience would run screaming from the theater.

As the lights came up, the audience applauded and August took the stage to bow. It was hearty applause, but not a standing ovation. Everyone was exhausted from 115 minutes of emotional torture. Lucy was confused, since she was a comic actress and her character was not funny, so she couldn't tell if she had pulled it off or not. Watching oneself onscreen is a disconcerting experience, like viewing your own colonoscopy while munching a tub of popcorn.

Perry said. "You are a great actress."

"You think? I'm not sure. I'll have to see it again. I'm sort of stunned. Is it a good movie?"

"Good, but depressing. Very American. It would never get made in my country. Women do not express themselves in this way."

"They should be grateful. After this, I feel like wearing a burqa and hibernating for a week."

"You should be proud."

"Well, August yanked it out of me."

"I am proud to be here with you. This is an experience I have never had."

"And you think I have?"

"Good point."

"What did you think?" said August, at the after-party in the theater's lobby bar, sipping his second scotch. "I'm finally calming down. That was nerve-wracking."

"Well, it could have used a couple of dancing girls and show tunes, but overall I enjoyed it, everyone in it is great. Not exactly light entertainment," said Lucy. She was still disoriented by it, but didn't want to rain on August's parade. "What do *you* think?"

"I like it, but I wrote and directed it. It's bloody hell. I've won an Oscar and I'm always one film away from total ruin. Thank God for Xanax."

Lucy was surprised to see this other side of August, who was a hyper-confident sadist on the set but, evidently, just as insecure about his work as the next poor showbiz sucker. It reminded her of how her first impression of Lonnie Jones so differed from what she knew now.

"Oh, August, this is my friend, Perry, from Morocco."

"Ah, the famous doctor. Thanks for rescuing her. You saved a great talent."

"I did not rescue her, I just took her vitals," said Perry, shaking his hand. "Very good film."

"Thanks. We'll see."

"*Lucy,* you're brilliant, *my God*, what a performance," said Audra, who popped up accompanied by three others. "This is Robert Caravetta from Richard Hagen's office, Easton Wells from Don Brantley's office, and Carlo Renato from Dave Bartee's office."

"You're great," said Carlo.

"Fabulous," said Easton.

"Nice work, both of you," said Robert.

Hands shook, tongues wagged and heads nodded. "Thank you, this is Perry," said Lucy. Perry did not extend his hand, instead slightly bowing to everyone: "How do you do?"

"So, August, looks like you have another prestige picture on your hands," said Easton, speaking in rapid-fire showbiz rat-tat-tat-tat. "The buzz is very good. Depends on how we market it, of course. Probably a slow build in Oscar season, open in New York and LA and then go wide after the reviews. Lucy, they're talking about campaigning you for supporting."

"Supporting what?"

"Actress. The Oscar."

"Oh, stop it."

"No, seriously. It's one of those breakthrough debuts, like Marlee Matlin or Mo'Nique or somebody. The press loves that crap. Hope you're prepared for the attention."

"Probably not," laughed Lucy, nervously.

"Can Perry here do some press with you? Always great to have a guy around," said Robert. "You two an item?"

"No, no, we're just friends. Perry lives in Morocco."

The three looked at him, obviously intrigued. Perry grinned at them, said nothing, then after an awkward pause said, "Yes. In Casablanca." His silence and enigmatic appearance had them riveted.

"Ah, the international long-distance relationship angle," said Carlo.

Lucy realized that, being press and marketing people, they were looking for dish for the press campaign about her, a new gadget to be introduced to the marketplace. She laughed a nervous laugh and said, "Well, um, you guys do what you have to do, this is all new to me. Those pictures all the paparazzi took, where are those going to end up?" asked Lucy.

"Oh, everywhere," said Audra. "We'll pitch them around and see who bites. *People, US, Star,* all the fan rags. *Women's Wear Daily,* definitely, for the Tatou angle. And with the Internet, you never know. They may end up on a blog in Antarctica. It's a great dress and you two look fabulous. Who are you wearing, Perry, so we can include that?"

"Sorry?" said Perry.

"Your designer."

"Oh." Perry was wearing an inexpensive tuxedo he wore on formal nights on the ship that he bought years ago in a

Morocco shop. He never thought anyone would ask him who designed it, but he sensed what these people wanted to hear, so he embellished.

"Well, it is by a very talented tailor, in a small shop in Casablanca, named Ahmed. He is a simple man who makes everything by hand and struggles to support his family. The vest was my father's, and this pendant was my grandmother's."

Expecting to hear the names of Giorgio Armani or some other chic designer, the press people were impressed with Perry's simplicity, not to mention his transcontinental veneer. "Very snazzy," said Robert. "You should give me his card. I get to Casablanca sometimes."

"I will see what I can do," said Perry.

"Does he have an agent?" said Easton.

"A what?"

"Representation."

"I doubt it."

"We could help him with that," said Robert, not realizing that "Ahmed" was probably a Pakistani sweatshop. These movie people and their pretensions amused Perry. He wondered how long they would last in the streets of Casablanca without a map.

Perry and Lucy stuck around for a while longer and chatted up a few assorted sycophants. Since neither of them knew anyone the conversations were all small talk, and both eventually had had enough of this showbiz blah blah blah. Lucy wanted to put on comfy clothes. Formal attire has a definite shelf life.

Back in Lucy's room at the hotel, as she was getting undressed, she said, *"Ahmed?* Really? Where did you come up with that?"

"It was the first name that popped into my head."

"Hilarious. You did really great with those people. My friend Zack would have lasted about ten minutes."

Lucy realized that this was the first time she had even thought about Zack since the day he had left her apartment. She had been too preoccupied, and every time she thought about him she stifled the thoughts, as if brushing unwanted lint off her clothes. She had assumed he had gone back to Texas, but hadn't heard anything and hadn't called him. She couldn't. Her mood abruptly shifted and her relaxed smile vanished. Perry noticed.

"Who is Zack?"

Lucy paused and then said, "An old friend, from college. He's um, a real small town guy and thinks showbiz people are full of it." She was torn between finding out what had happened to him immediately or just changing her phone number so she could close out that chapter and move on. Every time she had thought about him she was filled with an uncomfortable mixture of nostalgia, longing and dread. She put on her T-shirt and sweatpants, and began hanging the dress in the garment bag.

"Is he an old boyfriend?"

"Uh, yeah. Very old. It was over a long time ago. But, um…"

"What?"

"He's sort of…back in the picture."

Lucy was hesitant because she didn't know how a macho, possessive Arab man would react. Not that Perry was any of these things, but she had seen the news and heard Perry's stories, and didn't want a beheading.

She took a deep breath and essentially told Perry the entire story of Zack, ending with the surprise visit in New York a week ago. She left out the slap, lest Perry decide to personally fly to Waco and stab Zack with a Moroccan machete. Perry listened like only he could listen, his penetrating eyes never wavering from hers. At the end, Perry said, "So, obviously he is in pain. I am sorry for him. Texas sounds like parts of my country – stark, desolate and filled with small-minded people."

Lucy was amazed at his attitude. "Wow. I thought you would be upset with me."

"Of course not. I cannot come into your life and expect you to forget everyone and everything else. Even if we were married, I could not demand that. That thinking only brings misery. I have been through it, and never again. As you Americans say, no thanks."

Lucy looked at him and then gave him a kiss, which transported her to a Venetian gondola while being serenaded by an opera singer with a lute. Since she was in Italy, her fantasies had switched to Italian.

The next day, Lucy attended a press junket about the film with journalists who mercifully asked her simple questions in mostly foreign accents, until one said, "The scene with you in your underwear was very brave, especially since you are a full-figured girl. Did you have any hesitation about showing your body onscreen in that manner?"

Summoning every available ounce of self-esteem from the bottom of her toes, Lucy replied, "No. It was what the scene called for. The character hated her body. I don't. If anyone wants a nude scene, I'm there," she said with an awkward laugh.

Then, an American reporter said, "So, Miss Dixon, some say that you jumped off the ship to get publicity for your career, which was at a standstill at the time. Do you have a comment?"

Lucy took a deep breath and said, "When you think about it, I would have to be insane. Anyone who would jump off a ship as a career move deserves a career scraping barnacles off the hull of that ship." The journalists laughed. Lucy was getting through this inquisition, but it was getting old fast. Throughout the entire press conference she kept repeating in her head, *keep it light, don't get defensive, avoid bashing reporters in face with microphone.*

Later that day, as a needed respite from the chaos of the Festival, Lucy and Perry became tourists. The city was equally chaotic. They visited the Piazza San Marco, a tourist and pigeon infested square where she recalled Katharine Hepburn pining for Rossano Brazzi in *Summertime.* They took a boat tour of the canals, where she leaned against Perry and tried to be romantic, but the smell of fish and sewage was so pungent she had to put Kleenex over her mouth. It smelled like the water from the floor of a flooded porn theater. Venice was beautiful and unique, but the whole place seemed like a living museum where tourists clogged the drainpipes and where only old Italians wearing mothballs could possibly live.

That evening, they sat eating their entrees at the hotel restaurant, a gorgeous, marble columned salon that opened right onto the canal. Buildings gleamed in the twilight. Gondoliers lazily punted along, carrying tourists seeking romance. A vaporetto ferry sped by, causing the gondolas to wobble in its wake and a tourist standing inside a gondola taking pictures to lose his balance and nearly fall into the water. Lucy thought that this was probably the most elegant and romantic place she had ever been. She felt, for the moment, complete peace and tranquility.

Then Perry casually said, between bites of manicotti, "So, have you thought about it?"

"About what?"

"Marrying me."

Lucy's heart jumped, her peace and tranquility no more. It seemed enough that they were two people from opposite lands who had a rendezvous in a magical place, and the future was light years away. She took a deep breath and put down her fork. "Of course, and you're wonderful, but I have no idea how it would possibly work. You're here, I'm there, you're going back on the ship, etcetera."

"If we marry, I can live and work in America. It has always been my dream. You can continue with your career." He ate another mouthful.

Lucy, stunned, looked at him.

"W-what?"

Time stopped. Lucy felt like she came screeching to a halt in a car with a driver who couldn't work a clutch. "Wait," she said. "You want to marry me so you can work in *America?*"

"I would like to have a life with you – "

"Wait, wait, wait, wait, *wait,*" she said, her mood abruptly as curdled as spoiled milk. "You want to marry me so you can work in the States? What am I, a freaking green card?"

"No, you're a beautiful, wonderful, funny woman." Perry instantly knew he had said the wrong thing, yet again, and tried to pour on the charm. He smiled and reached for her hand. She didn't take it.

A huge wet towel had been thrown on her head. She saw the face of her mother wagging her finger and saying, *See? I warned you.* Every good feeling she had about this trip, Perry, their time together, Venice, the movie and life in general instantly drained out of her, as if someone had pulled out a stopper and her insides gushed onto the floor.

"Please, Lucy, my intentions are honorable," Perry said, with an expression that Lucy read as *uh-oh, busted.* "I may have plans to come to America anyway and –"

"Just stop. Just stop right there, doctor," Lucy said, wiping her vanished smile with her napkin and glaring at him. "Don't say anything else."

"Lucy – " Perry looked like he had just lost his dog.

"Don't," she said, shaking her head rapidly. "Just don't. I *knew* this, I *knew* it, but I kept believing, I really did. I thought, maybe a nice man just wants *me*. Maybe he's not a con man like my mother said, he just really loves little old *me*. I am stupid, stupid, stupid." Her eyes welled with tears, and she reached onto her left hand and pulled off Perry's grandmother's ring.

She looked at it with a mixture of longing, regret and resignation. It was indeed gorgeous. She said, "Boy, are you slick. You were even clever enough to make up a tuxedo designer on the spot. What else have you got up those black sleeves?"

"Lucy…"

She held the ring in her right hand, looked at it, looked at him, and then threw it at him. It hit Perry in the left cheek, he pulled back with a start, and the ring clattered onto the floor, noisily echoing throughout the restaurant and perhaps all of Venice. Other diners immediately ceased eating to witness the drama.

Perry's expression was that of a husband confessing to an affair or an eighth grader admitting he had rolled the neighbor's yard with toilet paper. Lucy had seen many expressions from him, but this was the first time she saw shame. He was, alas, just as beautiful. Perry looked at her a moment, then began searching for the ring on the floor. He found it a few feet away, picked it up, and said, "This is for you. I wanted you to have this. Please take it." He placed it on the table in front of her.

Lucy's cheeks were streaked with tears. She looked at him, took a breath, and choked out, "Have a nice life, Perry. I'm sorry this didn't work out for you. Maybe you can find another gullible gringo who will fall for it. Until then, enjoy the ship. Maybe some other idiot will fall off and you can show your fabulous bedside manner. Goodbye."

With that, she quickly wiped her eyes one more time with the napkin, took it in her hand, stood up, and walked away with a flourish that would have been highly dramatic and effective, except it wasn't the napkin she was holding, it was the edge of the tablecloth. She walked about four feet and then everything on the table – entrees, salads, wine glasses, salt and pepper shakers, utensils and a vase with a single orchid – came crashing to the ground with a loud series of clinks, clanks and jangles that echoed off the marble walls. Waiters stopped in their tracks. A few diners stifled giggles. Nearby gondoliers lifted their poles from the water and looked in.

Lucy, knowing that yanking a tablecloth off of a dining table was both a magician's trick and a classic comedy routine, even one featured on *I Love Lucy*, would have normally burst into hysterical laughter. But she didn't. She stood there a moment, surveyed the mess on the floor, looked one more time at the stunned Perry, and ran out of the restaurant.

She didn't wait for the elevator. She went to the stairs and ran up the three marble flights as fast as she could. She fumbled in her purse for her key card and opened the door to her room, slamming it behind her. Her clothes were everywhere. She quickly surveyed the room and in a kind of wild panic began to grab the clothes and throw them into her suitcase. She worked fast, choking out sobs, and once she had emptied the drawers and her suitcase was full, she opened the closet door and grabbed the garment bag holding her red gown, zipping it up so fast the bag almost ripped. She then ran into the bathroom, grabbed her toiletries, threw them into the plastic Ziploc bag and put it in the suitcase. She put the suitcase on the floor and closed it, easier said than done since the clothes were in wads. She pushed the top of the suitcase down with her knees and struggled to zip it closed. After a few tries, she manage to secure it.

She looked around the room to double check that she hadn't left anything, went to the bed and picked up her purse. Looking inside to make sure she had her wallet, phone, cash and passport, she snapped it shut. Her heart pounded and beads of sweat formed on her forehead. She went to the closet, grabbed her coat, put it on, took her purse, pulled the handle out of the suitcase, stood it on its wheels, slung the gown over her right arm, and opened the door. She ran to the elevator, pushed the call button repeatedly, and eons passed before it arrived. When it did, she rushed inside and pushed the lobby button. She felt like she was in a Hitchcock movie fleeing from a villain.

The elevator doors opened and Lucy walked quickly to the reception desk. She put her key card on the desk and said, "I'm sorry, I have to leave now. Dixon, Lucretia, room 306. Just put any changes on the card. Thank you."

"Scusa, signora?" said the startled clerk.

With that, she went towards the exit, down the steps and out the revolving door. Her suitcase got caught and stopped the door twice until she yanked it up, falling into the glass door and nearly breaking it.

"Taxi?" she said, to the valet. The valet nodded quickly and took the whistle hanging around his neck and blew it, the piercing sound startling Lucy. A waiting taxi sped up to the door, the driver got out, and Lucy said, "Aeroporto, per favore." The driver opened the trunk, took Lucy's bags and put them in. He shut the trunk and then moved to open the door for her. She got into the car and he shut the door and moved to the driver's side. She briefly glanced back the revolving door. In front of it stood Perry.

Lucy shook with a start and looked at him. To her he looked like a vampire staring down a virgin.

More sobs claimed their place in her throat. She barked at the driver. "Go, please."

The driver hit the ignition and the car sped forward. Lucy looked back and watched Perry recede into the distance.

18

A week earlier, after he had left Lucy's apartment, Zack stood on the sidewalk like a confused tourist, with no clue as to what to do next. He was utterly humiliated at his behavior, but oddly enough wasn't worried that Lucy would press charges, like Tiffany. He just hoped she would be able to forgive him. That he had behaved like a barroom drunk going after waitress made him feel like the dumbest hick in the stupidest town in the most backward state in the nation.

His entire reason for coming to New York had been to persuade Lucy to either marry him or at least resume their relationship, and he was staggered by her overwhelmingly negative response. His feelings for her, born again in California, seemed flushed down the drain on the sidewalk. He felt ashamed, thinking that unrequited love was usually the province of lovesick teenagers or fifty-something spinsters, not macho Texans. Nevertheless, here he was.

But maybe he wasn't such a macho Texan after all. He had been thinking about that a lot lately, bombarded by negative thoughts that show up unannounced, like Mormon missionaries. Those thoughts were partly what caused him to start drinking again. That, and the sheer mind crushing boredom he experienced day after day. He had many acquaintances but few close friends, no hobbies, and spent most of the time wanting to be anywhere but where he was.

His days were spent at the hardware store supervising his three employees and ordering exciting items like mulchers and leaf blowers. Lately, because so many had upgraded their home theater systems, he had experienced a run on extension cords, high-definition cables and multiple strip outlets. His nights were spent at home watching sports or surfing the Internet visiting the occasional porn site, infrequent bowling nights, or at bars frequented by tired cowboys, rednecks and butt-ugly women.

A year ago, he didn't think he was an alcoholic. After all, he didn't start drinking until after work. The problem was, he didn't stop. When one too many ghastly hangovers and a DUI arrest caused him to seek out his first Alcoholics Anonymous meeting in a dank Waco Baptist church basement, he was determined to do something, anything, to help alleviate the massive daily tedium that segued into melancholy before finally becoming rage. At least he might find someone to talk to.

In that meeting and in subsequent ones afterwards, he heard ordinary people tell of the desperate places their addictions had led them, places not on any map in Texas. At first he thought, *I'm not like these people, I'm just lonely and bored.* He sat through five meetings before he spoke a word, since hearing others candidly indulge in such emotional vomit was completely foreign. He finally spoke, saying, "My name is Zack, and I think I'm an alcoholic but I'm not sure, I just drink too much, and is there any way the program allows for one or two drinks a day or something?"

Some in the group reacted like he was a pedophile requesting permission to molest kids on alternate Tuesdays, but others chuckled and mouthed, "No." But as he continued his first share, long repressed truths poured out and tears ran down his cheeks. His feelings had shut down since his marriage. It had been a hell of a long stretch of telling nobody how he really felt about anything.

Eventually, he began to see how he used alcohol not as enjoyable relaxation but to anesthetize the debilitating shame he had felt most of his life. He had been ashamed of his poor upbringing, his family, his country accent, his adulterous marriage, and the hardware store. He was ashamed of his childhood home, which looked like Dorothy's house after it crashed into Munchkinland. And he had never gotten over the shame of the barnyard incident and never spoke of it until it was yanked out of him in acting class.

He continued to attend meetings and told the group everything about his life and, in fellowship, listened to their advice. These people had been around the block, even if that block was only downtown Waco. He was able to remain relatively sober and felt better about himself, realizing that the only person who could pull him out of his miseries was staring at him in the mirror. He remembered a mantra he heard over and over in meetings – *If you take simple action and reach out, help is there.*

That said, he decided to take action and impulsively visited Lucy in California, did not mention his problems, and thought, *what the hell, I might as well enjoy myself*. He drank on that trip, continued drinking when he returned home, stopped going to meetings, and returned promptly to square one.

Now, he walked the streets in a daze amid countless people but feeling totally alone, like Joe Buck cruising Times Square in *Midnight Cowboy*. He knew it was over with Lucy and realized that making the trip here was hitting some sort of bottom. Now all he could do was find a place to stay the night and then get the hell home.

He reckoned he was only man in the world who felt like this, his problems callously oblivious to passersby, but had no clue how many people walked the streets of New York in exactly the same mood. New York is good for that; easy to lose oneself in a crowd while stuck in one's head, indeed a more dangerous neighborhood than the slums of The Bronx. Even though this was only his second trip to New York, the sights and sounds that would dazzle a normal tourist left him numb and remote, like he was watching it all from inside an aquarium.

He found himself standing under the Hotel Edison marquee on West 47th Street between 7th and 8th Avenue. *OK, it says 'Hotel." And "Edison," Maybe it's one of them old hotels Edison stayed in or something.* He went into the lobby, which was filled with people of various ethnicities holding suitcases, speaking strange languages. It was an old hotel but it had a warm feeling, as if it could serve as a home away from home for lost souls.

He approached the front desk. A tired Indian desk clerk said, "Yes, may I help you?"

"Uh, you got a room for tonight?"

"How many, sir?"

"Just me."

"And how long will you be staying with us?"

"Just tonight. How much?"

"One moment, please." The clerk checked the computer. Zack looked around. So many people, from so many places, in town for God knows what reason.

"Yes sir, we have a nice room with a view of the street, $169 plus tax."

"You know where I can eat something?"

The clerk perked up. "Ah, yes, may I recommend our restaurant, the Café Edison, also known as the Polish Tea Room."

"The what?"

"Do you know the Russian Tea Room?"

"Uh, no."

"On 57th Street. Very famous clientele. Ours is where people from Broadway shows go to eat, not expensive, home cooking. They will give you a good hot meal. Maybe you can see some Broadway stars."

"OK, thanks." Zack was surprised. Here was a big city stranger with an odd accent telling him where he could get a good hot meal and perhaps watch some New York actors eat their soup. *If you take simple action and reach out, help is there.*

After he went up to his room, a decent hotel room with a view of sensational 47th Street, he took off his clothes and showered. He had not bathed in several days and felt shame about that, too. Drying off, he observed himself in the mirror. He still had a great body for a thirty-seven year old. In fact, if you divide all men into handsome vs. ugly, he was a knockout.

Dressed in the one pair of clean clothes he brought with him, he went down to the Polish Tea Room and sat at the bar. The large glass case filled with rotating desserts resembled those in Texas diners, and the waitresses milling about behind the bar made him feel less alone. The menu was filled with dishes he had never heard of, like kielbasa and kasha, but the meat loaf and mashed potatoes seemed harmless. A plump waitress with a strange accent took his order.

The restaurant was about half full, and Zack looked around. If there were any Broadway actors in here he wouldn't have the foggiest who they were, but he didn't care, since he had never given a damn about celebrities or social status his entire life; or maybe it was because he was raised in a lower class family and defensively derided anyone who thought they were hot stuff. Maybe he secretly *did* want an upgrade, part of which had led him back to Lucy. But if his AA meetings had taught him anything, money and fame were no guarantees of happiness whatsoever. One man in his group was a multimillionaire Texas oilman on his fourth wife who still felt like the same little fat boy everybody made fun of, and one day the poor sucker attempted suicide by attaching a hose to the exhaust of his Lamborghini and closing the garage door, a glamorous way to go if nothing else.

Seated two seats down at the bar was an attractive brunette in jeans and a blouse who looked to be in her late twenties, sipping soup. She was looking at Zack, and smiled when he turned to look at her. He turned away and then looked at her again. She was now staring at him.

"Um, excuse me," she said, "but are you Brad Pitt?"

Zack laughed. "No ma'am."

"Sorry. I guess you get that a lot."

"Uh, no ma'am. I'm from Texas, and nobody cares."

"Texas? Really? Welcome to New York."

Zack was taken aback at how forward she was, but this was New York and he was unaccustomed to local behavior. "Thank you. Are you an actress? They told me lots of show people eat in here."

"Not at all. I just came here because I was hungry and I have to go to a meeting in a bit. What brings you to New York?"

Zack paused, and then looked away and said, "Um, chasing after a girl, to tell you the truth."

The woman smiled. "And how's that going for you?"

Zack sort of smiled, took a sip of water, and then said, "Shoulda stayed home."

"None of my business."

Zack looked at her. She was very pretty. "Buy you a drink?"

The woman sipped her soup and then said, "No thank you, I don't drink. I'm an alcoholic."

Zack was shocked that she just blurted it out like that, but then remembered that some people in the program used this tool of admission to help them stay sober. "No kiddin'? You go to meetings and everything?"

"Every day I can manage. Sober two years now," she said, knocking on the Formica counter in absence of wood with her knuckles, with an unmistakable look of pride, like a little girl who had finally gotten an A+ in arithmetic.

Zack thought a minute and then decided to take the plunge. He extended his hand. "My name is Zack, and *I'm* an alcoholic, but I've been off the wagon for several months now, sad to say."

"Monica," she said, shaking his hand. "Sorry about that, but we all have our slips."

"Yes, ma'am, I reckon I'm in the middle of a really big one."

"Well, I wish you the best. Have you been to any meetings while you're here?"

"No ma'am, just got here today."

"How long are you here? Love your accent, by the way."

"It's a pretty hick town accent, sorry. Leaving tomorrow I reckon. You live here?"

"Yep, been here since I got out of college. I'm from Minnesota. I came here to be an actress, but that didn't happen, mainly because of my drinking. Now I work at a modeling agency."

"That's cool." The waitress put a plate of meat loaf, mashed potatoes and broccoli in front of Zack.

"Well, I'll let you eat, it was nice talking to you," said Monica.

"No, it's nice to have somebody to talk to, I've had a rough day."

Monica thought a moment, and then said, "I'm actually going to a meeting in an hour. Would you like to join me? It's at eight and it's right down the street, that's why I came in here. It's a good meeting to end the day with."

Zack was astonished. What were the odds of this happening amid millions of people? He thought a moment about the pros and cons of going somewhere with a strange New York girl, but then realized it was either that or a night of flipping through TV channels. "Yeah. I'd like that. I could use it. Thank you."

"Good, then. It will be my service for today. That's the only way I can stay sober – pray, and be of service. For me it's a daily thing. As long as I stay present and all that stuff – well, you know what I'm talking about. I was a wreck, and now, one day at a time, I'm not."

To have one of the first people he spoke to in New York say this seemed either a complete coincidence or a direct intervention of "higher power." He was suddenly filled with a sense of gratitude he hadn't felt in months, as if some angel was rescuing him.

"Would you mind telling me what led to your slip?" asked Monica. "It helps me to hear." Since she was enormously attracted to Zack, it suddenly became very important for her to humanize him so he wasn't a sex object. It was much safer. Thank God he spoke the language of the program. If not, she would have had to get out of here faster than a robber fleeing a bank, lest she get into dangerous territory.

"What the hell?" In between bites of his dinner for the next twenty minutes, Zack proceeded to tell her everything that had happened to him in the last months, his struggles at home and his impulsive trips to California and now New York. "It's just really hard for me to stay sober in Waco, 'cause it's so damn boring."

"Sounds like you need a big change."

"Yes, ma'am, but I'll be damned if I know how to go about it."

"Have you heard the slogan, 'Addicts hate two things – where they are, and change?'"

"No, but that's a good one. My, um, favorite slogan is what FEAR stands for – Forget Everything's All Right. Lately I've been totally forgettin' everything's all right. Totally."

"You know what else FEAR stands for?"

"No."

"Fuck Everything And Run."

Zack had to laugh. "Well, I reckon I done that today."

Monica also laughed. She reminded herself, once again, that this was not an appropriate way to get a date. One of the many things that had brought her to her first meeting was her habit of drunkenly hooking up with strange men and then beating herself up the next day for being such a slut. Her loneliness and need for companionship had gotten her into more trouble than a showgirl hitching a ride to Vegas. She liked this country boy immediately and somehow wanted to see him again, but in a sober way, so she thought a moment.

"This may sound stupid, but have you ever thought of modeling? You have a great look."

Zack nearly spit out his broccoli. "Do what?"

"Modeling, like for magazine ads and stuff like that."

"Are you kiddin?'"

"No, I'm not."

"No, ma'am. Not much call for that where I come from."

"You could do it. Really. Most models are pretty boys, and you're a handsome man. I can see you on a horse at sunset wearing Ralph Lauren or something."

Zack had to laugh. "Oh, what the hell, why not? Would beat the damn hardware store."

"Um, we need to go if we're going to make the meeting. You want to settle up?"

"OK." Zack put down a twenty on his check, which had been deposited by the waitress in the middle of his meal as a subtle reminder that turnover was how she made her money. They stood up and walked outside. A total stranger escorting him to a big city meeting was one of the surprising benefits of recovery: a whole underground network of people just waiting to help.

The meeting was in, of course, a nearby church basement. Zack wondered if church basements were used for anything else. It was easily the most crowded meeting Zack had ever attended, so he didn't worry about sharing until the end, when the leader asked if anyone had a "burning desire" to share. Zack's hand went up.

"Hi, my name is Zack, and I'm an alcoholic."

"Hi, Zack," said everyone in unison, a time-honored ritual that was either comforting or annoying, depending on one's mood.

"I just wanted to say that, um, I just came to New York today and I'm leaving tomorrow, but Monica here was nice enough to bring me, and this is my first New York meeting, and I'm grateful to be here. I've been struggling a lot lately but, um, I want to get back in the saddle and, um, I'm just – good to be here and it was good to hear everybody, thanks."

"Welcome, keep coming back," said many of the attendees. Zack was relieved, and a bit surprised, that this New York City meeting was exactly the same as Waco, albeit with more ethnicities. The program, evidently, was universal. If Bill W. had charged franchise fees, he would be richer than Bill G.

On the sidewalk afterwards, Monica introduced him to a few of her friends and they exchanged brief pleasantries. When someone asked Zack why he was in town, Zack replied, "Long story for another time." One man said, "Great accent, buddy."

Damn. Everybody always made fun of my accent, and now people are saying it's cool. What the hell.

As they walked back towards the hotel, Monica said, "Um, listen, when are you leaving?"

"I thought about goin' back tomorrow. Don't know, I'll have to call the airline."

"This is going to sound strange, but would you like to come up to my office tomorrow? I'd like to introduce you around, and have our in-house photographer take some shots of you. Who knows what it could lead to, but you really have a great look and I bet you could get some print work. Seriously."

"But, um, all I got are these clothes on my back."

"We have a huge wardrobe in the office. Here's my card. Call me first thing at the office tomorrow after 10 and we'll set it up. Please. Will you?" Monica handed him a business card from her pocket.

"And, for the record, this is not a pick-up. You should come to the office."

Momentarily disappointed that this *wasn't* a pick-up, Zack said, "OK."

"Good. It's taking action, if nothing else, right?"

They were at the entrance to the hotel. Monica smiled at him and said, "Tomorrow? Call me. Really."

"OK."

"And, uh, thanks for helping me stay sober tonight," she said, and leaned in and kissed him on the cheek.

"No, thank *you*, I think you saved my ass tonight."

"Tomorrow," she said, smiled, and turned and walked away. She looked very sexy walking down the sidewalk.

Zack walked into the hotel lobby, not believing what had just happened. The first thought he had was to sit down at the hotel bar and have a drink to calm down, but he stopped, looked at the bar, and then said aloud, "No. Not tonight." He went up to his room realizing that he was exhausted, like he had just worked all day on a road crew under one of New York's bridges.

In the bathroom, he splashed cold water on his face and looked in the mirror. *Everybody in Waco could just kiss my fashion model ass.*

He undressed, got in bed, turned on the TV and surfed through channels before stopping on a movie that he knew in five minutes was a waste of time. His eyelids began to droop and he began drifting in and out of sleep, thinking of Monica, the meeting, New York, and Lucy. He closed his eyes and said aloud the AA serenity prayer, said at the end of every meeting: "God, grant me the serenity to accept the things I cannot change, the courage to change the things I can, and the wisdom to know the difference."

He dreamed he was on a horse with a woman who looked like a cross between Monica and Lucy, wearing Ralph Lauren, riding off into the West Texas sunset.

19

"OK, see you tomorrow," said Lucy to Jon, the stage doorman.

"How was it tonight?" asked Jon.

"OK, audience a little sleepy. See you." As she walked out of the theater, a contingent of autograph seekers waited behind a guardrail. They thrust their programs forward. Lucy stopped, smiled, whipped out her Sharpie and signed every program offered her, saying, "Thanks," "Glad you enjoyed it," and so on. These people were here for Lonnie, but she was happy to oblige those who knew who she was.

One woman blurted, as she thrust her program into Lucy's face for a signature, "You should have won the Tony. That woman who won is a dumb whore."

"Uh, she's very nice, but thanks," said Lucy. She knew from experience to keep these conversations as brief as possible, lest one of these people be crazy. Such as this whack job.

Despite these occasionally exasperating audience members, Lucy praised the heavens that she was back on Broadway. It had been four months since she had returned from Venice in a state of shock. After she fled the hotel, she was not only afraid she wouldn't escape Perry; she was afraid she wouldn't get out of Italy alive. Her plane home was not until 1:30 PM the following afternoon and she had to get out of Venice, now, this minute. At the airline counter she was informed that there were no available flights and she would have to wait until her scheduled return.

"I need to leave, now. Where do you have flights going tonight? Maybe I could go back to the U.S. another way."

The befuddled clerk saw the panic in Lucy's eyes and looked at the computer. "Signora, the only other flight we have leaves tonight at 10:30."

"Where does it go?"

"Dubai."

Lucy thought a minute. New York via Dubai? She had just run away from one Arab, and now the only way to get out of here was to fly to an Arab country. "Um, is there a hotel near here?"

"Si, signora, the DaVinci Hotel, one half kilometer. A taxi will take you there."

Lucy limped to the curb and numbly hailed a taxi. It took her the hotel where she checked in, crawled into bed, took a sleeping pill, and died.

She struggled not to cry all the way on the plane home, but basically did. In the last two weeks she had lost both men in her life, one to domestic violence and the other to deceit. The excitement of her recent successes vanished in a wisp and she was stranded in the twilight zone, or in Italian, *il zona notturno*. Perry's betrayal had taken all her fantasies and squashed them like a watermelon falling off a skyscraper. Compared to how she felt now, her cruise vacation had been memories to be relived again and again.

She spent the next weeks in a fog, organizing her life between crying jags, long walks and channel surfing. She flew to Asheville for a few days to be with Ida on her seventieth birthday. Joan and her brood joined them, and most had a lovely time celebrating Ida's life with friends. Lucy faked enjoyment.

Noticing her sister's funk, Joan said, "Something's up. You're not right."

"Uh, yeah," said Lucy, washing her hands in the kitchen sink.

"Talk to me."

"Well, the fabulous doctor turned out to be a mercenary."

"What is that, Mafia or something?"

"No. He wanted to marry me to get his green card and live here. I was conned by the world's most stunning con man."

"Oh, crap." Joan's heart sank. Despite a distant relationship most of their lives, she loved her little sister. Joan had opted for unhappy domesticity while Lucy went off and followed her dreams, one of which had just smacked her in the face.

Joan paused and then said, "Listen, Lucy, you know I love you and I'm always here for you. I know I haven't always been, but really, I am. I'm sorry you've had so many disappointments. I can relate. Nothing turned out the way I wanted, and I'm stuck with it. My family could go on *The Jerry Springer Show* and the audience would yell at us."

Lucy looked at Joan and put her arms around her. "I love you, too." Then, she said, "Don't tell mom, OK? All she'll do is worry."

"Got it."

Later, when Ida asked about Perry, Lucy she said that they had had a lovely time in Venice but she didn't know when she would see him again. Actually, she did know: never.

One of the guests at her mother's birthday party, held in their home, was Reverend Tom from Ida's church, now in retirement, an old family friend and one of Lucy's favorite people. At a suitable break, she took him aside.

"Can we speak privately?"

"Sure," said the Reverend, wiping birthday cake from his mouth with a napkin.

They went into Lucy's room. Lucy told him what had transpired with Zack and Perry, and the Reverend nodded and listened. He was in his late seventies, but carried a beatific countenance known only to those of unshakable faith.

"I've never been religious, Reverend, but mom is, and I'm glad you were here."

"I wouldn't have missed it."

"Any advice?"

"Pray for guidance. None of what happened with these men is your fault. They have their own issues and you got caught in the crossfire. At least you weren't more involved. Learn what you can, and move on. Keep it simple."

Lucy listened, and then said, "I have to tell you something. That night, when I fell off the ship – yes, it was an accident, but I really did think about killing myself for a second. Only for a second. But the very thought horrifies me."

"But you weren't successful. You were given another chance. My opinion is that we do not have the right to end our lives. We were put here for a reason, and we owe it to the Almighty to find it. We all have moments when all seems lost, but it isn't. That's it."

Lucy said, "Then why should I even bother to try to succeed when it seems like something bad is always around the corner?"

"What choice do we have? We just have to be grateful for every moment we have on Earth, because there's no guarantee there will be a tomorrow. None whatsoever. Be happy with what you have, work for what you want, and deal with tragedy when it strikes, because it will. Sorry to mouth a bunch of shopworn clichés, alas, but true."

"Um, does - or do you think that - God really has a plan?"

"Who knows? I haven't the foggiest. If He does, I'd love to know it so I can organize my calendar. Most of what happens is a fluke, a coincidence. But some say coincidence is God's way of saying hello."

"Ah."

"I just have to believe that something better is around the corner, or I would never get up in the morning. My back is killing me, I have arthritis, I have melanoma. Old age is a cruel joke. Sometimes I think, *this* is what it has all led up to? I'm a wreck. But I get through it."

"But why do good things happen to bad people, and bad things happen to good people?"

The Reverend paused a moment, and then said, "Beats the *crap* out of me."

Three weeks later, God said hello. An actress in Lonnie Jones' show *Please Marry Me* abruptly quit and her understudy was getting the kind of audience reaction usually given a Botany lecture. Lonnie promptly called Lucy and asked her if she would be interested in stepping in and taking the role, a small but key role with one funny musical solo. Lucy didn't even have to audition, for the first time in her New York theater career. She assumed the part with one week's rehearsal and slipped into the show like a stripper into a G-string.

I just have to believe that something better is around the corner, or I would never get up in the morning.

It was a part Lucy could play blindfolded: a sassy lady along the same lines as her role in both *The Rag Trade* and *The Front Office*. It wasn't a stretch, but it was a fine way to make a living between more interesting offers and, being a replacement, she didn't have to worry about reviews. Being busy helped her get over her disappointments and concentrate on work. She was what she had always wanted to be: a working actress. Everything else was up to the Gods.

Perry had emailed her most every day since she returned. After reading the first, which contained profuse apologies, she hit "delete" before opening the rest. *Enough already. You're not going to snake charm me via cyberspace. Jump off the ship for all I care. Don't mess up your hair.* Perry, Zack, and indeed all men walking the planet could just go fuck themselves.

However, he was hard to avoid, since pictures the two of them in Venice were all over the Internet. None identified Perry by name, as most captions read, "Lucy Dixon and handsome escort" or "Lucy Dixon and friend." One breathlessly asked, "Who's the exotic mystery man behind rising star Lucy Dixon?" Her red dress was a hit, and she experienced the kind of mini-fame that fades after the initial zap, as a gossip hungry public moves on to the next series of computer clicks. She got many calls and emails from both friends and out-of-the-woodwork acquaintances she had no desire whatsoever to speak to again.

She thought about Zack constantly, but didn't want to talk to him any time soon. She just hoped he hadn't left her apartment and hightailed it straight to the George Washington Bridge and jumped into the Hudson River. He obviously hadn't; she would have seen it on the news, but not knowing his fate was odd. She wasn't the type who could easily wash that man right out of her hair and send him on his way, even though she had just done it twice.

Then, that night as she left the theater, she turned on her phone and had a voicemail. "Hey babe, it's me. Sorry I haven't called you back but, um, I'm OK. I'm in recovery and I've been going to meetings and all is well for today. Um…I just wanted to say I can't tell you how sorry I am for what happened. I hope some day you'll forgive me. I was drunk and scared. I love you and I always will, but, um, I think it's better if we don't talk for a while, and I continue my progress and get my life back. I have a lot of support and I just wanted to say, um, good luck to you, babe, you're gonna be a big star, I know it, and I'll be in touch some time, and I'll call you, OK? Uh, love you, bye." *Click.*

Lucy replayed the message to see if she could discern any desperation in his voice, but he really did sound all right, and evidently in the "making amends" part of recovery. She was relieved that he had gotten help that she couldn't possibly give. There comes a time in every friendship when the problems of the friend are mercifully out of your hands.

August's movie *Winter Of Our Discontent* was about to hit theaters, and Marvin's movie, now titled *Morocco Jitterbug*, was coming out in January. Lucy, incredulous that she had two movies coming out within a month and a half, had still not had any other offers but had meetings with five directors for projects still in development. Every time she went into a meeting she said a silent prayer of thanks that she wasn't dressed as a chicken.

At home, she began her nightly ritual of making herself supper, usually from whatever was in the refrigerator. Tonight it was sautéed salmon, string beans, corn, and sun-dried tomato pesto over linguini. She sat at the kitchen table eating and turned on her laptop to check emails and look at her favorite sites, usually entertainment blogs. The news of the day didn't really interest her, since she felt the best way she could serve the world was to entertain it.

These days were quiet, her routine returning to the same as it had been during her previous Broadway outing. Occasionally she went to Martell's but began to fit in less and less with the crowd, all struggling performers desperate for their first break, and Lucy felt she had *been there, done that.* When someone moves up to the next level, old friends are sometimes left behind.

The next night, after the show, Jon asked for the usual post-mortem of the performance. Lucy said goodbye and went outside, where the predictable phalanx of autograph seekers awaited. She went down the line and signed every one, with her usual assortment of *thank yous* and *glad you liked its*. These rituals gave her comfort. Doing the same thing every night can be a grind, but for an actress like Lucy who was grateful for the work after years of struggle, each moment was a godsend.

Then, at the end of the line, a man said, "Would you sign my program, Lucy?"

Lucy, looking only at the program, said, "Of course," and signed it, with her usual quick little glance into the person's face. But when she saw this particular face, she reacted as if she had pulled back her shower curtain to reveal Norman Bates in a wig holding a knife. She let out a yelp and dropped her Sharpie.

It was Perry.

What the freaking holy gold plated hell?

"How do you do, Miss Dixon?" He smiled. He was wearing a black sports jacket, a black T-shirt and black trousers, an informal version of himself at the Venice premiere. His hair grazed his shoulders.

"What the – " The autograph seekers looked at her, witnessing an actress in a real moment. One person snapped a picture, most likely of Lucy's mouth gaping like a Steven Spielberg character gazing at an alien. Thinking quickly, she took Perry's arm and led him away from the crowd, saying nothing. The film *Fatal Attraction* popped into her head, but this time it was reversed as an innocent Glenn Close being stalked by a crazy Michael Douglas.

When they were a sufficient distance away, she spoke. "What the hell are you *doing* here?"

"I live here now."

"You *what?*"

"For seventeen days. I'm here. Have you eaten?"

"No, I, uh, usually make something at home. I was – what? You *live* here?"

"Yes."

"Were you at the show tonight?"

"Of course, it was delightful."

"But – how did –"

"I Googled you."

"You what? Oh, right. Damn that Internet." Her head was wobbling like a bobble headed doll on the dashboard of a Pontiac. "You just don't give up, do you? You really, really must want to live here."

"Can I take you somewhere? I will explain everything."

"No, Perry. You scared me to death in Italy. I thought I was going to die. You took advantage – "

"Please, Lucy, let me explain. You are wrong about me. Just let me tell you what happened, and then you can say goodbye forever if you want. Allow me that, please."

She didn't want to succumb yet again to his irresistible charms, but succumb yet again she did. "Uh, sure, yeah, let's go…here." Lucy pulled Perry into the first restaurant she saw, which ended up being "Wahoo Bobcat Cookery."

He was literally the last person she expected to see waiting on the street, other than her deceased father or Jesus Christ. Perry was supposed to be back on the *Seafarer* in the middle of the Caribbean, for heaven's sake. This unsettling trend of former lovers showing up unannounced was getting *way* out of hand.

They were promptly seated, and given menus. "All I want a salad," she said, slamming the menu on the table. She was afraid that if she ate a full meal, it would end up in her lap.

"Same here," said Perry.

Lucy looked at him, exhaled, shook her head and said, "My, my, my. Dr. Bejravi. So what the *hell* brings you here?"

"You look wonderful. Have you lost weight?"

"Oh, yeah, thanks for noticing. Twelve pounds. It's easy to lose when you're doing a show, not sitting around eating, and miserable. And I've limited myself to one cocktail a day. I'm almost down to my old weight."

"You look beautiful."

"Yeah, yeah, whatever. OK, Perry, let's hear it."

The waitress appeared and said, "Something from the bar?"

"Hell yeah, cocktail time has arrived. Vodka tonic, please."

The waitress looked at Lucy, took a breath and said, "Excuse me, Miss Dixon, but I've been a fan of yours ever since *The Rag Trade,* and I just saw your show a couple of weeks ago and I'm an actress myself, and you're just wonderful and I'd like to offer you both a bottle of wine with my best wishes and compliments."

Startled by both the unexpected recognition, the presence of Perry and the offer of free liquor, Lucy said, "Uh, well, uh, sure, forget the vodka, we'll have, uh, Perry? What?"

"How about a Pinot Grigio?"

"Fine."

The waitress smiled and left.

Perry said, "Look at you, you're a star."

"Yeah, well, good for me, but let's hear it," she said, struggling to maintain her Grand Inquisitor persona. She wanted to be in charge of this conversation, and her semi-fame had just intruded. The fact that people actually recognized her was difficult to accept, conditioned from years of struggle to assume no one cared. Now, not only did it seem people cared, one of them was sitting opposite her, formerly 3600 miles away and now two feet away.

"Let me explain. I have been here for seventeen days. I am employed at Sloan Kettering Hospital. I have a visa. I had applied as a Physician Of Extraordinary Ability and three weeks ago it all came through. I resigned from the *Seafarer*. I had worked two months on the ship, and then this came to pass."

Who? "You're a what? A physician of what?"

"Of extraordinary ability. It's technical, but it means that the U.S. has specific need for my specialty, which is cancer research. I published a series in international medical journals before I worked on the ship. That was over a year ago and they started to get attention, and I had always wanted to do this and come to America, long before I met you. I interviewed at the hospital when I came to New York after I left you in Asheville. The whole process took about a year, but now I am here."

Lucy was astounded and confused. "Wait, you're this big cancer researcher but you were working on a *ship?* I don't get it."

"I was waiting until this happened, and, as I told you, I wanted to leave Morocco. Now I am here and I am finally able to do what I want to do."

"Why didn't you tell me this before?"

"I didn't want to, um, what's the word when you don't want to ruin your chances?"

"Jinx it."

"Yes, jinx. I thought if I mentioned it, it might not happen. But now it has. I was going to explain in Venice, but you left."

"Uh, yeah, I left. What about your wife, and son?"

"My son is with her. Our divorce came through. It is done. It is unfortunate that I am not with Luc, but I could not miss this. My being here may allow him to come study here. We are in contact every day. We talk more now than we did when I was at sea, since the ship's Internet is so slow. Luc is a very smart boy, very tough. I will also be flying back to see him. It has all happened very fast so it will take me some time to adjust. And how are you?"

Lucy's mind was trying to grasp that he was actually sitting across the table. His power in person had not diminished. His melodious accent still made her flesh quiver, and his eyes were even more piercing. But Perry had a new energy, as if his batteries had been recharged. He seemed much more casual, smiling like a big kid who had driven dad's car for the first time. Lucy took a breath.

"So, you're saying you *didn't* want to marry me so you could live here?"

"Of course not. I gave you the wrong impression and I apologize. I explained everything in my emails, but I assume you didn't read them. I had to come here to tell you personally. I am very, very sorry for any pain I caused you. That day you left me in Venice was the worst day of my life. I can't tell you how many sleepless nights I had on the *Seafarer*. The movements of the ship didn't help. Where did you go after you left me?"

The worst day of your life? Really? "To the airport. I stayed in the hotel and flew home the next day."

"I should pay you for your hotel. It was because of me that you ran away."

Lucy looked at him. Had he *always* been telling the truth and she was just a paranoid ninny, or was he the greatest shyster since Harold Hill, the Music Man?

"Please, tell me how you are," said Perry.

"Uh, well, oh gosh, I'm not going to lie, it's been rough, but basically I'm fine. Doing the show, just schlepping along."

"Schlepping?"

"It's a New York Jewish word, never mind, means walking slowly or something. Anyway, wow. You're here. And you're some sort of medical genius. Wow. How long are you going to be here?"

"At least two years."

"Two years?"

"If it all works out, I will have my green card. So I would be here whether I had met you or not."

Holy cow, holy mackerel, holy Moses, holy shit.

"Where are you staying?"

"In an apartment the hospital arranged for me. When I have not been going through orientation I have just been walking around. Amazing, a dream come true. I love New York!" He laughed a little laugh, almost a girlish giggle. She had never seen him giddy.

Lucy was as thunderstruck as a weather vane in Oklahoma during a tornado. Every suspicion she had about

Perry had just been tossed out the window. She was torn between wanting to slap him and exit the restaurant in a huff, or pull him out of the chair and grope him on the restaurant floor. She didn't know what to do, other than lift her glass of wine, which had just been poured in front of her, and say, "Well, cheers."

"Cheers." They clinked their glasses.

"You're not going to believe this," she said to Lonnie in her dressing room the following night, "but the doctor is in town."

"Who, the Prince Of Persia?" said Lonnie, making herself up while looking at Lucy in the mirror.

"The same."

"What the hell is he doing here?"

"He got a job at Sloan Kettering. He lives here now. He showed up last night outside."

"He *what?*"

"You heard me."

"My God, you're incredible. You leave them panting across the globe, and they stand below your window and howl at the moon. Are you OK? Want me to have him taken care of?"

"What?"

"I know people. They could keep him away from you."

"Geez, Lonnie, I don't want him *taken care of.* Who are you, Michael Corleone? We went out last night and he explained everything and he's some kind of medical genius or something, and he is working here now, and I went into a panic for nothing. He didn't need to marry me to come here. Unbelievable."

"Really? My *dear.* That couldn't be more convenient, could it?"

"He got a visa, and what can I say? The men just fly across the world and claw at the pavement for me. We went out, and after I got over the shock we actually had a wonderful time."

"And?"

"And *what?*"

"And then what happened?"

"Nothing. I put him in a cab. But he wanted to go out again tonight, so what could I say? What the hell, I'm Helen of freaking Troy. Want to meet him?"

"Are you kidding? I *have* to see this *specimen*. Make sure he comes around."

"It's so wild. My life in the last year – I can't believe any of it."

Lonnie spoke with the weathered assurance of a dame who had seen it all, buried three husbands and lived to tell about it, even though she had never married. She applied her lipstick. "It's in the stars, baby. It's *all* working out. Serendipity. Fate. Go for it. Get on the roller coaster, and ride."

"Roller coasters make me nauseous."

Lucy made it through the show with half of her mind on her performance and the other half in nervous anticipation of seeing Perry, like someone about to cheat on their spouse with a secret sex date. She even forgot a lyric, saying, "He gave me …something" when she should have said, "flowers." After the curtain call, Lonnie said, with a laugh, "Boy, roller coasters *do* make you nauseous."

"Oh, shut up."

In her dressing room, she got a call from Jon. "You have a visitor."

"I'll call back when I'm dressed, and then you can send him up."

"No problem."

She got out of her costume and into her street clothes faster than a quick-change artist. She was still in stage makeup so she wiped most of it off and then put on her street face. When she looked presentable, she called Jon. "OK, send him up. Thanks." She straightened up the dressing room, throwing underwear into a drawer.

Two minutes later, Perry appeared, holding a bouquet of flowers, sporting a smile that could only be called goofy.

"Oh, *that's* what I messed up tonight, the flowers lyric," she said, taking the flowers and then giving Perry a quick hug and a kiss. "I was so nervous about tonight I forgot the words to my song. Hello."

"It's just me," he said.

Lucy found herself just as jumpy as when Perry first visited her in Asheville, and struggled to get out the words as she threw old flowers in the trash and put the new ones in the vase. She turned on the sink's faucet so hard that the water splashed everywhere, including into her face. She nonchalantly wiped herself with a towel. "Wow. Well, we can talk over – wow, I can't - you hungry? There's someone who wants to meet you."

"Really? Who?"

"Lonnie, the leading lady. Let's go see her." She grabbed her purse and took Perry's hand, leading him down two levels to the star's dressing room. She knocked on the door, which was ajar. "Come in," said Lonnie.

"You decent?" They walked in.

"As decent as I'll ever get. Oh my, you must be the good doctor."

"Perry, this is Lonnie Jones."

"How do you do? I enjoyed your performance," said Perry, as he took Lonnie's hand and bowed slightly.

"I do just *fine,* thank you, welcome to New York. Well, Lucy. My, my."

"Wait – were you in *The Magician?*" asked Perry.

Lonnie laughed. "Guilty as charged."

"You were very good. But I saw it in French, so I will have to watch it again in English. "

"Wait, you speak French too?" said Lucy, incredulously.

"Of course."

Lonnie said, "This one can take your blood pressure *and* help you out when you do Moliere."

"It was very nice to meet you, Miss Jones."

"Lonnie, *please,* we're all family here," said Miss Jones.

Lucy and Lonnie exchanged conspiratorial looks that basically said, *Well!*

Lucy and Perry went out that night, as they did for most nights the following weeks. Perry seemed like a different man; his gentlemanly air and mysterious aura were still intact, but he was less serious, more playful, and at times flat out *funny*. America seemed to boost his spirits like a vitamin B-12 injection.

Perry felt like every day was a holiday, the Moroccan Revolution of the King and the People, *Thawrat al malik wa shâab*. At last getting the new life he had always wanted, he was thrilled to be a celebrated physician in a country everyone wanted to come to, where no one was forced into marriage or beheaded if father disapproved. And he was thrilled that Lucy would still see him. To him, she was the life force itself. He bounced along the sidewalks as if lifted by helium. If he had musical talents he would have tap-danced down the street crooning "Singin' In The Rain."

Lucy's suspicions of Perry gradually vanished, helped by the arrival of his apparently dormant sense of humor. She was amazed at how well they communicated and how protected she felt. It was altogether too much of a fairy tale and Lucy's cynicism, developed from years of rejection, finally got the best of her and one evening she said, "You know, there are lots of beautiful women in New York. What are you doing with me?"

"I love you is what I'm doing with you," Perry said, matter-of-factly as if stating a medical diagnosis, between bites of hummus and pita chips. "Do you want some of this?"

"He said he loved me again," she said to Lonnie in her dressing room the next night. "Why don't I believe it?"

"Darling. Listen to your mother. A great guy is evidently in love with you. A gorgeous doctor who speaks God knows how many languages. What the hell is your problem?"

"Well...I don't know. I've always known I'm talented. It's the other stuff I have no confidence in. You know, the body issues and – "

Lonnie, suddenly exasperated, launched into a tirade like when she tortured her director in *The Rag Trade*.

"Stop right there. Just stop it, Lucy. Am I going to have to call the *whaambulance*? If you were as grotesque as you seem to think you are, do you think you would have *ever* gotten a job? People *like* you, Lucy. You have a talent that inspires jealousy. Hell, *I* was jealous at first, I was threatened. I thought, *oh, no,* here's this hot young talent that's going to steal the thunder of the great Lonnie Jones. And you stole that show *right out* from under my skinny little ass. You're so much more likeable than me on stage I can't stand it. And I had to accept it. You can even *cook,* for God's sake. Just stop asking stupid questions. Acceptance is our *friend*. The guy says he loves you. *Accept it.* Truthfully, your self-esteem issues are getting really tiresome. They're talking about you for a damn *Oscar,* for heaven's sake. My *cat* has more self-confidence than you. Look, we all think that if the audience isn't so staggered by our very presence that they have a coronary, we're not good enough. Well, we *are* good enough, dammit. *Everything* is going your way right now, and if you don't just shut the hell up and enjoy it, I'm going to terminate your goddam lease and get someone who feels good about herself to live in my apartment. I'll even put a clause in – 'Subtenant must have decent self-esteem.' And *scene*. You *got it?"*

Lucy stared at her for a stunned moment, and then burst into tears that quickly became laughter. Lonnie embraced her. "Sweetie, *everything* you're going through, I went through. We work all our lives to be a success, and then when it happens, we can't believe it. We're pathetic, performers. Insane. We should be locked up. Just accept it."

Lucy pulled back, looked at Lonnie, and said, "Thank you."

Acceptance is our friend.

Lucy continued to see Perry, more relaxed with each passing day. She was thrilled that he seemed to like her just for herself and had no interest in show business whatsoever, one of the things she had liked about Zack. On weekends, they enjoyed New York in the fall, and Lucy found a new appreciation for the city she loved. Before she knew it, she found herself falling for him.

One Sunday in November, over lunch before her matinee, Lucy took a deep breath and said, "You asked me to marry you in Europe. You haven't even mentioned it the entire time you have been here."

"I have not."

"Have you lost interest?"

"Of course not. But you're not ready to be married. You have your career. Should things change, you know where to find me. Oh, and I still have my grandmother's ring that you threw at me, if you want it back."

Lucy, smiled, kissed him, and took another bite of her turkey sandwich.

20

Tom Hanks stood on the stage of the DeMille Theater in Hollywood holding the envelope, a huge Oscar statue looming behind him. The 5000 people in the theater held their breath as he announced the first award of the evening. "This category has showcased the finest actresses in Hollywood, veterans and promising newcomers alike. Tonight is no exception, as nominated are three previous Oscar winners, one with her third nomination, and one nominated for her very first film. The nominees for Best Supporting Actress are…"

Lucy tried to remain calm, as her face was about to be broadcast to a billion people, 999,500,000 who had never heard of her. She was wearing another Malan Tatou creation, this one of black and purple, and was resplendent in Harry Merrick jewelry. Perry sat next to her, in a Franco Batallia tuxedo arranged by Tatou, who was so taken with Perry when he measured him it almost amounted to molestation.

All night, Lucy had been trying to concentrate on the show, having felt nauseous all week, but her mind kept flashing to the mind-boggling sequence of events of the last few months...

In December, Lucy was cast in another movie. She continued with *Please Marry Me* until New Year's Day, when she left the show to film in Los Angeles, this time a slapstick comedy as the girlfriend of comedian Lenny Rogell, who had starred in the previous year's biggest comedy hit. It was another supporting role, but one that finally allowed her to use her comic skills to full effect. The director encouraged improvisation and sparks flew on the set. One scene, a fight between her and her boyfriend, was almost like a comic version of her rape scene in *Winter Of Our Discontent,* and required multiple takes because actors and crew kept cracking up. It was a fun shoot, and Lucy rented a car rather than depend on the studio to get her around, free to explore Los Angeles on her own should she feel like it.

Winter Of Our Discontent had opened in December in a small number of theaters to generally positive reviews, although one disgruntled critic said, "I felt like I had been trampled by stampeding elephants by the end of this emotionally exhausting ordeal. Not only do I never want to get married, I never want another personal relationship ever again." Another said, "The performances are amazing, but when they said 'discontent,' they weren't kidding." And another: "It's like spending the holidays with relatives you avoid the rest of the year. These folks make the Macbeths seem like the Partridge Family."

It was, indeed, the kind of snob art house hit Lucy had predicted. Among a certain type of cineaste, those who find waterboarding a laugh riot, it became the hot ticket du jour, its admirers proclaiming it 'devastating' and 'shattering.' It was a better film than the rough-cut shown in Venice. It was also fifteen minutes shorter, relieving the audience from having to beg for mercy. Lucy didn't know how anyone could get through it. That kind of domestic sturm and drang was just not her speed. She needed songs and laughs. Rick saw it and said, "You were great, but I wanted to stab myself." Ida watched it when Lucy sent her a promotional DVD, and said, "Lucretia, that was the most depressing thing I've ever seen in my life. Who are these people? Next time pick a musical."

Lucy's performance was universally praised, with words like 'breakout,' 'star-making' and 'painful,' and she was nominated for a Golden Globe award, along with two other cast members. She attended that ceremony in January in Los Angeles while still filming the comedy, seated at a large round table with the company, and drank club soda while the rest of them proceeded to get rip-roaring drunk. None of them won, and, miraculously, she didn't care. She was in the same room with stars she had watched all her life, and shook hands with as many as she could, *yessing* and *thankyouing* until she was blue in the face.

That proved to be one of the most incredibly entertaining nights of her life, marred only by the absence of Perry, in the midst of a project at the hospital. The whole night she schmoozed with the stars, as if this would be the only time this would happen and she better enjoy it. Everyone circulated during the commercials like a swarm of formally dressed bees.

But, for the first time in her life, she thought, *I belong here. Why not? It's either this or sorting veggies at Piggly Wiggly.*

Morocco Jitterbug opened "wide" in January, meaning in thousands of theaters at once. It got mixed reviews, but audiences enjoyed it and it seemed to be on the way to becoming profitable. Lucy thought it was a lot of fun, and Perry saw it in New York and was fascinated to see scenes he had witnessed filming finally up on the screen. Her role as a hapless tourist got good notices, including this one from *Hollywood Reporter:* "With this comic film and the searing drama *Winter Of Our Discontent*, as well as her Broadway credits and musical talent, Lucy Dixon may emerge as a talent who can do it all, in the vein of Bette Midler." Lucy almost soiled her panties after reading that one.

At the end of January, the Oscar nominations were announced. Lucy arrived on the set in Los Angeles as the cast gathered around a TV at five-thirty AM. Her category was one of the first, but despite all the talk she didn't think she had a chance in hell. When her name was called, the entire company screamed and applauded. Lucy burst into tears. She couldn't help it. As crewmembers hugged and kissed her, she was so overwhelmed with gratitude that she thought she would melt into the floor. *Winter Of Our Discontent* was also nominated for Best Actor for Charles McGuire, and Best Original Screenplay for August.

An article in *Variety* summed it up for her: "Many wags said that Dixon jumped off a ship to get acting work. It's ridiculous, but if that is indeed the case, she knew what she was doing. She is brilliant. Sometimes all it takes is a press-grabbing in incident. However, aspiring performers should be warned: Don't try this at home."

Then, as if things couldn't get any better, she got an offer to star in a Broadway revival of Cole Porter's *Anything Goes*, as Reno Sweeney. She wondered if the producers had any idea that she had played the role in high school, but now she was, at last, the right age for the part. The show would go into rehearsals in late fall and open early in the next year. Jared, her agent, said, "You're an Oscar nominee, baby. You're box office. I knew you had it when I got you that tour of *Fiddler*. Want to do it?"

"Are you *kidding?*" said Lucy. Not only would it be a starring role on Broadway, it would allow her to be home in New York with Perry, her friends, and her life.

When not filming, her days were filled with meetings, luncheons, and preparations for the ceremony. She tried not to read the usual press about Oscar predictions, since all of them put her chances of winning at zero. But she couldn't help it. This was her first time at the ball, and she wanted to know the buzz. An *Entertainment Weekly* article rated the nominees in order of their chances, and she was at the bottom with a fourteen percent likelihood of winning. The blurb next to her picture said, "Newcomer gives stellar performance, but film a downer, and she'll have to develop more street cred before winning." Veteran British actress Janet McEwan was considered the shoo-in in this category. But knowing that she wouldn't win lightened the load for Lucy, and she was able to relax and enjoy the circus.

The Oscar nominees luncheon was a highlight. A relaxed yet A-list affair, she got to meet her fellow nominees and exchange congratulations. Tatou had arranged for her to meet his Los Angeles counterpart, Sergio, who provided her with a suitable ensemble. Once again, Rick helped her deliver some quotable quotes to the press, such as, "I'm practicing my losing face. I already worked on it at the Tonys a few years ago, so I've got it down." Rick reminded her: *Never say that you think you might win. You're just honored to be there and blah blah blah. Hollywood loves that bullshit.*

Each of the nominees was allowed a brief speech, but front-runner Janet McEwan's speech lasted twenty-seven minutes, where she recounted the highlights of her long career and seemed to name every leading man she had ever worked with since The Blitz, all in a very to-the-manor-born British accent and Grand Lady demeanor like Olivia DeHavilland recalling highlights from *Gone With The Wind*. Lucy thought McEwan was eventually going to tell stories from her opening night of *Oedipus The King*, at the Theatre of Dionysus in ancient Greece, with the original cast.

Lucy, sensing the crowd getting restless, made a speech that was appropriately short: "Not only am I honored to be a nominee, I'm honored to be in the building, in this town, and on Planet Earth. This is all new to me so thank you very much, and forgive me if I fall flat on my face."

As she exited the stage, she did just that. She was smiling and watching the audience as she descended the stairs, keeping her head high for photographers, and misjudged a step and tripped onto the floor. An "Oooooh" rose from the crowd as an assistant rushed to help her up, but before he made it to her, she raised her nomination certificate into the air, waved it, and the audience laughed and applauded when they realized she was all right. She got to her feel, curtsied to the audience, shook her head and rolled her eyes, and exited stage left rapidly wiping the egg off her face.

The next day, the news of her fall was all over the Internet, and a picture of her on the floor held the top spot on the AOL home page. Some articles implied that she was drunk. One said, "If Dixon gets the Oscar, she might not be able to make it to the stage. This actress seems to have hit on a very novel way to get attention." In the end all she could do was laugh. She was certainly making a splat in Hollywood.

Later, as filming on the comedy drew to a close, fatigue and nausea began to plague her days, and at first she chalked it up to overwork and excitement. But, while filming one of her final scenes, she leaned in to kiss her co-star and promptly threw up all over his velvet jacket.

"Oh, God, I'm so sorry," said the mortified Lucy, as her co-star recoiled in disgust. Stagehands rushed to clean up the mess. "Did you get that on film?"

"I did," said Bruno, the director.

"For God's sake, don't put it on YouTube."

"You need to see a doctor."

"I've just been feeling bad, maybe the flu or something. It will pass."

"Nevertheless, I insist. You have one more scene and I want to make sure you get through it. Laura, make the arrangements for Lucy to see the company doctor, today if possible."

"I'm on it," said Laura, an assistant.

"The studio car will take you," said Bruno.

"I'm OK, really, I'll drive myself, because then I can just go back to the hotel rather than have to come back here and get the car. I'll be fine."

"Are you sure?"

"Yeah, yeah. Thanks, I feel better already. Sometimes all you need is just a good vomit."

In the parking garage, she sat in her car and took a few moments to catch her breath and map out the directions to the doctor's office. She felt alert but dizzy, like her stomach and head were in a boxing match. She turned on the ignition and slowly pulled out of the garage into the traffic, careful to not get sideswiped by one of the many homicidal maniacs who masqueraded as Los Angeles drivers. She drove towards the doctor's office, carefully taking her time and negotiating the traffic. It was almost as if she had tunnel vision, seeing only the car in front of her, the surrounding buildings in an out of focus haze.

As she drove up La Cienega Boulevard, she couldn't remember if she should turn right or left. At a stoplight, she fumbled for the Los Angeles map on the passenger seat and opened it, searching for the "X" she had marked above the doctor's office. Once she got her bearings, she resumed driving, the impatient honks of cars behind her reminding her to snap to it. Waiting at another stoplight, she then turned right onto Santa Monica Boulevard, and then suddenly saw the billboard looming above the street.

"WHAT?????"

She stared at the billboard in utter disbelief, the double whammy to end all double whammies. And then, she heard a huge crash as she lurched forward and hit the steering wheel with her forehead, as her car plowed into a parked vehicle on the right with a *wham*. The car behind her then smashed into hers, which pushed the parked car a foot up onto the sidewalk. Pedestrians yelped and scattered, birds in nearby trees flew away, dogs barked and horns blared. When Lucy realized what had happened, she held her forehead, blinked her eyes, looked in the rearview mirror, saw that she wasn't bleeding, and slowly got out of the car feeling like she was in a movie in slow motion with a dramatic swell of background music.

"What the hell is the matter with you, lady?" screamed the driver of the car behind her.

"Are you OK?" said a woman who ran towards Lucy from the sidewalk.

As if on cue, a police car's sirens blared. Lucy, oblivious to the cacophony she had just caused, stared at the huge billboard, shook her head in disbelief that this was the second time in her life that she had wrecked a car while staring at an advertisement for men's underwear, and grinned.

21

ACCIDENT-PRONE ACTRESS DIXON WINS UNEXPECTED OSCAR
By THE ASSOCIATED PRESS

HOLLYWOOD (AP) In what many insiders are calling the upset of the night at this year's Academy Awards ceremony, actress Lucy Dixon walked away with the Best Supporting Actress Oscar for the art-house entry **Winter Of Our Discontent**. The film was critically acclaimed but has performed poorly at the box office, its downbeat subject matter leaving many viewers in a state of suicidal depression. Dixon's performance was universally praised, but her chances of winning were not a favorite of odds makers.

The audience gasped and applauded as presenter Tom Hanks announced Dixon's name, as it was widely speculated the award would go to veteran Janet McEwan for her comeback performance in director Julie Taymor's avant-garde modernization of Euripides' **Medea**. McEwan's portrayal had previously won most of the major critics circle awards as well as the Golden Globe statuette, and the actress had recently recovered from a bout with cancer, which insiders suggested would win her the "sympathy" vote. Insiders also suggested that the Academy favors British actors because they have great accents and seem smarter. As for Dixon, a source inside the Academy said, "Hollywood loves a Cinderella story, and Dixon is it this year. She came out of nowhere and delivered. People just seem to like her."

Dixon, a New York stage actress new to films whose previous acting nomination was for Broadway's You Can't Take It With You, was thrust onto the national scene a year ago after a very public accident in which she fell off of a cruise ship into the Caribbean Sea. Tongues wagged that Dixon had either attempted suicide or jumped ship as an attention-getting device to revive a stagnant career, assumptions laughed off by Dixon in subsequent interviews. Director August Huff admitted that he cast her in Winter Of Our Discontent after seeing her appearance on CNN'S Doug Johnson Live explaining her accident, thinking her perfect for the role. "The good news is, she turned out great," remarked Huff at a press conference. "You can't help but love her onscreen, even when she's a wreck."

Dixon seemed genuinely shocked when her name was called, her hands covering her mouth and her eyes wide, and staggered to the stage mouthing "Oh, my God" repeatedly. Stunning in her black and purple gown by designer Malan Tatou, Dixon's delightful acceptance speech, punctuated by her brief bursts of laughter, was widely regarded as the funniest of the evening. Dixon said, "Thank you so much, this is unbelievable. I know that people at Oscar parties everywhere are looking at their ballots and screaming, 'Well, missed that one. Who the hell is this broad?' I have to thank August Huff, who took a big chance on an unknown, I have to thank the editor Eric Deane, for making it look like I gave a great performance, I have to thank all the people who *have supported me all through the years, especially Lonnie Jones. I have to thank the folks on the* Seafarer *for rescuing me from the ocean. I have to thank the LAPD for being fine, understanding police officers. And I have to thank my fiancée, Perry, who rescued me in so many other ways. I have to dedicate this to my dad, who didn't live to see this, but I know he's loving it. Thank you so much, what a surprise."*

Dixon's fiancée, identified as Dr. Perroj Bejravi of Casablanca, Morocco, was not available for comment. It has been reported that the doctor treated Dixon onboard the Seafarer *after her oceanic mishap.* Bejravi, a noted international cancer researcher, published a series of papers on radiation techniques imposingly entitled, "New Frontiers in Alpha-Fluoroestradiol." Sources say the dashing doctor was reportedly offered a role in the upcoming film Desert Assassins 4, *and declined.*

Dixon had recently received more unwanted publicity after falling on the floor at the Oscar nominees luncheon, and then after causing a three-car accident at the corner of Santa Monica and La Cienega boulevards. Dixon was at the wheel of a vehicle that rammed a parked car in front of her, which in turn caused her car to be hit from behind by another vehicle. No one was injured, but Dixon sustained minor head trauma and was treated at Cedars Sinai Medical Center. She was released after police questioning. An insurance investigation is pending.

That accident, as well as reports that she had vomited on a co-star while filming her latest opus, gave rise to a flurry of articles and jokes from late night comics about Dixon's mishaps. Comic Rudy DiCarlo cracked, "Actress Lucy Dixon was in the news again today – she made it across the street."

At the post-Oscar press conference, Dixon said, "I'm so sorry about the accident, but I was driving to the doctor and not feeling well, and I looked up at a billboard and there was my old boyfriend modeling underwear. I had no idea he was working as a model and he was the last person I expected to see looming over the street. You would have to know him to understand my shock. That's why I hit the car in front of me. As many people realize, I'm a klutz. I plead distracted."

Dixon's "old boyfriend" has been identified as model Zachary Bynum, who recently signed an exclusive contract with 4SQ Underwear. Bynum was unavailable for comment at press time, currently shooting an ad campaign in the Maldives.

Dixon also appears in the current Morocco Jitterbug and just completed filming an untitled comedy, starring comedian Lenny Rogell. When asked what's next, Dixon replied, "I'm getting married in May, and I'm supposed to do Anything Goes on Broadway next season, but that may change because I just found out I'm pregnant. That's why felt nauseous on the set. So we'll see. I never know what's going to happen next. A year ago I was working in a grocery store in North Carolina, and now all this has happened. But it could all change, so I just have to enjoy it. It's all a fluke."

When asked if she had any other interesting offers, Dixon laughed and replied, "Believe it or not, I was just offered a fortune to do a special show on a cruise ship. I said, 'Only if it's in dry dock.'"

YOU ARE INVITED

To a Fashionable Soiree!

Come and visit the new penthouse apartment of

Dr. Perry Bejravi

and

Mrs. Lucy Dixon Bejravi

and meet their twins

Frank Morocco Dixon Bejravi, called Rocky

and

Ida Rose Aswinkumar Bejravi, called Rosie

on June twenty-fifth

at seven PM

Cocktails, hors d'oeuvres and dinner served

Festive attire

623 East 68th Street Apt. 3D, New York, New York

Regrets only 212-228-3858 or ilovelucy@memail.com

THANKS TO

I am eternally grateful to friends and colleagues who read early drafts, offered valuable suggestions, and provided other assistance:

Kris Andersson, Cynthia Csabay Halloran, Paul Djirkalli, Leslie Doggett, Marni Fechter, Wayne Gibbons, Josh Gondelman, Gordon Heal, David Herder, Dennis Hensley, Cory Kahaney, Jon Krause, Eric Lyden, Charles Murdock Lucas, Terry Meerkov, Michael McFee, Denise Murphy, Georgeann Murphy, Nancy Rich, Nancy Sample, Steven Scott, Mark Sendroff, Tara Siesener, Tim Slauson, Bob Smith, Guy Smith, Mary Testa, Christine Turner, Jennifer Unter.

Martine Bellen provided invaluable editorial assistance and the book would not exist in this final form without her.

My parents, Charles and Nancy David, read an early draft, were not appalled, and provided more of the encouragement and support they have for my entire life. I was blessed with great parents who gave me the gift of humor.

Dan Rosenbaum provided great moral and financial support, and much needed assistance in maintaining the sanity of the author.

I also want to thank you, the reader, for reading my first novel. If you enjoyed it, please share it with your friends. If you didn't, share it with your enemies.

ABOUT THE AUTHOR

JIM DAVID is a comedian and writer seen on many television shows including his special *Comedy Central Presents Jim David*, *Tough Crowd With Colin Quinn* and many others. His comedy CDs, heard regularly on Sirius/XM radio, are available on Itunes. He has performed all over the world. His one-man play *South Pathetic* has been performed nationwide. A contributor to The Huffington Post, his articles have appeared in many publications. He has also been a teacher, waiter, photographer, office supply salesman and disc jockey. This is his first novel.

www.jimdavid.com